Also by

Veil & Shadow Series
**The Breaking*
**The Bleeding*

(**Prequel** to *The Anavrin Series*- Stand Alone)
**Little Red Rising*

The Anavrin Series
**A Kingdom Of Crowns And Malice*
**A Throne Of Chains And Fate*

Eventide Series
**Falling Even*
**Rising Tide*

Anexa O. Saphire
Little Red
Rising
Anexa O. Saphire

Entrance to Faery
The Den
WYLDER'S CABIN
Lupian Forest
Ritual Rock
To Town
Gram's Cottage

A uthor's Note:

Some Trigger Warnings

This book is a work of fiction. Any likeness to that of actual beings, living or deceased, is coincidental or embellished to tell a fictional tale.

It contains scenes that may be uncomfortable for some readers.

Including, but not limited to... violence, blood, explicit sex, alcohol abuse, and implied and/or unwanted sexual advances.

Some characters in this book are based off of real-world placement and classical works but do not strictly adhere to any one folklore.

The creative uses of such are fully fictional and not to be taken as fact.

Chapter One

Faelan

Coming in from another night of serving drunks and bussing tables, I tried not to wake my roommate who was already asleep.

All of my life I'd been a night owl. My mornings didn't exist until well after noon.

Fitting in with everyone else was much harder considering the majority of people lived their waking hours opposite of mine.

The blaring music of my latest ringtone made me jump out of my skin. Who the hell was calling me at two in the morning?

Digging my cell from the pocket of my hoodie, the contact's name, "The Womb" flashed on the screen. Biting the bullet, I pushed the talk button.

"Hello, Mother." Not wanting to have to listen to a lecture on what it meant to be a good daughter, I also didn't want to give my mom any variance. "To what do I owe this late-night intrusion of cellular bliss?"

The other end of the line was quiet except for a few hushed sobs.

"Mom?"

"Oh Faelan, it's your Grams." Her tone left little room for positive thoughts. "She's gone."

The racing of my heart and blood rushing in my ears drowned out whatever else my mother was still trying to say.

A glass of whiskey had been left on the coffee table next to my roommate's keys and purse. Downing the liquid, I barely felt the burn.

Somewhere in the recesses of my mind I vaguely registering that mom was still speaking.

"Faelan, did you hear what I said?" she half shouted.

"No, Mom. I was a bit in shock." The copper tang on my tongue pulled me from my spiraling thoughts. Wiping at my mouth, I realized that I'd bitten through the side of it. "When's the funeral?"

"She's not dead honey. That's what I was trying to tell you." The sounds of walkie talkies in the background now drew my attention. "She's missing. The police are here now, but they say it happened a week or so ago." *Way to bury the lead, Mom.*

One deep breath. Then another. In through my nose and out through my mouth. Just like my Grams had taught me for when the panic attacks took hold.

My mother's voice became muffled, and I realized that she must be cupping her hand to talk into the phone more privately.

"You know that your Grams believed in a bunch of claptrap. They are saying that her cottage was ransacked, but that nothing appears to have been taken... other than your grandmother." She sobbed again. "I know what you're thinking, Faelan, but I loved your Grams very much."

"Love, Mom! She's not dead, remember!" I wanted to hang up, but I couldn't bring myself to do so just yet.

"I know, honey. We never saw eye to eye because I didn't want to follow in her footsteps. Not because she spoke her truth." She cut off abruptly and I could hear the officers telling her that the odds of finding Grams alive were slim to none.

They'd found blood but couldn't determine who it had come from.

"Mother, I have to go." My heart was so heavy, I felt like it might push through my chest.

Grams was the only person, other than my roommate, Alayna, who I was comfortable enough to be myself around. My whole life I'd felt like an outcast, but Grams made me feel special.

Hanging up the phone, I poured another glass of whiskey and made a decision.

I'd set off to the cottage after I got some sleep and look for clues myself.

Chapter Two

Faelan

Morning came earlier than expected. Alayna was bustling around the apartment chaotically.

Normally, she tried to be quiet as a church mouse so I could sleep in peace, but something was off with her energy.

Remembering last night's call, I jolted straight up in bed.

Panic seized my system again. Struggling to get air into my lungs, half of the room was a blur. My body was shaking from head to toe.

With my hands trembling, I reached for the water bottle on the nightstand and wrestled with the cap.

"Here," Lanie said, coming into the room. Taking the bottle to open it, she handed it back. "Focus on the lamp shade, Faelan," her voice placating.

There was an underlining tension in her tone. Something was awry in her world.

With my Grams missing and my best friend not seeming to be herself, the air simply would not stay in my lungs.

Several minutes and a lot of deep, long breaths late, Lanie guided me enough to calm down and get up out of bed.

The first step was shaky. I'd had my nails done just two days prior and they were already grown out. *Weird.*

I'd brought my laundry into the room to put away a few days ago but it was still in the chair next to the bed. As simple as it was to put it away, I hated to do it.

Rummaging around the closet instead, my favorite shirt snagged on my newly sharpened nails.

"Damn it!" It made a small hole, but it would definitely be noticeable.

"I need to go," Laynie said. "I may not be home tonight. I don't know yet."

"Wait! I have to tell you something." Wearing my emotions close to the surface, tears began to swell but I didn't let them fall. "My Grams is missing. I'm going to her cottage to look for anything that might help find her."

I had expected Alayna to be concerned or make a fuss, but she was distracted. The blood in my veins pounded loudly in my ears.

"Okay. Be safe." Laynie made to exit the room, but I grabbed the top of her arm.

"Did you not hear what I said?" I didn't even recognize my own tone as I yelled. "My Grandmother is missing! The police found blood at the scene."

Lanie turned her concerned eyes stared into mine for a brief second. The next, a mask of indifference pulled down in its place.

"That sucks, Faelan. I'm sorry that you're going through this." She turned again to the door, stopping but not turning around. "Remember, I probably won't be here tonight."

I couldn't believe that that was all she had to say to me. Where was the comforting best friend I'd come to count on? She took another step into the hallway.

"Where are you going?" She didn't stop.

Betrayal gripped at my heart. I'd come to think of Alayna as family.

The red heat of anger burned through me and my pulse raced with anxiety. "Stay here!"

Again, the tone that came out of my own mouth rang out hollow. Like a double sounding echo.

"I need you, Lanie."

She stopped in her tracks. Turning slowly to face me with her head hung, she sighed.

"What would you have me do, Fifi?"

The nickname was one that I relished, but only from my Grams. Whenever Lanie used it, it was to annoy me. And it worked.

"I don't know what is going on with you, but I need my best friend right now."

"I know." Coming back in, her arm wrapped around my shoulder and the half hug did its job. "I would go with you if I could, but I can't." She went on before I could interrupt. "I can't tell you where I am going or what I am doing. I want to, but I can't. Can you please just let me go do what I need to do so that I can get back and be there for you?"

Finally hugging her back, some of the tension lifted.

"Go on. Get out of here. Be safe, whatever you're doing."

Her lips turned up at the corners, but the smile didn't reach her eyes. With a quick squeeze of my hand before leaving, my muscles relaxed a bit.

My friend cared. She was just otherwise obligated at the moment. I could live with that.

Getting dressed and grabbing my red hooded shawl that Grams had given me last year on my 25th birthday, I headed out the door.

Chapter Three

Faelan

With wandering thoughts, I strolled through the entrance of the Lupian Forest. My red hooded shawl covered my head and shoulders.

It was usually welcoming in its warmth whenever I walked the dirt road trail. Today it felt stuffy and hot, though the temperature was hardly above fifty degrees.

Traveling to Grams cottage had always brought me feelings of peace and a sense of belonging but now, my perception was slightly askew.

The forest had a nuance of darkness attached to the atmosphere knowing Gram's disappeared from its depths.

The trees were silent. The normal sounds of leaves ruffling in the wind were muted. No noise of animals scurrying in the underbrush reached my ears. No birds chirping. No crickets rubbing their songs into existence.

The forest was in mourning.

My steps faltered with that realization.

As her cottage came into view, I could see a lantern lit next to the sheer curtained window. *That's Odd.*

There were a lot of footprints around the front door. The police either didn't secure the crime scene properly or they simply didn't care enough to not track mud into the house.

The local sheriff's office in this town knew of all the rumors circulating about these woods.

They'd had an unspoken arrangement with Grams. Not asking many questions allowed them to sleep more soundly at night.

As I approached the entryway looking for the spare key, the door pushed open.

Not only did they not lock up when they'd exited, they'd left the cottage open to any woodland critters that might wander in.

I didn't know if I believed all the tales my grandmother spun throughout my childhood.

Stories were told to me every night before bed when spending time here in my youth.

Regret colored my thoughts as I remembered the last time Grams had called.

She'd wanted me to visit so that we could talk about the future and what path I might want to follow. Life got in the way and days turned into weeks.

Looking back, Grams did seem a bit distraught. That recollection stung my eyes.

A crash sounded in the front room and just before calling out to see if someone might be there, I heard a gruff voice swore. "Fuck."

Creeping in to take a peek, I tried to be extra quiet.

The male was half hidden in shadows, but his huge frame dominated the whole space around him.

The room was in disarray. Drawers opened, emptied of their contents. The coffee table was smashed to splinters. There was blood on the floor next to a fallen vase.

I couldn't see what he bent down to pick up from just under the front of the couch, but it must not have been that important as he answered his phone.

"There's nothing here to go on," he growled out. "We're no closer than we were a few days ago and the Blood moon is only a few weeks away. If I can't find Inara, they'll have to proceed without her."

After a long minute of conversation on the other end of the line, he hung up with a huff. "Useless scabs."

I had no idea who or what he meant by that.

Letting out a breath that I hadn't realized I'd been holding, the air in the room felt charged.

A split second later, the beastly brute had me dangling by the shawl I wore.

A single scream left my lungs before a strong forearm pressed against my windpipe. Stars dotted my eyes as I struggled for air.

"What are you doing here?" he demanded. The eyes of a predator stared me in the face.

I'd always been unusually strong and scrappy, but the surprise of the attack left little room for any defensive tactic.

How was I supposed to fight back against this behemoth block of muscle holding me hostage? *Think.*

Just when I'd about given into the darkness threatening to pull me under, a man with an axe in hand, came crashing into the room.

"I suggest you put her down," he said. "Now!"

Muscle man dropped me without so much as a glance in my direction, taking a step towards the newcomer in the same motion.

"I wouldn't do that if I were you," the axe wielder said. "It could get very messy." His smirk promised as much.

As the intruder took a step back, light from the lantern cast his face in stark relief.

The hair on his head was as dark as a moonless night. Scruff covered his chin and added to his rugged look. Handsome was an understatement.

If I'd happened upon this guy while out at a bar, I'd have made it my mission to feel that facial hair, up close and personal.

As it were, however, I didn't meet him on a night out. I'd come across him tossing my grandmother's house.

The axe man returned his weapon to his hip holster and offered a hand to help me up. I only took it because I didn't want to be at the feet of these testosterone driven males any longer than necessary.

His silver blonde hair glimmered in the moonlight.

"You'd best be on your way, Wylder." Keeping one hand on mine, he kept the other firmly gripped on the handle of his axe. "We wouldn't want any accidents to happen, would we?"

Chocolate gold eyes bore a hole into me. Moving backwards towards the rear entrance of the house, regret radiated off of him, but his eyes never left mine as he spoke.

"This isn't over, Loxias."

They know each other. *Interesting.*

Before turning to leave, a growl rumbled from the depths of Wylder's chest. A low, throaty sound that I felt deep within.

Warmth traveled the length of my body and gathered low in my belly. *What the hell?*

With jumbled thoughts, I turned to thank my savior. He was staring down at me, and his expression gave me pause.

This male, Loxias, was painfully handsome too. The cut of his jaw, the arch of his brow, the bow of his lips. *Get a grip, Faelan.*

Nothing that I'd wanted to say left my mouth.

The curl of his lips lit up his features, twinkling in his eyes.

He must have realized why I hadn't spoken. He knew he was good looking and understood how it affected people.

Just great, I thought, but what I said was, "Thank you for chasing him away."

Chapter Four

Wylder

Walking out that door had been a lot harder than it should have been.

The look in the girl's eyes was one of surprise.

I could have sworn there was a bit of longing in them too.

While tossing the house for the ritual stone, I'd let my guard down. A lot could be said for someone being stealthy enough to best me.

An overreaction was an understatement. It felt wrong from the minute I'd lifted her off the floor.

The fact that the huntsman barged in was a bombshell I still couldn't figure out.

Loxias shouldn't have been there.

Him showing up at that exact time, threatening me or the girl, was definitely a shocker. It had question after question bouncing through my head.

Did he play a part in Inara's disappearance? Was he after the stone? *Shit.*

The girl had a quality about her. The resemblance to her grandmother was uncanny.

Any other time, I might have made time to find out why she appealed to me so much... but now wasn't that time.

I had my own mission. The Blood moon was approaching quickly.

If the ritual stone wasn't found before then, fighting for the spot of leader would be a free for all.

That was something that needed to be avoided at all costs.

With all of the things that go bump in the night running around the Lupian Forest, the ritual to keep them in check was more important than ever.

Though, if Inara fled and was in hiding, I needed to find her first. I owed her a life debt. *Double Shit.*

Being alone for the last several decades made for an interesting life, but it was not the way I would choose to live out my remaining days. Loneliness does get the better of me sometimes.

I've been craving purpose, and I needed responsibilities to thrive.

Inara had given me a sliver of hope to cling to. When she'd found me beaten bloody, and near death, she saved my life.

If there was one thing that could be counted on, it was that a life debt was binding. It was old magics. And magics demanded to be fulfilled above all else.

Ugh. With that thought, my objective shifted, and I knew what must be done.

Doing it would cost me, but it was painfully clear what my new mission would have to be.

The magics pulled the strings. I was just their puppet.

Chapter Five

Faelan

"**N**o problem at all." The huntsman flashed a charming smile, and my legs went weak.

Swooning, really?

"How did you happen upon this cottage?" he asked in his husky voice.

That should have been my line. What was this god of a man doing this far into the Lupian Forest? And with an axe?

Noting his fine threaded attire, it made no sense to think he was simply on a hike.

The overcoat he wore was deep crimson, nearly black, giving the illusion of dried blood. The Givenchy style boots definitely didn't belong in the woods. He wore them as if they were simply utilitarian, an afterthought to his outfit.

I had the sneaky suspicion he didn't just "<u>happened upon the scene</u>."

There was some undercurrent to the way he and Wylder spoke. A conversation that was said in what they didn't say.

"This is my Grams house." Looking down at the ransacked living area, I sighed. "She's missing. I wanted to come to see if there was any way that I might find clues as to what happened to her."

Glancing around the room, he took in every detail. I didn't like it. The scene was not for prying eyes or curious spectators.

Gesturing him towards the kitchen, he followed my lead.

A cup of tea was what Grams offered whenever a "<u>lull in life</u>" presented itself.

Her cabinets were full of various homemade teas in colorful jars. Each had its own label, telling what they did. There was one for sleep. One for calmness. One for health and one for invigoration.

And behind those were some that I'd never asked to sample. One of them was for truth. One for immobilizing. And one that had simply been labeled **The Long Sleep**.

Rumors and whispers had always floated around about our family.

The thought they may not be rumors after all entered my mind. *Was Grams really a Witch?*

The thought was surprisingly... intriguing. I'd always said that I believed her stories. In reality, however, what I meant was that I Wanted to believe Gram's fables.

She'd spun masterful spiderwebs of folklore. Fairytale creatures played a dominant role in every weave of one of her colorful tales.

When werewolves, witches, or fae were the focus of her story, Grams' tone would become more serious.

It didn't matter if it was a tale of intrigue or a fun & cozy short story. She'd focus more, conveying a sense of imparting wisdom as I looked back on it. *Well, damn.*

"How do you take your tea?" I asked Loxias as nonchalantly as possible.

To hide the bitter undertones of the Truth tea, I hoped he took two lumps of sugar or, at least, a bit of honey.

"I like my tea like I like my women." The side of his mouth drew up, eyes twinkling. "Bold and tenebrous." *Was he serious?*

His eyes dimmed with the incredulity of my reaction. "Straight tea... Miss?'"

"Faelan. Faelan Callileach." Holding out his hand to me, Loxias kissed my knuckles.

Sexy Weirdo. My face heated. Blushing always brought the pink to my cheeks rather easily.

"Charmed to meet you, Miss Callileach. Even if the circumstances are not ideal." A full lipped smile that reached all the way to his eyes and I couldn't help but to grin back.

Bringing him over his tea and a few biscuits I'd found in the cupboard, the tension eased between us as I took a sip of mine first.

Loxias's bottom lip jutted out in a pout when he tasted the tea, my first instinct was to apologize.

The tongue between my teeth itched to do just that, but Grams had always warned me never to say "thank you" or "sorry" to a being unless you knew for certain that they were human.

If you happened upon a fae, they would consider those phrases a tantamount to a debt and no one ever wanted to be indebted to those tricksters.

Whether I believed all her stories or not, I was hardwired to uphold all those superstitions.

"You never said... What were you doing this far out in the woods?" The words casually rolled off of my tongue.

I was hinging all of my hope on them not giving away my desire to know the full story behind this axe wielding, man god. *Luna, help me.*

"Ah," he hesitated. "Right to the point, I see."

What the hell point is he talking about?

I took a deep breath, refusing to have a panic attack in front of this handsome stranger sitting at my missing grandmother's table.

Not giving an inch, lips pressed together tightly, I waited for him to continue.

The sound of his fingers drumming the table was driving me nuts. Even that small sip of tea should have kicked in by now. *Out with it already.*

His smile slipped ever so slightly as he fought against the tea. Clearly, he was hiding something.

"Well," he said. "Miss Callileach, is it? Not Lupa-Callileach?" *How did he know that?*

I kept my mouth shut, waiting for him to press on in my silence.

"I came to acquire something from Inara, but seeing as she was not here, I left."

He brought the mug to his lips again and paused. Thinking better of it, he set the cup down and reached for a biscuit instead.

"I wasn't that far away when I heard a woman's scream." Inclining his chin towards me, he bit the tip of the biscuit and chewed slowly.

I stood and went to the sink to rinse out my mug.

Hearing his cup clatter to the floor behind me, not bothering to turn around, I spoke over my shoulder.

"Those biscuits pack more of a punch than I remembered," I mused.

Walking over and bending down to look him in his large, wide eyes, I continued.

"Let me get this straight, Loxias... You came here looking for something from my, now missing, grandmother. Saw the disarray of her house and presumably the blood and shattered glass. Noted she wasn't home. And then simply left, only to be near enough to assist me when I screamed?"

Shaking my head, my eyes roamed the kitchen until I found what I was looking for. The double thick butcher's twine.

His eye's remained open but the biscuit immobilized the rest of him, including his cursed tongue. *No talking for you, Mister Fabulous.*

Retrieving the twine, I set to tying all four of his limbs to the table legs.

He was too big for me to try and position upright in one of the chairs.

"Your shoes are too expensive for a quick trip to the inner depths of the forest. Did you think THAT would go unnoticed?" I turned up my nose, mocking my offense. "I had wondered what drew the Sherriff's department out this way in the first place."

Pausing momentarily, I rummaged through what thoughts bouncing around my cluttered brain.

"After the initial shock of the situation wore off, I went over that conversation you had with the beastly male fishing around the house."

His eyes closed in a slow blink and then widened when I was in front of him again as they opened.

I didn't know what his deal was, but I had this itching sense of wrongness under my skin that wouldn't let up.

"It was you who called the authorities, wasn't it?"

Why though? After wracking my brain for another moment, I leaned down to study his face.

"Who, exactly, is Wylder?"

The feeling must have started coming back to his limbs already. His fingers and feet began moving in small wiggles, trying to get free.

My time for questioning had run out too quickly.

"I'll let you in on a little secret before I go," I said, placing a quick peck on his cheek. "I read... a lot. I'm going to figure out what's going on. And when I do, if you've played some nefarious part in this, you'd better hope that my grandmother's genes of **turn the other cheek** were passed down in our bloodline."

The feeling must have started coming back to his face now too. With a grin, he slurred his words as he tried to speak. "Yoouurr bloodline is sooiilled."

Not having any idea what he was talking about, I sat up, needing to put distance between us as quickly as possible.

"At least I'm not some pompous ass parading as a hero."

With that, I patted his head. tightened my shawl and threw up my hood.

Running out the door into the cool air, I didn't look back.

Chapter Six

Faelan

Fleeing the cottage into the darkening woods might have been a mistake but I didn't trust Loxias.

The way he had said, "it could get very messy" played over and over in my mind.

In the moment, I'd thought that the threat was directed towards the massive male, Wylder. Now looking at it, he'd backed away the second harm was inferred.

Surely, he could have taken Loxias. *Right?*

Was the threat about me? None of this hindsight gave me any clear direction to go in.

I needed to regroup and think it through. Maybe if I bounced some ideas off of Lanie, she could figure it out.

Getting back out of the forest, unscathed, was my biggest issue at the moment.

Sticking to the main dirt road would be a mistake. Who knew how long it'd be until Loxias was fully mobile? Running the trails was still a bit risky.

I'd venture to say the only way out was through... through the brushwood, that is. *Oh, goody me.*

The sun was just starting to go down. The dark never bothered me, but the creatures I feared called these woods home were a different matter.

Movement from my left had me frozen in place.

Crouching down in the underbrush, golden eyes stared back from between the thickets. The bushes moved as the creature shot forward.

"Nixie! ... You nearly gave me a heart attack."

Grams' cat slinked closer and came to rest at my feet.

I didn't know the last time she'd been fed but Nixie was a mouser. She could probably fend for herself.

Bending down to pet the precocious feline, I scratched behind her ears. She purred and wound around my legs.

"I'm sorry, Nix. I don't know when she'll be back."

I'd always felt connected to animals. They didn't speak to me, but I felt as if every non-verbal communication were exactly what they would have said if they could, whenever I interacted with them.

Nixie was no different.

Standing to get as far away from Mister Hot Mess as possible, Nixie followed. "I'm not coming back for a bit. Are you sure you want to come?"

The frisky feline twisted her head to look at the cottage one more time and then trotted towards the unmarked trail that led to the east, away from the way she'd originally come.

An hour of walking turned into two. The cold crept in with every degree that fell as evening settled around me.

My shawl kept snagging on limbs and bushes as the hike dragged on.

The light of the moon was bright enough to see by, though it was a good two weeks from full.

Crickets chirped from the bushes as the owls announced their awakening. Nixie flittered in and out of the trail chasing moths.

It was peaceful and yet eerie this far into the forest. *Am I going the right way?*

A change in the atmosphere and sudden silence halted me in my steps. The air was still, like right before it snowed. October was early for it, but not unheard of.

Gloves would have been nice. I hadn't thought past going to Grams. Being out this late, after the sun went down, had never entered my mind.

"Nixie?" I whispered. "Where did you go?" *Damn cat!* She could have at least given me some kind of warning before she darted off.

Squinting down the darkening trail, I had the hair-raising feeling that I was being watched.

Trying not to panic, I resumed hiking in the direction of the lake.

A twig snapped, freezing me in place once again. "Who's there? Show yourself."

The squeak in my voice gave away my nerves.

A figure came out of the darkness from behind a tree just off the path. The sheer size of this male was massive.

Thoughts of running were quickly squashed when he made his way in front of me in less than three strides, raising his hands in surrender as a patch of light from the moon shone across his face.

"Don't hurt me," he said. The breath that I'd been holding pushed out in a huff. "I come in peace, Red."

My mind raced as I processed the fact that the man who'd held me off the floor by the throat was standing in front of me asking for mercy with a grin on his face.

"Wylder?" Watching as he perched his one eyebrow higher, I took a casual step back.

"You know me then?" His feet shuffled, ruffling the fallen leaves. "Did Inara mention me?"

Before I could speak, Nixie bounded from the bushes, sauntering right to him.

The sight of her helped pull some the tension from my limbs.

"Hello, Beasty." With a gentleness I didn't know someone of his size could master, he picked the cat up like they were old friends.

She purred loudly and rubbed her chin all over the scruff on his face.

Remembering my earlier thoughts about that scruff, I blushed. *Damn, kitty. Ya beat me to it.*

That thought startled a laugh from me before I could reign it in.

"She seems to know you," was all I managed to say.

"Nixie?" His voice was deep with a velvety gruffness to it. "Yeah, she and I go way back."

"Why were you..." "I'm sorry about..." We both started at the same time.

"You go first," I said.

The big lug looked bashful. And that was a feat to see on those rugged features.

"I'm sorry for scaring you earlier."

It sounded sincere but it irritated me for no good reason. Now my former ire raised its nasty head.

"What, exactly, are you sorry for?" My hands planted on my hips without giving them permission to do so. "Are you sorry for breaking into my Grams house?" Taking an absentminded step towards him, I continued. "Or are you sorry for scaring the crap out of me out here the dark forest?"

Uh-oh. I was on a roll but couldn't stop myself.

"Or perhaps you're apologizing for manhandling me after rummaging through my childhood sanctuary?"

Rubbing the spot where his forearm left its mark on my neck, I stepped forward.

He smirked. He actually smirked. The tiny lines around his eyes and mouth crinkled with delight.

"All of it, I guess." That deep voice did things it shouldn't to me.

If I had to put a name to the expression he wore, it'd have to be discomforted.

I was close enough to see the smile in his eyes. Smell the manly scent of him. I had thought that he was huge before, but up this close... *Oh, for crying out loud. Luna, save me.*

"Well, isn't that just great." It wasn't a question.

Annoyed with myself for allowing my mind to wander to places they definitely shouldn't be while out here, alone with this stranger, I through my hands in the air.

Walking away from him, I called, "Come on, Nixie," over my shoulder.

Glancing back at them to see if she was following, the cat hung her head.

She looked affronted, perhaps realizing that she had been acting like a traitor.

Jumping down, she threw a backwards mew towards Wylder.

"Wait, where are you headed, Red?" He took a few steps in my direction but didn't allow himself to catch up to me.

Why does he keep calling me that? I was ditching the coat at the first chance I had to get a different one.

"Not that it's any of your business, but I am on the hunt for what happened to my Grams."

That brought him up short. Grabbing my arm and spinning me around, I startled at his touch.

Hey. Hey. Hey. No hands Mister tall, dark, and devastating.

"You should let the authorities handle it. These woods are no joke, sweetpea." There was an edge to his tone giving me the impression he knew more than he was saying.

"No." I didn't elaborate or give him anymore to decipher.

Letting go of my arm and staring at me like I'd grown two new heads, his mouth gaped open.

"No?" he asked. I almost smirked but held back. "May I ask what a small, young woman like you thinks she can do all alone in these woods?"

Small? Was he referring to my size or did he think I was some fragile female in need of protecting?

Anyone would be small compared to this behemoth.

Annoyance washed over my tongue. I knew where my smart mouth was leading but couldn't stop it.

"Listen up, Buttercup!" *Oh boy*.

My finger was pressing on his chest now of its own accord.

"I may be small compared to your ogre size." *Great Luna, here we go.* "But good things come in small packages! And if I were you, I'd be..."

"Would you like to?' he interrupted my tangent.

"What?" The sides of his mouth turned up in a playful smirk, but a lustful spark danced in his eyes.

"Would you like to?" he repeated.

Taking my hand off of his chest, I took a step back to look him in his stupidly handsome face.

"Would I like to what?" The annoyance in my tone turned to mild uncertainty.

"Cum." The casual way he said it was like he was asking about the weather. *Is he seriously asking me that*?

Before I could think of anything to say, crunching leaves and the snapping of twigs drew our attention to the woods.

Wylder discreetly stepped in front of me, blocking me from whatever was coming towards us. *Oooh, manly*.

Five silhouettes enter the trail just ahead of us. They were fanning out in a U shape. *What in the formation?*

"Give us the girl, Wylder, and you can be on your way."

Chapter Seven

Wylder

id these asshats actually think I would do that? *Well, that's insulting.*

"She's free to do whatever she wants, Reed."

Faelan took a step closer to me. Her scent of wild berries, cardamon, and cloves was distracting. *Focus, damn it!*

All five of them inched closer. The growl that escaped my throat did so without thought.

"We just need to talk to her," Reed said. " "Inara's bloodline must be acknowledged."

Faelan took another step towards my side. Chancing a glance in her direction, the perplexed look she wore made me huff a laugh.

It wasn't until I looked down at her hand clutching tightly to my arm that I realized how frightened she was. And that thought set my hairs on end.

"What do you know about my grandmother?" The spunk she had was all Inara.

The warmth from that small point of contact was distracting.

All of my instincts screamed at me to throw her over my shoulder and run her far away from this.

I couldn't be sure of the circumstances around Inara's disappearance, but I'd just sworn to protect this wee one to honor my life debt.

Now wasn't the time to let pack politics get in the way.

"Your grandmother was our Alpha. We need to get to the bottom of this quickly, " Reed pushed on. "The Blood moon is only a few weeks away. We Must have a new leader in place before the end of the Lunar cycle."

"What, in the actual fuck, are you talking about?" she let fly like a sailor. *Good Luna. This girl.*

Her nails biting into my upper arm where she clung to me.

Her face said it all. Inara may have told her the lore but never filled her in on the details of her heritage.

She had no idea of the shit storm that was placed at her doorstep when Inara went missing.

"How about you back off, Reed?" I barked out. "Clearly, she has no clue what you're saying. Look at her."

"Surely, Inara has given her the rites. I can smell it in her blood," Zito said.

He was third in command of Inara's pack after Reed.

Speaking directly to Faelan, he calmly asked, "Did your grandmother not tell you anything?"

"I don't know who you all are or what you have to do with my Grams, but if someone doesn't start filling me in fast, I'm going to lose my shit!" Her chin held high, anger leaked through her voice.

She might have been scared but she wasn't backing down.

I could feel how fast her heart was racing through the fingertips and palm dug into my skin.

Reed growled and both he and I automatically went into a semi crouch.

Reed's Beta side felt the challenge ringing through Red's blood. I was barely resisting it myself as I remained primed to counter the attack if needed.

The rest of the pack whimpered in response.

"What the hell? What is wrong with you all?" she said.

Straightening up, Reed and Zito stepped forward, followed by Piper and Blaze.

Inara's last pack member still stood in the shadows, and I couldn't figure out why.

Finally stepping into the light of the trail, Alayna let the hood of her jacket fall.

"Lanie?" Faelan started forward but I held her arm as she tried to pass.

She didn't brush me aside as she stared at the female.

"Lanie, what are you doing here? Who are these people?"

I knew that look. The one that Alayna wore now.

Whenever I was at Inara's and any of them would happen in, it was the look of mistrust. The look of disgust.

Pack members didn't take kindly to Sigma's. They felt the pull of the pack and couldn't understand the lone wolf lifestyle.

And what they didn't understand, they feared.

"What are You doing with Him?" Alayna thrust her finger in my direction.

I couldn't contain the smirk that came to my face, but I kept quiet. The pack didn't care for me, but Inara was a true friend.

"I was where I told you I'd be going today. I found him rummaging around Grams' cottage." The blush on her cheeks sent my insides squirming. *Get a hold of yourself, damn it.*

It was Reed who now looked murderous. I knew what it must seem like to them all.

I was in Inara's house, rummaging through her stuff. She was missing and so was the ritual stone.

I couldn't blame them. I would have been suspicious too.

"What were you doing at Inara's, Wylder? Where's the stone?" Zito asked without accusation.

I'd always liked him. There was never any ill will or contempt in his tone. Simple and direct. It was refreshing.

"I was looking for clues to Inara's disappearance... and the stone."

That did it. The hackles of every member of the pack were up.

Of course, it was Blaze who lunged.

Reed caught him around his middle and let off a deep growl in his face that had him lowering his head and averting his eyes.

I couldn't blame the pup. He was young, as far as Lycan go; maybe twenty-three or twenty-four Luna cycles.

Werewolves didn't age like normal humans. They only aged during the daylight hours. And the less daylight in their area of the world, the younger a werewolf could stay for longer.

It allowed them to maintain their youthful years and live a lot longer.

It didn't help that Blaze's personality leaned towards being a dick.

In the space from one breath to another, Faelan had dropped her fear. It was replaced by something I'd seen on Inara's face time and time again. Pure domination.

"I am going to repeat myself just this once," she said.

I heard the double ring in her tone and knew that everyone else did too. She probably had no idea that she was doing it.

"Who are you all? Where is my grandmother? And what the fuck are you talking about 'rites, stones, & smelling my blood'? Nobody so much as move but answer me now!"

Heat rose up inside of me. Pride? Lust? I couldn't tell. Maybe there wasn't even a difference.

I was a lone wolf for a reason, but the draw to her called to me from deep within.

They would have no choice but to answer her questions. The Alpha in her blood dripped in every word.

Crossing my arms over my chest, I waited for the show to begin. This was about to get interesting.

Alayna spoke first. She didn't approach yet. Faelan still stood with her back straight. Chin high.

Straight and by my side. *Interesting.*

Raising both hands in surrender in front of her, Alayna finally stepped just out of arm's length after Red gave her a small nod to go ahead.

"We are your Grams' pack, Fifi," she said.

The way Faelan's nose scrunched up made my heart skip a beat. *Luna, have mercy.*

"Inara was our Alpha. She was a witch... but she was also a werewolf."

Chapter Eight

Faelan

The burst of laugher that left my body was nothing short of hysterics.

Lanie and these others thought Grams was a witch and a werewolf leader. *Seriously?*

The male in front spoke next but the panic attack threatening to come on shut out his words.

Wylder reached over and laying a hand on the small of my back. It calmed down the jitterbugs skittering over my body instantly.

How the hell did he do that?

Focusing in on what Reed was saying now, I tried to absorb the reality around me.

Grams was missing. She was half witch, half werewolf. And she was the leader of this pack.

Reality was far from what I would call this. *Where are the men in the white coats when you need them?*

"So, why are you here with Wylder?" Zito asked this time. I appreciated his lighter tone. "Do you think he was involved in…"

The question hung there, unfinished as his eyes landed on Wylder's face.

"I did. He was in her house, looking around, and then had me held up by the throat against the wall."

The growls of all five pack members loudly broke the silent night around us.

Inching closer to Wylder, he crouched in a defensive posture at my side. *Why do I care? Geesh.*

"Stop." It surprised me when they all immediately straightened out of their crouches.

Glancing over at the hunk of man meat beside me, I noticed only he remained ready to fight.

"Like I was saying… I did, until that arrogant huntsman came in and Wylder left without incident."

A thought occurred to me… had he been waiting there to follow me down the trail? *Well, damn.*

"Wait, Loxias was there?" Reed directed his question to Wylder who was studiously studying the trees to our left.

His finger slyly came to his lips and then motioned to his ear.

Zito and Piper headed off on that course after a slight nod from Reed. He headed in the same direction but from a different path.

From my other side, Alayna and Blaze positioned themselves on my flanks.

Wylder stepped up behind me and his hand found the small of my back again.

A shuttering thrill went through my system as the charged atmosphere had my invisible hackles standing. *By Luna. I really might be part wolf.*

After a few tense minutes, Reed, Zito, and Piper immerged holding a male I didn't recognize by the scruff of the neck.

Thrusting him forward, they pushed him to his feet in front of me.

"Who is this?" Something about him looked familiar but not placeable.

"The other one got away," Reed said. "They work for Loxias." The confusion must have shown on my face because Zito took over explaining from there.

"Loxias isn't a huntsman, not exactly," he said. "He does hunt. The creatures of the Lupian Forest make up the majority of the trophies for him and his family."

He must have sensed my annoyance after I didn't say anything, so he went on.

"Loxias is a Prince. A Prince of Faery. He is something like fifth or sixth in line to the crown. Thus, he doesn't mind getting his hands dirty in the sport of hunting mythical creatures... like witches, werewolves, or even other fae."

Thus? Geesh. How old were these people?

"Oh, sure," I spit out. "We might as well include the Abominable Snowman and Bigfoot while we're being delusional."

Wylder tried to hide his laugh, but I saw it out of the corner of my eye.

"What are you laughing at, Sasquatch? Are you throwing your lot in with these," I thumbed over my shoulder to the pack, "farcically furry fucktards?"

His mouth popped open and then snapped shut. Apparently, he wasn't going to answer. *Traitor*.

It was Lanie who grabbed onto her chesticals and stepped up to the plate.

"Look, Faelan. Your Grams told us that we couldn't divulge any specifics to you." She hung her head. "We're roommates, but it was Inara who put me in your path... to keep an eye on you."

"Is that what we are, Lanie?" I was getting more heated by the minute. "Roommates? I kind of thought we were best friends."

Walking in a circle around the group, I stopped in front of the male still prostrated where I had been standing a few minutes ago. The points of his ears on full display.

I hadn't noticed Loxias' ears. Perhaps he'd hidden them somehow.

"What are you here for? Why did Mister Haughty Hotness send you?" My boldness surprising even me.

Wylder raised an eyebrow. *Stop looking at me like that.*

"We were meant to intercept you." His breathing was labored. "His Highness wishes to speak with you about the witch."

"The Witch, as you put it, is my grandmother. And I bested Luscious Loxias fair and square." Anger threatened to bubble over from my chest.

Wylder huffed. Whether in reference to the nickname I'd given the huntsman or for besting the bloke, I wasn't sure.

"Makes no difference. His Highness wants the heir. He will have the heir."

Wylder's booted foot came down hard on the male's head. Blood and grey matter spattered the front of my pants, not jumping back fast enough.

"No." Wylder said. "He won't." *Hubba hubba... Damn it, focus Faelan.*

That was disturbing. He'd just squashed a guy... faery... whatever, for threatening me.

Why was I always attracted to the bad boys? *Ugh.*

"My sentiments exactly, Sigma." Reed said the word like a slur.

I didn't know what the term meant but Wylder smirked like it was a badge of honor.

"We'll keep you safe, Faelan." Reed said. "Come with us and we will fill in all that we know about your grandmother's heritage: Your heritage."

Taking my hand, Lanie gave me a meek smile. "I am still your friend, Fifi."

A snarl ripped from my throat. The sound surprised me, and I dropped Alayna's hand, stepping back into Blaze.

Strong hands grabbed the tops of my arms and flung me to the side, but I managed to stay standing.

Wylder was in Blaze's face a second later.

"Don't touch her, Pup!" Wylder seethed.

Growls and whimpers ran around the group. Blaze's snarl sounded like a non-verbal string of curse words. Reed yanked Blaze back and took his place.

I was frozen, not daring to move.

Just when I'd thought they would tear each other apart, Nixie came strolling out from the underbrush, wrapping herself in and out of Wylder's legs.

Reed straightened up when the cat hissed at him.

"My bad," he said. He was talking to the damn cat. "Emotions are running high, Wylder. There's no need for posturing."

"I make my own decisions, or have you forgotten *that*, Beta?" Wylder came back to stand at my side after picking Nixie up off the ground and cradling her in his arms.

Alayna reclaimed my attention. "Come with us. We'll help you."

I didn't know if I should go with them, go home, or follow Wylder but I knew I needed protection from the fae prince who was apparently not giving up his hunt for me.

"Can you take Nixie back to the cottage for me?" I asked Wylder.

His eyes tightened but that was the only indication of his dismay.

"Of course. She'll be fed and taken care of, I swear it," he said, making a criss cross over his heart with his free hand. Something else lingered in his expression but I couldn't tell what it was.

"Thank you, Wylder." Turning back to the pack, I said, "Okay. Where are we going? I want to know everything."

Piper spoke for the first time. Her voice was a low, sultry alto that went well with her beautifully feminine features. "This way, Blood Red."

I raised an eyebrow at the name but didn't ask any questions. Not yet. I followed the pack's lead.

After one more glance back at Wylder and the dead fae laying at his feet, I gathered my nerves and went to find answers.

Chapter Nine

Wylder

Letting her leave my sight felt wrong. It went against every instinct screaming in my whole body.

The life debt I owed to Inara was ringing in Red's blood now with Inara gone. Did that mean the witch was dead? *Shit*.

Nixie had been content enough to follow me back down the trail to the cottage. Her black fur was swallowed up in the shadows of the bushes as she wound in and out of sight.

As we approached the house, it looked empty enough. Whatever Faelan had done to Loxias, he was gone now.

The door was still wide open, and the light was left on, but all was quiet.

Nixie purred as she passed me on her way to the kitchen.

Cold tea and a half eaten biscuit laid discarded on the table. Picking it up and giving it a sniff, I smiled.

For all of Red's protesting about not believing in the super-natural, she'd relied on Inara's handmade potions to help her get away. *Smart girl.*

The cat food cans were on the top shelf in the cabinet, but the bag of dry kibble laid curled up closed on the counter. *Strange.* Inara never left Nixie's food out.

Opening the bag and giving it a shake, Beasty jumped onto the counter and bumped my arm, spilling kibble everywhere.

After fetching a broom, I bent down to retrieve the dustpan, and a folded piece of paper caught my eye from just under the edge of the bottom cabinets.

It was completely covered in blood on the outside but as I opened it, not a trace had made it inside. *Not eerie at all, Witch.*

Opening the note, Inara had written it directly to me.

<u>Wylder... If you are reading this, my visions came to pass. I tried to get Faelan to come see me so that we could talk about her heritage, but she'd never managed to make it here.</u>

<u>She will be lost, dear friend. I never intended to call in your debt, but I find that I have no other choice now.</u>

I charge you with her safety. I burden you with her enlightenment. I entrust you with her life.

Three by three

The words are read

The bond created

Three by three

I dub thee

Guardian of the Blood Red Heir

The spell is cast. I know you would do this for me if I could have given you a choice and I hate having to force it upon you.

If you meet her before you find this note, you will have felt a pull towards her already.

The Blood moon ritual is fast approaching, and with me gone, Faelan must use the stone to keep the balance of the Lupian Forest creatures in check.

My Book of Shadows is hidden in plain sight. It is her birthright now. *Damn it, witch*!

You really are the best of us!

Be the Sigma you were meant to be but protect my Alpha heir with your life.

May Luna guide you...

Oh, and feed my cat.

Your friend, Inara.

A stinging zing flashed through my system as the spell spread from the top of my head, down to my feet, and straight back to zap me in the heart.

Grabbing my chest, I collapsed to my knees.

Fuck me. The urge to find Red intensified.

I struggled to my feet, panting like an out of shape marathon runner.

It took a few minutes for the pain to subside. An ache would be a more accurate word than pain.

Making it to the sink, I splashed cool water over my face and the back of my neck before stoppering the bottom and filling the basin with water.

If I was going out to get Faelan, I wanted to make sure Nixie had plenty to drink. Who knew when I'd get back?

"Sorry Beasty, but this will have to do."

After dumping all of the hard kibble into the biggest bowl I could find and popping the top of a cat food can, I headed out the door in the direction of Red's pull.

This was going to get old fast.

I couldn't blame Inara. I even understood, but that didn't mean I appreciated being tied to anyone again.

It almost felt like the same strings that tied pack members together, only stronger. Much stronger.

If I was right, knowing the witch, my life force was now tied to Faelan's.

If I failed, I'd died. *Fucking great.*

Chapter Ten

Faelan

The walk felt never ending.

I wasn't out of shape exactly. I just hadn't had to hike for any extended length of time in quite a while.

Lanie walked behind me a few steps. I don't know if I'd have come with them if she hadn't been a part of this group.

Reed had been on my right and Zito a step behind on my left for most of the trip.

"If you don't mind me asking," Zito said. "What all do you know about Inara?"

Before today, I would have thought that to be an odd question.

Grams was the best person I knew. In many ways, I'd wanted to be like her.

Now, however, I realized that I hadn't known who my grandmother truly was at all.

The thought squeezed my chest. *Damn, Grams. This sucks.*

"She used to tell me fables about all sorts of mythological creatures. I loved her stories, but that's all that I thought they were," I could hear the melancholy coloring my tone. I was sure he could too.

It hurt to know that Grams kept the whole truth hidden.... *but did she, really?*

She had wanted to talk. She'd ask for a visit several times.

"Are you okay?" Zito had been talking to me, but not a word he said had penetrated my thoughts.

"I'm not. I love my grandmother fiercely, but I am realizing that I don't know her at all."

Alayna reached forward and took my hand, giving it a squeeze.

"She loved you, Faelan," she said. "All she ever did was try to protect you."

"Loves!" I snapped. "Not loved. She's still alive. I know it." They all exchanged a look that I didn't miss.

What in the actual hell? What did they all know that I didn't?

I stopped walking, halting them all where they stood.

There would be no more secrets kept from me. Enough of these games.

"What is it that you lot know about her disappearance that I don't?" The group all glanced to Reed but said nothing when he gave the smallest shake of his head. "Well, you can either tell me, or this is where we part ways."

"You're awfully cocky for someone who is in the midst of a pack of werewolves," Blaze snarled. "We don't know you and you don't know us!"

"Blaze," Reed's voice was calm but I could feel the tension coming off of him. He angled his body a slight step in front of me. "Tone," he said.

"No, Reed. He's right." I stood straight and stepped out from behind his shadow. "We don't know each other, but that doesn't mean I should be kept in the dark. If my grandmother was the leader of this pack, "... *Am I really going along with this nonsense? ...* "would she want your silence... or your allegiance?"

Chancing a glance in Lanie's direction, my best friend gave me a slight, barely there, dip of her chin.

"I am of her blood. That has to mean something to the pack, does it not?"

Motioning for them all to continue down the path, Reed stepped to Blaze's side as the males silently stare each other down.

Zito took my elbow to usher me forward, but I pulled out of his grip with a weak smile, and he instantly dropped his hand.

I liked Zito. He was non-assuming, kind, and thought through each action.

Blaze, on the other hand, was brutish, loud, and volatile.

Getting to the bottom of all the secrets Grams kept was what was most important. Only then would I be able to start seeking her out. *The old bitty better be alive.*

The sound of growls getting louder by the minute focused my attention.

Turning just in time, I saw a blur of fur where Blaze had stood a moment ago.

Before I even had time to raise my hands to cover my face, a swish of wind flew past me from out of the copse of trees.

I followed the line of sight to the snarling sounds and bared teeth of two enormous wolves circling each other a few paces in front of me.

Howls tore through the night air from the throats of every person standing around me.

Every instinct of my humanity screamed for me to run away and hide, but there was a stronger part of my subconscious that wouldn't allow it. It gripped my mind like a vice.

A roaring growl ripped its way from my chest and out my mouth in the direction of the two wolves. *Holy shit*!

The smaller, sandy colored wolf coward, whimpering as he straightened from his fighting stance, but the larger black wolf snapped his jaws in his face before striding over to sit at my side.

Strangely, I wasn't afraid. I was in the midst of wolves and not an ounce of fear to be found.

"Go change," Reed said to the sandy colored wolf. "Piper, go with him to get his clothes. Make sure Blaze has his head on right before he returns to the pack."

There was no malice in his tone. It was simply a command.

He turned back to face the wolf at my side. "Are you going to stay in shift or are you going to change so we can talk?

Another bunch of snarls, which sounded a lot like a string of profanities, came tumbling up from the black wolf's throat.

I blinked and before me stood a very naked Wylder. *Oh, dear Luna*. Not a hint of embarrassment or modesty in him.

"You had better get that pup in line before he gets his throat torn out!" he said. "She hasn't even truly known about the supernatural world for a full day and already been challenged!?... by a lessor at that!" *Hubba, hubba big boy.*

I tried to not look at him standing there in all his glory. Tried and failed. *Get it together, Callileach.*

After a few seconds, I found my voice.

"Would somebody please explain to me what in the name of Luna is going on?"

Lanie stepped forward and Wylder growled at her. Slapping his arm before I'd thought it through, his incredulous eyes bore into me, but he didn't chastise me for it.

Alayna spoke softly. "Blaze is the youngest, wolf wise, in our pack." Some understanding was starting to resonate deep in the recesses of my mind. "He loses control the easiest still. And since you aren't exactly at full Alpha aspect yet, he challenged you when he lunged."

A ripple slid down my back, just under my skin. He'd been willing to attack me because he could right now, in theory, challenge my Alpha status.

I didn't even want it, but his teeth and claws would have killed me anyway.

"Why the fuck didn't you put him in his place, Reed?" Wylder demanded.

I chanced a glance down at his rather endowed package. A small smirk turned up at the corner of his lips that I knew was meant for me. *Well, damn.*

Reed brushed a stray piece of reddish-brown hair from his face.

"I don't see how pack business is any concern to you, but Blaze had every right to challenge her." Wylder snarled louder this time. "If he'd have won, I would have challenged him in turn."

Silence followed. Wylder's face lit up with dark amusement a moment later.

"Inara had you make a Place Keeper oath, didn't she?" His expression remained guarded. "You can't directly challenge Faelan?"

"Not until after the Blood Moon Ritual," he glanced at me. "Then I have every right to take over the pack."

This had to be what Grams wanted to talk to me about, why she wanted me to visit so badly. This guy wanted to fight me for my birthright. One that I hadn't even known existed.

"Were you ever even taking me somewhere to school me on what I don't know about all of this?" Bile rose in the back of my throat, and I watched Lanie's eyes widen.

"Reed?" she prodded. "Answer her. Were you going to tell her everything or not?"

Zito's chin dropped. "Honestly, Reed. Did you think we'd let you bypass Inara's wishes?"

The air felt heavy. It had already been a long day and now, where was I left to turn?

A thought rebounded in my mind over and over again. *He came back for me*.

A tug behind my ribcage startled me. It wasn't metaphorical. There was an actual tug in my heart. *What the fuck was that*?

"Nice, Reed," Wylder said.

He walked towards the tree line, and I panicked for a moment, thinking he was going to leave me.

Reaching into the brush and grabbing a knapsack, he began tugging on a pair of grey sweatpants. They did nothing to hide his manhood.

"You are definitely the asshole Inara always thought you to be," he said.

Wylder was quickly becoming one of my favorite people.

"Inara wasn't as smart as she thought she was. Otherwise, she'd have foreseen the ways around her Place Keeper Oath pact." Reed's insolence grated on my nerves.

I lunged for him, but Wylder caught me around the waist in midair.

"Easy," he whispered a breath away from my ear so only I could hear. "His time will come, Red."

"Let's go." Reed headed for the trees without waiting to see if Zito or Alayna followed.

After another few awkward moments, Zito hung his head and went into the woods after him.

Lanie gave me one of the most heartbreaking looks I'd ever seen from my best friend and then ran into the forest without a backward glance.

I couldn't believe she'd left me. *Seriously?*

"Don't take it personally," Wylder said. "The pack mind isn't something easily detached from."

His bare chest melted the sparce snowflakes as they fell on his muscular form.

"You came back for me," was all I managed to say.

Chapter Eleven

Wylder

"What?" Standing there looking at Red, I'd forgotten everything else. "I mean, yeah." *Get a hold of yourself.*

Faelan shifted her backpack from one shoulder to the other before looking up to meet my eyes. Her long lashes batted once. *Oh, Fuck!*

"Why would you do that? You don't even know me." Her voice had taken on a sultry tone.

The fuzzy vibration in my brain blocked out my good senses.

"Look," I made up my mind right there to give her at least half the truth. "I owe Inara a life debt and I plan to see it through."

Her expression was crestfallen. That's the only way I could describe it. *Real nice, asshole.*

Picking up my knapsack, I started back down the trail. I didn't turn but I walked slowly until I could make certain she was following me.

"So, helping me is the debt? Nothing personal, right?" *This girl.*

"I would have helped Inara if she'd asked me to, regardless. She and I were good friends." I didn't tack on that from the first time I saw her, I couldn't keep away.

Noticing the sound of her footsteps stop, I swiveled to see why.

"Are," her words came out in a huff of frustration.

"I'm sorry, what?"

"You **Are** friends, present tense. I refuse to believe that she's dead." Her tight eyes rimmed with unshed tears.

Geesh, I really am a callous prick. Wondering how I was still this much of an asshole after all of these years, the breath pushed from me in a long blast of self frustration.

"Right. I didn't mean anything by it." Stepping back, I put my hand on her chin, forcing her to look up at me. "I miss her, and I am not giving up on her either."

Staring her down, heat built between us in the moment. Her lips were only inches away. The moisture in her eyes became raw emotion. *Well, shit.*

Dropping my hand, I stepped out of her personal space before I did something Inara would castrate me for.

"We'd better get going. There are a lot of things in these woods that are looking for their next meal."

Not missing her desire scenting the air, I tried to keep a level head.

She was my charge. It wouldn't be wise to get involved. *Don't do it, don't do it, don't do it.*

Walking at a snail's pace to match hers, it'd already been over an hour since time we'd spoken a word.

"Did you and my Grams have a relationship?" Her first question went off like a bomb, making my feet falter.

"What kind of relationship are you asking about?" I said, realizing where her mind had been.

Faelan gave me the side eye as she walked past without stopping.

I caught up to her, grabbing her by the elbow to halt our progress.

"If you're asking whether or not we were involved sexually," her nose crinkled in disgust. *Aww, Cute.* "...then, no."

It had never been a thought with Inara. She'd loved her husband. When he'd disappeared, she'd never had any interest in anyone else as far as I knew.

"She saved my life, and I owed her for it, but somewhere along the line, I found myself coming to rely on her for wisdom and friendship." Saying it out loud felt odd. "I found myself seeking her out for guidance." *Geesh, shut up now.* "And eventually she became family."

That look. *Gods, help me.*

It was Inara's contemplative look. The one she had whenever I'd voice a quandary. It was her ruminating look.

"Okay," she said after a few minutes.

One word. She didn't ramble on. "Okay what?"

"Okay. I can live with that." I let her go with an incredulous eyebrow raised. "I don't think that I could have handled it if you'd been bumping uglies with Grams."

"Geesh, Red. That's a visual I could have lived my whole life without." *Yup.* Gonna have to burn my eyes out.

She had the audacity to smile up at me.

"That's the image I've been walking around with for the last hour, so, you're welcome." *This girl's gonna end me.*

Inara would owe me after all this was over. I was sure of it.

We were almost to my place on the far end of the forest when a glint of light caught my eye.

With a quick jerk to her wrist, her mouth opened to protest but I brought a finger to my lips, shushing her.

Reaching for the dagger at my belt, I noticed another two shadowed figures from the opposite side and one closer to where we stood.

"Show yourselves!" Calculating the odds of defeating three foes while protecting Red weren't the best.

My cabin was only a hundred yards away. We could make a run for it, but she was slow.

I could throw her over my shoulder and make a dash for it, but I didn't know who else was stalking us.

The wind shifted and the scent hit my nose full on. *Fae.*

Loxias stepped from the vegetable patch growing in the only spot between the trees. Two of his lackies came into view from the other side of the trail.

All of them carrying crossbows. Wolfsbane and fae venom tipped, no doubt.

"What do you want, Prince?" I could smell Red's fear, and it tugged on that bond, reminding me to keep her safe at all costs.

"I thought she might come your way, Sigma. Pity she didn't have better taste."

Barely able to hear over my own growl, I assumed a defensive stance, crouching slightly and blocking her from view as best I could.

Two more were in the trees still out of sight. *Freaking fabulous.*

The two fae on the trail darted forward and I exploded in a fit of fur and teeth. They tried getting past me to lay hands on Red as she stood there motionless.

Turning my attention back to the fight, a net swung towards me, and I ducked just in time.

One of them jumped onto my back, fangs biting deep into the soft spot between my shoulder and ear.

Another fae shooting me with a bolt to the shoulder, just missing my heart.

Snarls ripped from my throat as the other one tried again to swing the net over my body but with a quick swish of my strong tail, the fae guard went flying into the underbrush.

"Come with me, Faelan." I watched in horror as Loxias stepped forward to take her hand.

Blood trickled from the vein that had been bitten in my neck and my rage lit up like a bonfire at the sight.

Throwing the fae from my back, I stomped mercilessly on her neck with my gigantic paws. Grabbing the other one in my massive jaws, I crushed his head to splinters.

Loxias usually hunted with his two best friends but kept an entourage of lesser fae with him to do the dirty work.

Faelan cried out in pain as Loxias twisted her arm. The snap echoed all around us.

A wicked grin lit up the prince's face and he leaned into whisper in her ear.

I was still too far away to stop him. The faery venom and wolfsbane that the bolt carried was working its way through my system.

Red's eyes met mine and widened in horror.

The ground came up to meet me, but I fought against the darkness.

Sound exploded all around me.

The last thing I saw before darkness overtook me was a large white wolf.

Chapter Twelve

Faelan

If anyone would have told me that I came from a long line of werewolves before a few days ago, I would have had them committed.

Fairies, and witches, and all the other supernatural beings belonged in books, not the Lupian Forest.

Yet here I sat. At the bedside of a werewolf who'd been at death's door due to fae venom.

I'd dragged him to the cabin and into bed but had no idea what to do or who to call for help.

After a massive panic attack subsided, I'd found his knapsack, Grams book and rooted around the area for the ingredients to make a cure.

A witch's potion. *Yup. Totally a witch. Thanks Grams.*

Not only was I a witch myself, but there was no denying that I was a werewolf now either.

Loxias had snapped my arm, and the pain was unbearable. He'd whispered in my ear that Wylder was my bonded and that I was going to watch him die.

I remembered the fear first, then the white-hot rage that flowed through me and the sizzling energy just below my skin.

The next thing I knew was pain, anger, and a need to sink sharp teeth into the threat.

And the hair. It was everywhere.

Strange way to get it but, I've always wanted a faux fur coat. Now I have a real one.

Loxias barely escaped with his life. The only thought that had run through my mind was getting to Wylder. Nothing but the tug in my chest mattered.

Wylder had transformed back into his human form, but I couldn't figure out how to do that.

The strength of my white wolf was twenty times that of my own.

It helped to carry him to the bed. Naked and bloody and scarcely breathing, but alive.

Those couple of hours after I'd finally changed back were surreal.

The shock of everything burned off quickly. Much quicker than I would have expected.

My arm was healed as well. I could feel it healing when I was still in wolf form. Bizarre was an understatement.

With a task to focus on, it kept me calmer than I would have thought. I put all of my energy into saving his life.

All I could do now was wait... and read.

Grams had left a book of witchcraft and familial notes, called a book of shadows. And a book of spells and potions, called a Grimoire.

They had appeared as one book until I opened the cover, and my breath brushed the first page. A shimmer of light surrounded me, and it split into two separate books.

For the last four days, sitting by Wylder's bedside, I'd been dripping water with honey into his mouth every few hours and reading through the books the rest of the time.

He was still naked. *Mmmmm.*

The sheet I'd laid over him hadn't kept my mind from wandering while cleaning up the blood. The cuts around his neck, arms, and face healed fast once the wolfsbane and fae venom were out of his system.

He needed to wake up soon. Eating was going to be a problem if he didn't.

After I'd changed back into my human form, the hunger consumed my every thought.

With him on the mend and no longer the focus of my attention, I'd ate through nearly everything that was in his cold box and half of what was in the cabinets.

Yesterday, I ventured out to the vegetable patch but most of the things there weren't ready to be eaten yet.

The thought of Loxias coming back again had me scampering back to the house quickly and bolting all of the windows and doors.

Warmth stirred in my chest as he began to stir. Setting my book aside, I went to his side.

"What day is it?" he whispered; voice raspy from disuse.

"You've been out for four days... well, five if you count that today is nearing sunset."

I had saved a can of soup that was in the pantry in case his throat still hurt. He'd need to eat to bring back his strength.

No awkwardness laid between us. Even with him still naked, the space was comfortable. "Can I fix you a bowl of soup?"

"I'd rather have steak and a glass of scotch." *Geesh. Now it was awkward.*

He must have noticed the sheepish expression on my face. "What? You don't approve?"

"It's not that. I sort of... ate most of the food you had here." Feeling my cheeks flush, I looked back down at Grams book.

"I see." The smirk on that handsome face sent butterflies skittering around in my belly.

Sitting up slowly, he kept one hand on the sheet as his muscles firmed in all've the right places. *Yum-meee.*

"I'll go hunt us some game in a bit. I don't think traveling all the way to town is a good idea right now," he said.

As he stood, the sheet dropped to the ground and his length was on full display.

My eyes didn't want to look away. I couldn't find the mechanisms to make them work.

I didn't think my cheeks could get any hotter without combusting. *It's a damn tree.*

Noticing where my gaze landed, the crook of his stupid mouth curled up.

Leaning in and over my shoulder, IT brushed against the top of my forearm.

"What are you...?" I started to holler but he pulled back with a pair of sweatpants that had been sitting on the dresser behind my chair.

"Don't get your panties in a bunch, Red. Unless it's because you want me to walk around in the buff." With a quick wink, he walked out of the bedroom, leaving me flabbergasted. *Sexy jerk.*

I set the book on the dresser and followed him out.

A pot was already heating on the stove, and the smell of stew hit my senses like a smack to the face. *Where was that hidden?*

"Grab a seat. We need to talk," he said, gesturing to one of the stools at the breakfast bar.

I did as he suggested just as my stomach growled, loudly. *Oh, good lord.* It was loud enough that I knew he'd heard it.

"Should I just fill you in on everything that happened while you were sleeping?"

The quirky way his left eyebrow raised at my choice of words sent a slight shiver up my spine. *Damn it, Faelan. Focus.*

If I took the driver's seat now, then I wouldn't feel so at a loss about everything I'd come to do and read about over the last few days.

After he didn't say anything, I took that as my cue, so I went ahead and filled him in on all of it.

Getting to the part about pulling the sheet over him and cleaning the blood off, I felt the flush of my cheeks and hurried past the awkwardness of it all.

"Wait, you pulled up the sheet with your snout? Impressive."

Confused by his admiration, I asked, "Why? Isn't that what you would have done?"

"It is, but I've been wolfing out for decades. New pups..." It was my turn to raise an eyebrow. "Sorry, wolves newer to changing aren't usually in control enough to do most anything but the basics... like growling, biting, fighting."

He placed a bowl in front of each of us. It smelled divine.

"It takes years to master that kind of control." Taking a bite and chewing over more than the stew, a shrewd gleam appeared in his eye. "It may be that you're half witch or maybe it's because of your bloodline... but I have another theory too." *Well, this should be good.*

"Which is?" The spoon hit the bottom of the bowl and came back empty far too quickly.

My belly grumbled again, and he pushed his bowl towards me.

"No, no. You've been asleep for days. You need that," I attempted to protest.

"I'll live." When I still wouldn't take it from him, he added. "We'll go hunting right after we talk, Red. I'll be full by bedtime."

With a rueful grin, I snatched the bowl and devoured it in three gulps.

Embarrassed by my own gluttony, I looked away. *Oh geesh. Real lady like.*

"Don't be bashful. The first few changes made me eat an entire elk, all the food I had in the cold box and pantry, and half the food Inana had on hand." Seeing my look, he added,

"Yes, we were friends before she saved my life. We grew up in different packs, but we've known each other since childhood."

"Really?"

That was new information I overthink about later, but I was a relieved to know it wasn't just me who ate like a bottomless pit after changing.

"That does make me feel better. I thought it was just nerves when you were out. I tried to ration myself, but my stomach kept gnawing." My voice tapered off as our eyes met.

"Yeah, so... after you had me naked in bed?" The unfazed sarcasm he used would have worked if not for the mischievous gleam in his eye.

"Oh, right," picking up where I'd left off, I told him about the panic attack and then the book.

Remembering that he'd had a theory before I'd eaten his stew, I asked, "So, what was your theory about why I have more control normal?"

He stood and walked the bowls to the sink before turning that chiseled body around and leaning casually against it.

My eyes traveled along the vee that led to his sweatpants and land on the bulge just below the surface. *My, my.*

Crossing his arms over his chest, he said, "My eyes are up here, Red." *Oops.*

"You're not going to like it." Wylder uncrossed his arms and ran one of his hands through the scruff on his face and up through his tussled dark hair. "Hell, I don't like it either... but Inara had her reasons, I guess."

That snapped me out of my growing desire. "What are you talking about?"

He held up a finger for me to give him a minute, then walked out the door.

When he came back in, he was holding a piece of folded paper that looked to be covered in dry blood. *What the fuck is that?*

"I found this in your Grams kitchen when I went back to feed Nixie. I swung by here on my way back to find you so that I could stash it in a safe place."

Taking it gingerly with my fingertips so I wouldn't accidentally rip it, I unfolded and spread it out on the bar top.

My grandmother's writing brought a tear to my eye, but I pushed past the emotions threatening to mangle my resolve.

It was straight forward. After all that I'd read while Wylder was still unconscious, I recognized this for the spell it was. *Damn it, Grams.*

It was a strong one. It bound me and Wylder together at our very core.

That must have been the tug I'd been feeling ever so often since we'd met. Thinking that this gorgeous guy liked me for me only made the realization that the attraction wasn't real that much worse. *Ugh, fuck my life.*

"Do you understand what that note means, Red?" All of his attention was focused on my lips. *Well, that's not confusing.*

"It means you don't want to help me, but you have to." My heart sunk a bit at the thought. "Grams gave you no choice."

He took a step forward and placed his massive hand under my chin, drawing my eyes to his.

"It means that we are in this together. I had no idea about the bond when I set out to find clues on Inara's disappearance.

And I sure as shit didn't have a clue about the bond when I followed you into the woods after you encountered Loxias that first time." He was staring intently, studying my face.

"Yes, but the first part of the spell was already in place. The tug was already there." I tried to pull my chin from his grip, but he wasn't having it. *Just Lovely.*

Placing a hand on each side of my face and looking deep into my eyes, he leaned in just above my parted lips. I could feel his breath in my mouth as he whispered.

"So what if it was? That doesn't negate the fact that you're worth protecting."

He brushed the scruff of his chin against my bottom lip.

"It doesn't undermine the fact that you're beautiful."

The tip of his nose stroked against the side of my face tenderly.

"And it sure as hell doesn't stop the courage I'd felt pride in when you were facing down a group of strangers."

The heat from his hands traveled to the base of my neck, pulling me impossibly closer. "No, Faelan. The attraction I have for you would have been there with or without Inara's spell." *Luna, have mercy.*

Without another word, he brought his mouth down on mine with bruising force and I was putty in his hands. *I'm screwed.*

Chapter Thirteen

Wylder

The kiss was frantic, my hands roamed everywhere. Pulling back to catch our breath, my forehead pressed against hers as she placed her hands lightly on my heaving chest.

"That was..." she started.

"Intense," I finished. *What am I doing?*

I trailed my long, calloused fingers lightly down the side of her soft face, coming to rest on her exposed neck.

Wrapping my hand around the back, I brushed a chaste kiss to her swollen lips.

"I shouldn't have done that." I'd spoken softly in a non-repentant tone that didn't match my words. She tried to push me away, but I only held tighter. "I shouldn't have, but I don't regret it one bit."

Reaching up to rub her bottom lip with my thumb, I placed a gentle kiss to her forehead.

"We're both at fault. I wasn't exactly stopping you," she said, giving me a timid smile that I returned.

Clearing my throat, I dropped my hand. Inara was going to have my head if we ever found her.

I wasn't a pack member and rarely played well with others.

The pull I'd felt was undeniable. *That has to be the bond, right*?

I'd meant what I'd told her. She was definitely my type and more alluring than anyone I'd ever met... but the way I longed for her was so intense.

The spell that tied us together was doing its job.

"I'm supposed to protect you." Shaking my head in self-frustration, I meant to take a step back but couldn't get my feet to co-operate. "I can't even protect you from me."

"Who says I want your protection? I'm not some innocent little girl, dude." *Dude*? "I can take care of myself."

Moving back into my personal space, she reached for my face.

A snarl ripped from the back of my throat, but Faelan didn't flinch. *She'll be my death.*

Standing on her tiptoes and taking my face in both of her hands, she placed light kisses to the side of my throat. Nibbling her way to my ear and sending a shiver up my spine, the longing in my groin became increasingly heavier.

My hands found her waist. First to nudge her away. Then to pull her closer.

She kissed each side of my mouth with a feather light touch. *Fuck it.*

Lifting her off her feet and slamming my mouth down on hers, I carried her back into the bedroom.

There were two options.

Option one, take her to bed and risk the witch alpha's wrath if she returned.

Or option two, carry her into the shower and douse us both in cold water.

Go with option one. Go with option one.

Faelan wrapped her legs firmly around my waist as I walked. Her soft tongue had forced its way into my mouth and wrestled like an Olympian fighting for the gold. *Damn, this woman can hold her own.*

Trying not to fall behind, my fingers wound through her long hair and yanked her head back.

The need to breathe didn't seem important to her but I wanted access to her ear. Sucking the lobe into my mouth, a moan escaped her lips.

"This isn't what you want but it's what we need," I whispered in her ear.

The cold water hit us a second later.

Peeling her off of my middle and setting her down, she growled at me. *That's so fucking hot.*

The frigid water was doing nothing to help my raging hard-on. Now we were dripping wet and still ready to rip each other apart.

"What the fuck are you doing?" she yelled.

The drenched sweatpants I wore clung to me like a glove.

She was quick and ruthless with her need. Lunging forward, she wrapped her hands around my waistband and yanked them to the floor, dropping to her knees in the process.

"Red, stop. Inara will kill me." *This girl.*

Her hands moved slowly like she was afraid I was a mouse ready to bolt.

Looking up into my eyes, she cupped my balls in one hand and wrapped the fingers of her other around my hardened girth.

"I'll stop if you really want me to." Her tongue darted out, licking the pre-cum from the tip. "I'm a grown woman." She stroked me once from shaft to head. "I make my own decisions."

A moan of pleasure rumbled from deep withing me. *She's definitely that.*

It was harder to speak the words than I would have thought. "Is it really your decision though? The spell, the bond..."

She silenced me by taking my cock into her mouth and down her throat in one move.

Knees wobbling, my cry of pure elation echoed off the shower walls. One hand using the faucet for support, the other wrapped in the back of her hair again as I closed my eyes.

Gagging and slurping noises filtered through the sound of the running water. *Is this really happening?*

Chancing a glance down at her taking me into her luscious mouth, with dripping hair and on her knees, I was done in.

I tapped her shoulder to let her know I was going to lose control.

Faelan smiled up at me with her eyes but never stopped her assault. *Oh fuck.*

Heat built at my core. She worked the shaft and never relented once.

The explosion shook me violently. An electric tingle sizzled throughout my system.

Holding onto the walls for support, I found her eyes and what I saw in them I knew was the same thing I was feeling...

Mine!

Chapter Fourteen

Faelan

Standing as the water cascaded over and around us, I reached up to touch his face, but he snatched both of my wrists in one quick motion.

The seconds ticked by as we stared each other down and lustful snarls made their way up from the back of Wylder's throat.

Putting both of my wrists into one of his large hands, he grabbed the top of my shirt and ripped it down the middle, exposing my bare breasts.

I didn't bother putting a bra on this morning while reading. Now, I was even more grateful that I hadn't.

A dip of his head and one of my erect nipples stung as his teeth grazed against the sensitive surface. His tongue flittered in and out, circling around and around before sucking the nub into his mouth. *Oh, dear Gods.*

"Mmmm," he whispered. "The things I'm going to do to you..."

Gulp. I've gone and done it now.

Not waiting for my response, he hauled me up into his arms and tripped over the pants that he'd forgotten were around his ankles. We came crashing to the floor of the bathroom.

Trying to catch myself as we fell, my hands unintentionally slid over every part of his wet, naked body before they landed.

"Shit," he exclaimed. "I'm so sorry." It was the first time Mister Sauve looked embarrassed.

The vulnerability written on his face had me biting my bottom lip. *Aww, he's sensitive.*

"It's fine. Only..." I teased, leaving it open ended to bait him.

Arching his brow, the humility oozed from him at my chastising. "Only what?"

A sheepish grin crinkled the corners of my eyes, and my mouth tugged up at one corner.

"Well, if I were part Fae, you'd be in my debt now... saying you're sorry and all." I giggled.

"You little shit." His playful tone did funny things to my core. *Oops.*

He stood, taking his pants from his ankles and throwing them back into the shower.

Turning swiftly, he scooped me up off the floor, walked three paces to the bed and unceremoniously tossed me on it. Wet clothes and all.

"Hey!" I protested. "That wasn't..."

With his nakedness on full display, he pounced on top of me. "Play time's over," he growled. *Double gulp.*

Yanking both of my feet towards the bottom of the bed, he made quick work of taking off my pants... but he left my panties on. *Damn it.*

Wylder looked up from in between my legs and the valley of my breasts.

"My turn.... and Red, just so you know," he slid his hand over the material that restrained my throbbing nerve bundle. "This is going be torturous."

Waggling his eyebrows, he bit his bottom lip. That smirk made everything inside of me turn liquid. *Dear Lord, have mercy.*

I put the heal of my hand in my mouth to stop the quiet moans at his every pass over my clothed folds. The torturous pleasure threatened to rip me open.

His teeth gingerly bit at the panties still covering my most sensitive area. The heat from his breath presented its own pleasure.

Using the palm of his hand, he cupped my mound and rubbed circles in time with every nibble. Over and over again.

Arching my back with every turn, I begged for more contact. *Oh, come on!*

"Wylder...please," my breathless voice implored.

"Now who's indebted to Faeries?" he teased.

Seriously? Pushing myself into his hand harder, he chuckled.

In one swift swipe, the cloth ripped away, and he plunged his tongue deep inside me.

"Oh, gods!" Undulating under his touch, my body was coming undone.

I was almost there... almost. Wylder pulled back with a knowing smile.

"Ah ah ah, Red. Not until I say so." *No. No. No. No. Noooo!*

I couldn't contain my frustration. Grabbing for his ears, he shot just out of my reach.

A stinging swack to my engorged bean made me come out of my skin at the sudden pain. "Hey!"

"It seems to me that you need to learn discipline."

Sliding an unexpected finger inside... "I say when you find pleasure."

Adding a second finger to the first and pumping harder... "I say when you lose control."

Sliding his fingers out before I could even muster a response. In the next instance, he was on top of me, sliding all the way in and filling me to the brim. "I say when you cum." *Ohhhh, yes.*

Pulling all the way out, the head of his cock rested at my entrance, teasing me with it as he kissed up my neck, to my ear, and landing on the side of my mouth.

"Do you understand me, Faelan?" he whispered.

The way he'd used my name tore at my defenses. *Yes, sir! Wait... what?*

His tongue edged its way between my lips as he slid himself in fully to the hilt, taking my breath away.

When he'd stopped the kiss to stare into my eyes, that tingling feeling welled up in my center. All thought processes ceased.

"I..." I was at the fringe of ecstasy. *Luna, help me.*

His slow, agonizingly pleasurable strokes were driving me mad.

"Say the words, Red." Another slow stroke. "I want to hear you say it." Another hard pump at each word. "Tell me that I... Own... Your... Rapture..." A hiss escaped through my teeth.

"Yes," I breathed. "It's yours. Take it!" *This moment will be my undoing, for sure.*

No sooner had the words left my mouth before he was in full stride. Pumping harder. Faster, but still too slow for my need.

It was too much and not enough. I dug my nails into his back and just when I was about to cum, he pulled out.

"Nooooo...." was all I managed before he flipped me onto all fours and slammed into me from behind.

I saw stars. His length and girth were large enough to satisfy without being too big to find pleasure in, but the sudden change of position left me little time to adjust to his massive size.

A smack to my round bottom sent a tingling sensation all the way to the top of my head.

With both of his hands on my hips and him pounding into me from behind now, I didn't have to care about the weird faces I'd always made during sex.

It was liberating to be in the moment. *Wolf style. Hot damn*!

My release would not be delayed much longer. The lines between pleasurable euphoria and tormenting agony were beginning to blur.

Threading his fingers through my hair and pummeling my insides with his cock as his balls slapped skin to skin, I knew he was at the door to bliss as well.

"Scream my name, Red," he demanded. "I want you to come with my name on your lips, sweetpea." *Oh gods.*

"Wylder... yes. Yes. Fuck me, Wylder!" Bringing his wishes to life unleashed something primal I hadn't realize had been bound within me.

As my orgasm rocked through me, tightening and releasing over and over again, juices slipped down the back of my legs. I could feel my muscles clenching around his cock.

"By Luna!" he exclaimed. "Faelan!" was all he could say before his orgasm overtook him. *That's right. Say my name.*

Pumping faster and faster, the drenched area of my entrance quivered in the wake of my explosion. The slipping and sliding of his cock as he expended himself felt amazing.

A sense of rightness hit me in the chest. In that moment, he belonged to me.

Mine!

Chapter Fifteen

Wylder

What in the hell just happened? One minute, I'd been in control. I was my own pack. Not an Alpha, but a Sigma. A lone wolf.

After she'd relinquished control... telling me to take it... something inside of me splintered. I felt an immediate convergence with her.

The bond bound us in the way of a spell. It had taken hold of me from the minute I'd read Inara's words.

This... this was different. A soul connecting different.

There was no other way to explain it. I was sure that she was mine and I was hers.

Mated pairs hadn't existed in roughly two centuries. My great- great grandparents had been mated.

The natural mating bond had been extinct since modern travel was made more easily available. *Why now?*

Faelan laid naked in my arms, stroking up and down my wrist. All felt right with the world.

I should tell her about my suspicions but what if she rejects me because I'm a Sigma? She was a born Alpha. *Damn it.*

I didn't need that kind of loss again.

To lose your pack was an awful loneliness for a long time. It was a hollowness that couldn't be filled. Pack connection bindings tethered all members together.

When those bindings were snapped, it left an emotional wound that took years, if not decades, to get over.

I ran my fingers through her hair, brushing the loose strands from her face. I wanted to stay in this moment forever.

No sooner than I'd had the thought, she sat up with a "Let's talk" look. *Well, shit.*

She leaned forward, placing a chaste kiss upon my lips. Veering back to look me in the eyes, I worried at what she might be thinking. *Here we go.*

"You're mine." Her words knocked me off kilter.

I hadn't been expecting a declaration. There was no judgement, no condemnation. It was a simple statement of fact, like, water is wet.

"You felt it too? The connection?" My mind raced while my heart stopped beating, waiting for her response.

Pushing that stray piece of hair behind her ear again, my fingers trailed the length of her neck. A flush of heat immediately rushed to the surface of her skin. *Mine.*

"I felt something. I'm not sure how to explain it but I know that you and I are more than just spellbound," she said. The sparkle in her eyes lit to full-on flames as I watched.

"I think it's a mating bond. There hasn't been one in nearly two hundred years, but this feels like how my father had described his great-grandfather and great-grandmother's mated connection." I drew Faelan's hand to my lips. "It's primal. There's a need to protect and cherish you that goes beyond reason. I mean, we just met for crying out loud!" *This is crazy.*

"Are you upset that we're mated?" The hurt in her voice brought out an irrational need to lash out at the cause of her pain.

"Gods, No! I'm just surprised. Look Red..." I didn't know how to put into words what I was feeling. "You're... everything I would have asked for if I'd known what I wanted." I hung my head, not sure how to continue. "I can't get this right." *Idiot.*

Faelan smiled weakly, but it genuinely reached her eyes. I grinned back in response.

Propping herself up and straddling me again, I felt the rising heat within myself and growled. She snarled back. *Fuck. That's hot.*

A crash from outside startled us both. We jumped up and apart and instinctively crouched. Naked and protective.

Throwing my arm out in front of her to block any danger that might be present, I realized my mistake almost immediately.

She may be new to the supernatural world, but it was born in her. And as an Alpha, her primal instincts took the driver's seat, shoving me to the side.

Grabbing her clothes that had been scattered around the room and throwing them on haphazardly, she was the first out the door to assess the situation.

"That sounded like a tree falling onto the outbuilding. They must be back." The worry in her tone tugged at me to keep her safe.

The guess was a sound one. Loxias wouldn't stay away for long. And according to her, I'd been unconscious for a few days. *Well, fuck.*

"Would you listen if I asked you to stay here?" I asked, already knowing the answer.

"Hell no." *Just swell.* "I'm not going to hide away while you take on a fae prince and however many other fae he's brought with him!"

She looked ready for battle but the spell that bound her life to mine only worked in one direction.

"I'm only asking because if you die, I die." My words landed like a blow. Her eyes went wide, and she took an involuntary step backwards. *Real smooth, asshole.*

"What do you mean? Because of the mating bond?"

Now wasn't when I'd wanted to have this conversation, but we were given no other choice. *I'm gonna kill Inara for this.*

"No. Not the mating bond." Reaching forward, I put a finger under her chin, tilting her face up to mine. "The spell that your grandmother cast tied my life to yours. You don't have to worry about it being vice versa." I didn't want her to worry for me in that way. "If anything happens to me, you'll be fine."

She yanked free from the grip I'd placed on her chin. "Fine?" she said. "You think I'll be fine if anything happens to you?"

I was taken aback. No one but Inara had cared about what happened to me for an extraordinarily long time. It was all I could do to keep the smile from taking over my face.

I grabbed her by the waist and my lips crashed to hers with a bruising force. *This woman.*

Another crash sounded outside the window. Breaking our kiss, she walked over to the cupboard and pulled out a bow and a few daggers.

"Let's take care of this threat..." She threw me the crossbow. I didn't even know if she knew how to use a weapon. "Then we can discuss all of the things that are wrong with your definition of Fine"

Rolling her eyes, she headed towards the door as I stood there. Staring. *Yup. I'm screwed.*

Striding over and placing a kiss atop her head, I stepped over the threshold and looked back at her one last time, smiling.

Purpose. Finally.

"Alright Red. Let's go hunting."

Chapter Sixteen

Wylder

Loxias sent an arrow whizzing past my head and embedding in the frame of the door the minute I'd opened it. Faelan jumped to the side but didn't back down.

"You're still a lousy shot for a fae." My voice was casual but the tension I felt at having her in danger was palatable. It brought a metallic taste to my tongue. "Did daddy not teach you anything? Ya know, with not having a real shot at taking the throne, maybe he thought it a waste of his time."

Taunting the prince came naturally.

Faeries had gifts and were more formidable than regular humans. The Lupian Forest was home to many different supernatural creatures.

Fae didn't even merit a second thought in my book, but Loxias was becoming more of a nuisance with every encounter.

"I just want to talk to the Blood Red Heir. That's not too much to ask, is it?" Loxias smirk had anger rising through my entire being.

Faelan came to stand by my side. Touching my elbow and staring up at me, she silently reminded me that she was not leaving my side without a fight.

Without missing a beat, she turned her witty attention to the prince.

"I see you didn't learn your lesson the first two times you came to talk to me. I'd heard fae were smarter than that." Her dazzling smile left me breathless. *There's my she-wolf.*

That fire in her eyes lit me up from the inside.

"I simply have a few questions for you regarding your grandmother and a certain stone." He took a nonchalant step forward and a growl grumbled from my chest.

"The affairs of werewolves are none of your business, Faery," I said. "It wouldn't be wise to interfere with full moon rituals if you want to live."

Loxias raised his hands in mock surrender. "I am a hunter, Wolf. And the fae are the true rulers here."

There was no jest in his words. *What the fuck was he talking about?*

"If you fancy a night of delusion, I'd suggest taking a tour of the city. That's where the world has forgotten the natural order of things." I took Faelan's hand. "The forest belongs to us."

"I would say that you are half right," he said.

I couldn't discern the dark expression that passed over his face. It was gone a second later.

The smirk on his face had my nerve endings itching. "The humans have forgotten their roots... but so, it seems, have the creatures of the forest."

"What's that supposed to mean?" Faelan asked.

Loxias gave her an appraising look. If his answer were anything threatening, I would end him here and now.

"I am a few centuries older than your... partner," he said, inclining his head knowingly. The smugness rolling off him made my teeth grind. "My people still remember the true hierarchy. The one before the curse."

"Curse?" Faelan turned to me with new questions written on her face, but I didn't have any more clue as to what the prince was talking about than she did.

"The fae were cursed by a highly powerful Halfbreed witch nearly two centuries ago."

He raised an eyebrow and stared down at our intertwined hands. I didn't understand the yearning in his expression.

"When she cursed our people, the balance of the magics was placed upon her own people. The mating bond was the cost." I began to interject but Loxias held up a hand and continued. "Those who were already mated, stayed mated. However, no new pairs have been bound since then... to our people or yours."

"And you believe this has something to do with Red's ancestorial line?" It was a sound theory. *Damn.*

The smell of rain in the distance felt ominous. A storm was brewing.

"We've had our eye on Inara for a while, since a few years after her birth but, the power she wielded from her wolf side and witch side wasn't as potent as we would have expected." He looked to Faelan. "You, on the other hand... unknowing and untrained, were still able to take us on. Twice."

Lightening stuck a few miles away. Somewhere over by Ritual Rock. The crack resounded throughout the forest.

"Let me get this straight," she said. "You're saying that the fae ruled all? And that my, however many greats, grandmother was powerful enough to curse an entire species? The curse is still in place to this day, and you think that the full moon coming up, combined with this missing stone, will break the curse?"

The scent of petrichor swept in on the breeze as the trees rustled all around us.

"Yes, to all of that." He looked to his left and to his right, checking the placement of his guard. "We will need you and the stone to come with us, Deliverer." *Um, what?*

The rain began to fall gently. Faelan's hair hung in her face, water dripping off her nose.

"Did you hurt my Grams?" Her poignant question left her lips in barely a whisper.

"She was injured in our altercation but is alive. That is all I will tell you for now." *Fuck.*

Before he was finished his words, Faelan lunged, shifting between one moment and the next.

Her jaws snapped and snarled inches from Loxias' throat. Two of his guardsmen rushed to dislodge her while the other four charged at me.

High fae strength was legendary but these were low fae. I still never made the mistake of underestimating them when it came to brute force.

I knew I had to trust her. The Alpha in her would demand nothing less than pure dominance. I only worried that Loxias would use his gifts if he got his hands on her.

Throwing two of the guard to the ground, the other two managed to get a large, silver net over me.

Reaching for the iron dagger at my side, my strength waning, I managed to lash out at the ankles of the fae in front of me.

The silver taking its toll, I dropped to my knees. The last guard jumped out of my reach. My only hope at helping her was shifting.

When I looked over, guards were standing over Faelan with silver shackles. They wrapped them around her neck and were yanking with all of their might, the strain clear on their faces. *That woman.*

Pride swelled inside my chest and my flesh melted away into fur.

Loxias fought to keep her jaws at bay as slobber dripped onto his face.

A yelp escaped her when one of the guards brought a silver sword down, narrowly missing the side of her throat, grazing her front paw instead. *I'll kill him!*

I threw the net off as my rage hit a new high. Teeth snapping, I bit the arm clear off of the sword wielding fae. Blood squirted in all directions.

A shadow passed in front of me in a blur of movement. Looking up in time to see the cause, my heart relaxed slightly.

The other guard dropped the shackles from her neck when he felt the snout of a wolf a breadth from his ear. The growl menacing.

I didn't hesitate as I passed the wolf, changing back to my human form, and placing a tender touch to Faelan's paw.

The rustling of trees and menacing growls reverberated off of the surrounding cliffs and forest. Four more pairs of eyes from nearly horse-sized shadows stood in the copse of trees.

Loxias jumped to his feet and swiftly ran away, his men following the best they could.

"Thanks, Reed." My eyes never left Faelan's as I spoke. "The packs timing is impeccable."

The rest of the pack emerged from the forest in wolf form as Reed shifted back. "We aren't here for you... but duly noted."

Alayna shifted and ran towards Faelan, but I stopped her with a snarl. "She just needs a minute," I told the pack.

I knew she was having trouble transforming back. Reaching down and rubbing the back of her ears, I gave a quick kiss to her snout.

"You were amazing," I said. Shock shown through her startled eyes. The surprised look was still there on her face as she looked back at me with her human eyes. "There's my girl."

"How... how did you know that would help me change back?" Faelan dipped her chin, looking down at her naked body. "I was stuck. I..." *Poor newbie.*

Lifting her chin with my forefinger and thumb to look at me, I placed a gentle kiss on her forehead.

I could feel the rest of the pack staring daggers at my touch, but they said nothing. As long as their Alpha didn't protest, it wasn't their place to speak out.

"You're mine," was all I said.

One side of her face pulled up before she realized that there were five other people standing in the clearing with us.

Faelan darted out of my grip and behind me, trying to block their view with my body. All five, plus she and I, were naked. My chuckle left me before I could think better of it.

"Modesty goes by the wayside when you're a werewolf, Red." That earned me a playful smack.

Slowly, she stepped out from behind me and reached for my hand instinctively. Every eye of every pack member followed the action.

Howls rung out through the forest.

It felt wrong to leave her exposed to them like that. I wanted to take her, right then and there... but this was her pack. And she needed to own it.

Addressing them for the first time since they arrived, she dropped my hand and took a step forward.

"Go to the cabin and make yourselves a drink. We need to talk." The double ring in her voice made it clear that it was an inexorable command. "We'll be along in a minute."

Reed didn't appear to want to leave her alone with me, a Sigma, but the command gave him no choice other than to follow orders.

Once we were alone, Faelan wrapped her arms around my waist. Having her naked body pressed against me was everything and still mildly embarrassing in the light of pack life.

My immediate hard-on was on full display for all to see. *Well, shit.*

"Thank you, Wylder. I lost myself for a minute there." She squeezed around my middle, and I kissed the top of her head.

"Anytime, love." *Love?* The term felt too natural.

My hands found the bottom of her ass and pulled her up to wrap her legs around me.

"I have to say... it was hot watching you attack that fae." That earned me another playful smack.

Tamping down my need to fuck her here and now, I did as Inara had suggested many times in the past and used my words to communicate my feelings.

"I am, however, finding it difficult to let you be naked in front of others and not take you right there in front of them. This mating bond has me fiercely possessive." My mouth came down on hers before she could protest what I'd said.

Breaking the kiss only after running out of breath, I pulled back and set her on her feet.

"Well," she said. "Let's just hope that I don't catch any of them eyeing your junk." A few steps before the cabin, she turned around with and wink. "I'd hate to have to off one of my own pack members to protect what's mine." *Fuck, that's hot.*

I was left standing there. Watching her perfect ass sashay away. The stiffness of my cock stinging in the chilly air.

Stopping in the doorway, she turned back when I hadn't moved. "You coming?"

Not yet. That was all I could think but I didn't say it.

Walking back to the cabin and into the wolves' proverbial den, I came to stand by my mate's side.

Chapter Seventeen

Faelan

Everyone was dressed again as we came through the door. I needed to find some clothes and collect my thoughts before addressing the elephant in the room.

Wylder walked in behind me and the sight of his member on full display had an aching deep within my walls. *Dear Luna.*

The fact that Alayna and Piper were there to see him made an irrational snarl burst from my chest. *Geesh, get it together.*

Catching up with me, his hand found its way to the back of my neck. The panic attacks I'd always been prone to were nothing compared to the jealousy fits I suspected would become a regular occurrence.

With his firm, reassuring grip, the claim he placed on me was clear.

I was naked in front of Reed, Zito, and Blaze and he was doing his best not to overreact.

A tug on the bond and I relaxed ever so slightly as we approached the bedroom. *Close the door, close the door, close the door!*

When it closed, his grip on my neck tightened. Spinning me around and kissing me fiercely, I opened my lips to allow him more access.

His passion lit me from within, but we were not alone. I had to get this under control before desire overruled our senses.

Not wanting to do it, I pulled back anyway.

"Wylder, we have to get dressed." There was little to no breath left in my lungs as I spoke.

His hand cupped the side of my face, but he said nothing. For a long moment, he just stared.

"We need to tell them everything. About Grams. About the curse. About the stone and my ancestor's involvement." Swallowing once, I stammered out, "and about the spell and mating bond."

Finally dropping his hand from my face, he stepped back. Running his fingers through his matted hair, the crazed look he'd had faded just a bit.

"I could have lost you out there." His words threw me off track. "I've only just found you and I could have lost you, Red!" Taking a walk around my still nude form, his eyes trailed me from head to toe. "If Reed hadn't shown up when he did..." he trailed off. *Aww, he really cares.*

"Hey, I'm right here." Closing the distance between us, I wound my arms around his middle. "I'm fine. We're fine."

Feeling the kiss on top of my head, I released him and headed over to the wardrobe.

"I know we haven't seen the last of Loxias. You're no mere trophy for him to display." Coming up behind me and shifting a stray piece of hair behind my ear, he kissed the side of my neck. *Oh Gods.* "You're a living trophy that has the power to break the curse of his people. He won't give up with that much on the line." *Well, that's just an awesome thought.*

I knew he was right but hearing it said out loud that way made me cringe.

From my grandmother's stories, I knew that Faeries were tricksters and could be cruel. Words meant much more to them than any other creature. And if they could mislead you by deceitfully clever phrases, the magic was binding.

"I know. That's why we need to tell the pack everything." I turned in his arms and placed a gentle kiss to his lips.

This magic was the strangest. It felt like we'd known each other for decades, not only a few days.

Thinking it through, I said, "We need a plan. Defense clearly isn't working so we're going to have to take the offensive."

He rested his forehead against mine. Huffing out a long breath, he nodded. "Well, I guess we should get this over with."

"Don't be so glum," I said with a wicked smile. "I might get to bite somebody." *Did I really just say that?*

The tension in his muscles relaxed slightly. Pulling me close, he rubbed the sides of his face all over me.

"What the hell is that about?" I asked.

Waggling his eyebrows with a devilish grin, he replied, "Scent marking."

Mine was all I could think as I smiled back at him.

Chapter Eighteen

Faelan

Entering that room was much harder than I expected it to be. Everyone was looking to me. It was unnerving.

No one had ever given my opinion much thought.

Even as a bartender on busy weekends, the crowd tended to flow around me as if I weren't of any importance.

Alayna jumped up and came to my side the moment I entered. Blaze tsk'd. Zito shook his head in exasperation before turning his attention back to me.

Wylder's hand came up around my waist and a few growls ran around the room.

Stepping away from Lanie to Wylder's side, I intertwined our fingers.

"Let's get this straight right now... and for the last time," I said. "Where I go, he goes."

Taking each pair of eyes in turn, never blinking, the point sank in.

"Why? You barely know him." Blaze couldn't be more obvious about his contempt for Wylder... or for me. *Just great.*

"Well, here's the thing?" I started to say. Wylder's arm tightened around my middle with gentle, reassuring pressure. "My Grams, Inara, she... well, she cast a spell on him. It bound him to be my protector."

"When?" Reed demanded. "Was this before she disappeared?"

Zito interjected in that intelligent, calm demeaner of his. "I think the better question is how, Faelan?"

He was really growing on me. There was no judgement in his tone, no fear or accusation. There was only a quest for knowledge.

Wylder was quicker with the answer. "I felt a pull towards her from the moment I saw her. And I'll admit, it was a strange feeling. That's why I pinned her against the wall."

It was Piper who growled this time. Giving her a small smile, the wolf quieted down. *Hmmmm, very interesting.*

He stepped out from behind me and directly in front of Reed.

"When I went back to the cabin to investigate some more after you led Red away, I found a piece of paper with blood on it. And after reading it... boom. The spell was completed."

"There's more." Looking up into Wylder's eyes, I said, "We're mated."

"What the fuck? No!" Blaze was fuming. "There are no mated couples. It's impossible." *Yeah, 'cause I get my jollies off lying to strangers for no reason.*

Reed placed a firm hand on the young wolf's arm. With a quick squeeze, Blaze backed up.

The whole wolf thing was going to take time to get used to.

"What my young friend," Zito said, inclining his chin towards Blaze, "is trying to say is that mated wolves went extinct centuries ago. Why do you think you might be mated?"

Taking a deep breath to calm myself, I instinctively began rubbing Wylders muscular arm with my fingertips.

"There is no might about it. We are mated. Loxias as much as said it himself," I said. "The Fae curse is why wolves are no longer mated. Neither are the fae. It's not because of the rise of technology outside of the forest."

My words sunk in around the circle and a mummer ran through the pack. Everyone turned to Zito. He was, apparently, the smartest of them. They waited for his conclusion.

Deep in thought, with a finger and thumb practically rubbing a hole in his chin, he finally looked back to me and Wylder.

"Loxias is several centuries old." *That's not mind boggling or anything.* "He would have encountered mated pairs in the past." Walking around us in a circle, he sniffed, appraising our smell. "Their scents are definitely mingled." *Ewww, creeper.*

An immediate blush flooded my cheeks and Wylder cleared his throat. He'd been quiet during all of the discussion and this assessment.

Zito stepped a foot closer to me and Wylder growled. The pack, in turn, all whimpered or snarled and I burst out laughing.

Every head snapped in my direction.

"I mean... seriously? I know I'm new to all of this but... can't you see how ridiculous some of this posturing is?" My smile faded when there wasn't a single one of them who agreed with me. *Well, damn.*

Zito walked back to the group, gesturing for them all to take a seat around Wylder's small crowded front room.

"Okay, Faelan, tell us everything. And try not to leave out any detail, no matter how small it may seem to you."

Perching myself on the arm of the recliner that Wylder sat in, I began. An emboldening hand was placed on the small of my back. He knew just what I needed.

I gathered the courage to muster through everything, beginning from the night my mother called me with the news of my grandmother's disappearance. Whatever I didn't know, Wylder filled in.

After saying it all out loud, some things I'd read in Grams's book while waiting for him to recover, made a lot more sense.

"I think she may have been trying to find a way to undo parts of the curse but leave some precautions in place. It didn't make any sense to me at the time." Bringing my finger to my lip and tapping it like I'd always done when thinking things through, I added, "But it's kind of obvious now. She knew that the Fae were on the track of hunting down a way to reverse it completely. And that would mean that they needed either her or myself."

Though, I'm not sure what I'd be able to do.

"Didn't you say that she was trying to get you to come see her for a few weeks before everything went to hell?" Lanie asked.

Zito templed his fingers under his chin. "So, maybe she knew... and by knew, I mean that she had a vision of something happening to her." *What visions? Damn, Grams. Who are you?*

Zito was quick with his calculations, and I appreciated that.

Shaking his head slightly, he added, "Maybe that's why she was working on precautions. She'd have wanted you protected at all costs. You're the last Blood Red Heir."

I turned back to look at Wylder. "Is that why you call me Red?"

The wicked grin on his face said it all. My playful smack that he'd caught mid strike, and a waggle of his eyebrows had my insides melting.

"I was going to ditch that red coat Grams had made me because I thought you were poking fun at me in it." His eyes smoldered as he batted his lashes at me in mock embarrassment.

"Oh no, babygirl. I only intend to poke you in one way." His hand trailed a path of heat in its wake as he slid that ever stray piece of hair behind my ear. *Hubba, hubba.*

A collective gagging noise ushered us out of our little bubble, bringing us back to the reality of the situation.

Rain pelted harder against the living room window. The room was too small for all of these body, making it a tad too warm. My thoughts muddled in a haze.

"So, what would you have us do?" Lanie's question brought me up short. *Shit, I'm in charge. Just great.*

Looking to my new mate for answers, his lips were sealed. Pack politics didn't involve his input. And while I understood that he couldn't interfere, a small part of me wanted him to take charge.

"How about this?" Reed chimed in for the first time since I'd started talking.

He hadn't said a word. Not about the curse. Not about the spell. Not about the mating bond. And not one word about the ritual stone or what it might mean to us all in the long run.

"If you think it wise, of course, then we should proceed towards the known area around the Fae lands entrance. I'm positive that Loxias or some of his guards will try to intercept us but that's what you want, right?"

It was a good goal but what would be the actual plan? One without the other was a recipe for disaster.

If books, movies, and television had taught me anything, it was that you needed a clear, step by step, plan to achieve any dangerous objective. *Ugh.*

"Okay. Here's the thing. I have no idea what I am doing." Blaze barked out a disgruntled laugh and Piper gave me a weak smile. "I'm just winging it. Up until last week, I was a bartender. Well tipped, but yeah, not much in the way of plotting any kind of offensive."

"It was your idea to go after them first!" Blaze yelled. *Well, geesh. When he puts it like that...*

Wylder tapped me on the shoulder, seeking affirmation in my eyes before addressing the rest of the pack. *Oh, thank Luna.*

With a small nod, my shoulders relaxed a bit.

"It's a smart goal. If we take Loxias out of the equation, we'll have a better shot at prolonging the fae's attempts to break the curse." He rested a firm hand on my shoulder. "They need

Faelan. And if the curse is broken, then the fae will be our superiors again."

Hurt flashed in a few of their faces, but anger was written on others.

"I'm not saying that we'd see them that way. That's just how it was a long time ago. Their magic was stronger than any other supernatural being on earth. And for an immortal being, not having access to their full magics for so long, they're surely going to want to unleash the reins once they get it back. That would spell disaster. Not only for all of the Lupian Forest, but for the humans of the world as well."

"He's right, ya know." Zito looked to Reed when he spoke. "The fae have strong magic now. Can you imagine what their cruelty could be like if they get it all back?"

Lanie walked over and rested her head against Piper's arm and whimpered. I missed my best friend. This person wasn't her.

The person I'd been close to was all an act. Hollowness at her loss filled my chest.

"I say we find Loxias. Dismember him if necessary. And start looking for that damned stone!" It was the most I'd heard Piper say since we'd met.

I liked her reserved demeanor. There was more to Piper than she let on. I could feel it.

"I might have an idea how to go about it, but I don't know enough about magic to do it without help." Retrieving Grams book from where I'd stashed it earlier, I'd opened it back to the page I'd left off on. "She left clues in here, but it's in riddle form and I'm just no good at those."

Zito took the book from my hand. "You can read this?"

Raising my eyebrow, I tried to puzzle out why he would ask such a ridiculous question. "You can't read?"

"I can't read this. No one but a blood descendant of the Isbith line of witches can."

His words clicked in an unfamiliar way, an unreachable itch.

"That's not our family's name though. What's the Isbith line of witches?" I had the feeling I knew before he'd even answered.

Lightening crashed not far from the cabin. The rain poured, making the thunderous deluge of rain deafening as it hit the roof.

Zito had to talk louder just to be heard over its onslaught.

"The first witch. She had three daughters. Those daughters had three daughters each. We all believed that Inara was a descendant in the direct line to one of them, but?" Zito paused.

"But what?" I waited on bated breath.

"The First Witch had one son. He was her only namesake; Isbith." He began to look uncomfortable as he spoke. "It is said that he had magics too. And when his sisters were given their mothers blessing for theirs, he was denied it."

"So, what happened?" My nails were bitten to the quicks.

Another loud crack. I jumped in response and Wylder chuckled, drawing me closer to his side.

"The story goes that he found his mother's book of shadows. Gathered them all for a celebratory dinner. After the last of the wine he'd cursed was drank, in her weakened state, he killed the first witch. Thereby, stealing her powers, her book, and any magics lingering to the surface of his sisters."

I still didn't understand. The whole supernatural realm was making my brain exhausted from simply take it all in.

"Then how did the sisters and their descendants have such strong magics still?" Wylder asked before I could. I wasn't the only one flummoxed.

"Tobias Isbith underestimated the feminine line of magics. There was a reason that only the females were given the ritual blessing. Males were not stable vessels for Earthen magics."

Looking at the confusion on all of our faces, he continued. "Magics shift and churn. While the feminine gene is adaptable to change... such as it is needed for birthing children, the masculine gene is constant, inflexible. When he gave them the cursed wine, it limited their access to its well. He stole all that had remained on the surface but unknowingly left them a full pool of the divine magics that lay in the well's depths when he had spelled them."

He shook his head. Dismayed at the situation or the old witch, I couldn't say. After another few minutes of rumination, he went on.

"Males always seem to overestimate their own prowess. When the effects of the wine wore off, his sisters set off to end him with their combined magics. And end him they did, but they hadn't realized he had already fathered three daughters with three different women. Pure fae women. His line lives on."

"So, what? I'm the descendant of some pyscho male witch?" *Wonderful.*

"Yes... but more importantly, you hold all of the power of the first witch within your reach. And being a descendant of the male line and a full fae female, you hold the ability of true change within you as well. Magics are about balance. True change is exponentially rare, if not non-existent. You hold within you the female masculine and the male feminine, and the flip side of both."

His proclamation wasn't comforting. Wylder tensed at my side. The pack sat on the edge of their seats.

Zito continued as if he hadn't noticed the charge in the atmosphere.

"It means that Inara is most probably alive, out there some-where, waiting for you to step up." *Seriously Grams*? "Your werewolf half isn't merely a gene passed on from your grand-mother. It's THE gene that gave all of us," he motioned around the room, "the shape-shifting abilities we have in the first place."

He slouched as if suddenly tired.

"It means that you're the answer."

"Lovely. And just what am I supposed to be stepping up and being the answer to?"

"Your destiny, love." Wylder said. "You are the one foretold to change everything. You are the Deliverer."

Chapter Nineteen

Wylder

*W*ell *fuck*. Of all of the new information I'd been hit with over the last week, my new mate being the legendary foretold Deliverer was the biggest bombshell.

The term had been thrown around in every shape-shifting group and every witch's coven for many centuries. It had become a running joke eventually.

Whenever packs clashed or different supernatural beings warred with each other, they'd jest, "*You'll meet your end by the Deliverer or Deliverer save us.*" It hadn't been something anyone believed would happen in their lifetime.

And here she was... all wrapped up in an untrained, unskilled, and unknowing human package. *Shit.*

"Are you sure about this, Zito?" Reed asked. My face reddened as he clenched and unclenched his fist.

Piper spoke up. "It makes sense. Inara barely had to think before she knew a spell, sure... but she'd also had impeccable control over her wolf."

"True," he said. "She could even change just a small part of herself with hardly any effort at all."

Feeling a loss for words, I turned to Faelan. She wasn't making eye contact with any of them.

Placing my hand on her cheek to help provide her some comfort, I asked Zito the question that no one else wanted to.

"If Inara's line is the key, what makes Faelan the Deliverer and not Inara?" She looked to me in a way that could only be described as gratitude. *Anytime, Red.*

"Good question. Why should we think she's this special Deliverer person, Zee?" Blaze's flippantness was beginning to grate on my nerves.

Before I could retort a smart-ass answer, Faelan jumped up, lunging at the pup before anyone registered her moving.

Knocking him off balance with the surprise of the attack, she landed on top of him. He growled and lashed out at her with a closed fist.

As difficult as it was to watch, I knew I couldn't interfere. Red needed to prove her role as pack leader.

Blaze's fist never connected. She'd dodged it and threw her elbow at his throat like a cage fighter. *Damn woman, that's hot.*

The blow made the pup gasp for air. Watching her snarling in response to Blaze's disrespect, her mouth, and now elongated teeth were less than an inch from his exposed neck.

Every person in the room whimpered, including me.

She may not have realized what she was doing or that she'd even changed just that small part of her body, but even Inara never had that kind of Alpha response and control.

When Blaze's whimpers became more and more submissive, howls went out around the pack.

Faelan looked up in surprise at what had just transpired.

As one, the group lowered their heads in supplication. They were asking her to lead them with all of their allegiance now truly earned and not just inherited.

While I wasn't part of her pack, I was still bound to her in more ways than one. Instinct had me beginning to lower my chin but when our eyes met, she gave a subtle shake of her head.

I was a Sigma, and as such, I didn't have to follow an Alpha's orders.

And it was instinct that had her baying towards the sky in the next breath. Her pack following suit.

After several minutes, they all quieted down, and she addressed Zito with the question again.

"It must have something to do with your father. If he were from a line of shifters, you would be the same as Inara," Zito said. "Or perhaps the fates determined the timing."

"My dad had never let on that he had any inkling into the supernatural world. I'd always just assumed he was a logic brained human with no time for my Grams' non-sense." The melancholy in her voice made me ache.

Recalling a period of mourning that Inara had a few years back, it clicked into place as to why Red was suddenly so sad.

Squeezing her hand, she leaned into my comfort.

Zito scratched at his chin in contemplation like he always did when thinking things through.

"It has to mean that your father comes from one of the first witch's daughters' lines and your mother and Inara come from Tobias Isbith's line. Perhaps it's something altogether different, but regardless, he would have to be pure fae."

"Well, that's just gross," she said. "Like some kind of cousins?"

He laughed but answered respectfully. "Over the centuries, every path crosses. All families are inter-mingled to create new generations."

Scrunching her nose up, she continued looking repulsed. *Freaking adorable.*

Not able to help myself, I pulled her closer.

"Listen, Red. You have to think of it this way... You have a dollar. That represents the first witch. She had four children. Think of them as quarters." She gave me an amused smile but kept quiet. "If you break it down into dimes and nickels first, and then into pennies, it gets easier to forget. One hundred pennies going through circulation over hundreds of years still all go back to that one dollar that started it all."

Her biting at her bottom lip did something to my heart. The cute faces she'd made when she was thinking, the frustrated faces when she didn't understand something, and even the blissed-out pleasure faces she'd made when we'd been together all tied an unbreakable knot around my core. *Luna, help me.*

It was Lanie who broke the spell on my thought trail. "So, Fif... sorry, Faelan. What is our next move?"

"Wylder and I need to head back to the city." I wasn't the only one looking at her in puzzlement. She held up a finger to stop the onslaught of questions before they could start. "While he was recovering, I was reading over Grams' book, and I believe she sent me that stone months ago. I just didn't know what it was at the time."

"Are you talking about that pendant she sent you around your birthday?" Alayna asked. Inara had been smart planting her in close proximity to Faelan.

"That's the one. She knew I'd never get rid of something she'd gifted me, even if it wasn't my taste in jewelry." Smiling at her roommate, she then turned to Reed. "I'm going to need you to split into two groups. Reed and Lanie, you need to find the trail that leads into Faery, but do not be seen and don't go anywhere near any fae or the opening. Just find out where it is for us." *That's my girl. Take those reins.*

"And then what?" Reed was taking her status as Alpha better now than I'd expected but his disdain when addressing her still made me want to punch him in the throat. "We just wait around for you to run your errand?"

"No. I expect you to meet up with Zito, Piper, and Blaze after they track Loxias and his guard's whereabouts. Then you will wait for the two of us to return." Her tone brokered no room for argument again.

My chest rose in pride at how well she was doing with all of this. It made me want to take her, right there, in front of everyone. As irrational of a thought as that was, I couldn't help the need to claim her then and there. *Damn it! Get a grip.*

Shaking my fingers out to dispel some of this energy, I cracked each side of my neck in turn to bring my focus back to the room.

Zito nodded in affirmation and the rest of the pack grumbled but didn't question her. Blaze inched towards Reed and Red didn't miss a beat.

"Blaze, you're going with Piper and Zito. Not Reed," she said calmly. "There will be no discussion on the matter. We will all meet up at Grams tomorrow, around noon. Any questions?"

I chuckled when Zito raised his hand like he was in grade school. She didn't laugh but she did smile broadly as she pointed to him.

"Are we allowed to engage if the fae do find us snooping and attack?" His voice was quiet but there was real concern for her orders underlying his tone.

Thinking back to my time with a pack, I remembered the feeling of strings attached to my Alpha's commands. *Gods, I don't miss that.*

"Of course," Faelan answered right away. "You always have the right to defend yourselves. Even from each other." Her eyes roved over Blaze and then Reed. "I don't want to control you. Geesh."

Running a hand over her face, she looked to me. She wouldn't find any answers here. I was a Sigma because I didn't play well with others.

"Look guys, I'm new to all of this. Grams' book gave me a lot of insight to the witch side of things but this wolf stuff... I'm just winging it here."

She walked around the room and touched each one of them on the arm as she went.

"I realize that it's my job to give us direction and to break up any discord, but as long as you tell me or ask me something in a respectful manner, I definitely want your opinions and insights. I can't seem to stop myself from the challenge when one of you are insolent. And I'll work on that, but you're going to have to be obeisant." *I think I'm in love.*

"Understood. And thank you, Faelan," Zito came forward and nuzzled his head under her chin and she jumped back. He whimpered and moved forward again. "It's a show of respect in a pack," he said.

When her eyes met mine with a clear question in them, I gave her a small nod to reassure her.

Lanie and Piper made their way up to her and nuzzled in too. Blaze and Reed chose not to nuzzle but they did move forward to show a unified front. *Well, that's a start.*

"We should get going. We each have our assignments." Taking out my phone, I noted the time. "Don't let Loxias touch you if you can help it. His ability is to persuade you to see things from his point of view, but he needs touch to do it. If the fae curse is broken, he'll have the full range of his gifts back."

I looked at each of them in turn. Loxias' power was something of nightmares to a pack mind.

"That means he won't even need to be near you. He could pit each of us against the other from across a field. And the humans won't stand a chance." My eyes met Faelan's for a moment longer than the rest of them. "Stick to the plan. We will meet at Inara's in roughly fifteen hours."

"If anything goes wrong," she added. "You **Will** listen to Wylder." *Um, what?*

Reed and Blaze began to protest but she held up her hand to silence them.

"Let me clarify... this bond we have gives us a direct link to one another. You will listen as if the words came out of my mouth. Understand?"

After some hemming and hawing, they all agreed, and the whole pack headed to the door.

The storm had blown through quickly. It was no longer raining but there were puddles everywhere.

It'd been a long day, and we were about to make it even longer with this mission.

The urge to be with her overwhelmed me again.

Grabbing Faelan's arm to hold her back, I shut the door behind them.

I needed her all to myself.

Chapter Twenty

Faelan

My back pressed against the door's hard surface. Wylder's arms created a cage as he looked me up and down, hunger written in his eyes.

Biting my lip to hide the satisfaction his lust brought about only intensified his gaze. Grazing his nose along my neck, breathing me in deeply, a chill went down my spine, lodging itself low in my belly. *Oh, heavens help me.*

"I'm going to fuck you senseless," he growled. "You have no idea how hot all of that posturing was, do you?"

He brought his lips to my ear and the warmth of his breath made my toes curl. Dropping one arm and sliding his hand around my ass, I felt his arousal press into me. *Down boy.*

Breathless, I managed to get the words out with great effort. "We have to get going. I gave them a deadline, remember?"

"Hmmm. Is that really what you want? To leave me hard as granite, wanting to make you cum as you scream my name?"

He bit down on my shoulder and an involuntary shudder tore through my system.

Gathering my resolve to nudge him away was more difficult than I'd expected it to be.

"No, but we have to go, Wylder. If Loxias finds a way to break the curse, it's not going to be only supernatural's at the mercy of the fae."

Straightening up, he stepped back in the same motion. Reaching past me to reopen the door, his woodsy scent hit me full on. *Mmmmm. What the hell was I saying?*

"We should be going then. I wouldn't want our lechery to doom the world." His mouth curled up at one corner as he smirked down at my motionless body.

Smacking me on the ass, I jumped. *Oofff.*

"After you," he said as he motioned towards the opened door.

Internally I groaned but proceeded towards the trail that led to the dirt road. Following closely enough that his scent was nearly overwhelming, I found my ability to put one foot in front of the other difficult at best.

After fifteen minutes of walking, I finally spoke.

The silence hadn't been awkward. On the contrary. It was peaceful, but a nagging question wouldn't let me continue on without voicing it.

"I take it you've known Loxias for a while?"

"Yeah. He's been a thorn in my side for a few decades." The atmosphere changed with his mood. "Go ahead, ask it. I know it's weighing on your mind."

Stumbling slightly at being so easy to read, I caught myself before blurting out all of my preconceived notions of this new world around me.

Grams had only told me half-truth stories and what I'd assumed were trumped up myths. All of it was a lot to take in, let alone believe.

I was a werewolf and a witch from the line of the male betrayer.

The term warlock was often thrown around with humans, but they didn't understand that a male witch wasn't necessarily one. Warlock was a term given to the male betrayers of witches.

Grams had made sure that if I knew nothing else, I knew that. *She knew. She knew our heritage and never said anything.*

"Well, if Grams and I come from Tobias Isbith's line, does that make us bad witches?" Anxiety beat heavy drums in my chest while I waited for the answer.

"No, Red," he said quickly. "It just means that, because of his betrayal, your line is extremely powerful. It has no bearing on you or what you choose to do."

Feeling comforted by that, my thoughts turned to the other thing weighing on my mind.

Dodging a puddle, I skirted the edge of the trail. My coat wet from the leaves it brushed against.

I had a million question, but I settled on the one that was jumping to the forefront every few minutes.

"Do wolves age like regular humans?"

A plethora of emotions flickered across his face. They were there and gone again in a fraction of a moment, but I saw them. Doubt, wonder, desire, dread. *Dear Luna. How bad is it?*

"Not exactly." Giving him a perplexed look, he took the hint and continued. "We age slowly. The more we stay in wolf form, the slower the wrinkles and other tell-tale signs of growing older show in our human form. And we only age during daylight hours."

Well, shit. "So, how old are you, Wylder?" I didn't want to hear the answer but felt that I should know. "Oh, gods. How old does Grams appear to the rest of you?"

Placing his forefinger and thumb under my chin and tilting my face to look into his eyes, he placed a chaste kiss to my lips.

"I don't think you're ready to know that yet, sweetpea. There are some things that are going to take time to wrap your mind around."

"If I don't know, it'll just fester in my brain like a grain of sand in an oysters' mouth." I knew how easily I could fall into the labyrinth's trap of my own mind. It was better to just rip the bandage off all at once.

Taking a step back and glancing around, his lips pursed with anxiety. *Geesh, how bad can it be?*

"Inara is an old witch. She has the ability to glamour her appearance, but the rest of us don't." It was unsettling how the bottom of my stomach fell away. It knew before he'd spoken that this was going to be a shock. "She didn't have your mother until she was in her late nineties." *Holy fuck!*

My eyes went wide, and my mouth snapped opened with an audible pop. *That can't be right.*

He waited a few seconds for me to recover, and I was grateful.

The math became a complex obstacle as my logical brain tried to make sense of the word problem he'd presented.

I'd registered the panic attack that was at the edge of my nerve endings, buzzing in response to the dilemma.

Reaching over and touching the small of my back with one hand, a comforting zing from the binding spell pull me away from the edge.

It wasn't the mating bond that had him making contact with me when I felt out of sorts. It was the spell that Grams had cast.

From the information I'd gathered in the book of shadows, it was an unconscious action. Whatever mental anguish I felt would be perceived by his body as pain and he'd act, without thought, to stop it.

I didn't know how to feel about that. I'd rather it be an awareness for my needs from the mating bond, but in this moment, I was grateful for the contact.

"My mom is in her mid-sixties. I was supposedly a late life baby." Shaking my head at the absurdity, the realization hit me like a sack of potatoes, and I huffed out a humorless laugh. "My mom didn't want any part of all this, but she still looks amazing for her age. I take it her genes have everything to do with that. Wait until I tell her."

"You can't, Faelan," he said vehemently. "She can't know about all of this unless she's willing to accept her place in the pack. It's supernatural law."

"And who in the forsaken makes up this bullshit?" It was one thing not to be close to my mom. It was a whole other thing to be told that I couldn't talk about whatever I wanted to with whomever I wanted.

"The gods, I suppose." His mouth turned up at the corner.

I was beginning to think I was the only one who ever got to see the softer side of Wylder and it gave me a satisfying thrill.

"The fact of the matter is, if she knew about all of this and still refuses her pack, the natural order of things would play out. She's aging slowly now, but if natural order reared its ugly head, your mom would age like a normal human. And the stress of all of the years she hasn't aged normally would catch up to her all at once." His eyes filled with despair. "She would most likely die shortly after, Red."

I swallowed the lump in my throat.

Somewhere along the way, I'd accepted all of this. I'd taken my rightful place.

My mom had flat out refused to acknowledge any of it. Always playing it off as Grams being eccentric.

I couldn't bring myself to be the nail in my mom's coffin.

This was now my life, and I felt a sudden loss. No longer did I have a place in modern human society.

"And how old are you, Wylder?" He placed a chaste kiss upon my forehead. "Should I be calling you grandpa?" I teased.

Grabbing me firmly by the back of the neck, his voice a lustfully, rough whisper.

"The only familial name you will ever be calling me is Daddy."

Chapter Twenty-One

Wylder

Faelan's lips parted, allowing me the access I craved.

Reaching down to the heat between her legs, I cupped her mound, feeling the wetness that soaked through her panties. Our kiss was long and passionate, and I didn't want it to end. The smell of her skin so close revved my motor to a frenzy with every pass of our tongues.

Too soon for my liking, she pulled away. *Damn.*

"We have to get going. Loxias isn't the only fae with abilities, right?" she said. "If we're going to be able to locate the stone & perform the ritual and hold the curse in place by the Full Blood Moon, then we need to get going."

Why does she have to be so logical? Ugh!

Forcing myself to step back, I adjusted my painfully hard cock and glanced down at the tent in my sweatpants. I noticed her doing the same and smirked.

"Alright, sweetpea," I couldn't keep the longing out of my voice. "Let's get going."

She turned around and began heading towards town again, but I pulled her back against my chest, wrapping an arm around her waist.

Allowing my hardened length to press firmly against her ass, I whispered tauntingly in her ear. "After we retrieve the stone, I'm going to have you regretting making me wait."

Letting her go abruptly, she stumbled, and I chuckled. The way her throat bobbed as she swallowed my meaning had me waggling my eyebrows and biting my bottom lip.

"We'll see if you can make good on that promise once we get to my apartment."

Her tone was playful, but there was an undercurrent that I didn't quite understand. Seeing my confusion, she clarified, "You'll have to be mindful of my neighbors and not to break my apartment to bits. Do you think you can you give me all you have portended with those rules?"

That damn face. I started to jog ahead of her.

"Hey!"

"Keep up, Red," I hollered back. "You haven't really seen what I am capable of yet." Smiling a toothy grin, I relished the blush that colored her cheeks.

"What's with all those teeth showing?" she teased.

Now she's done it. I began running but not before shooting back...

"The better to eat you with, my dear."

Chapter Twenty-Two

Faelan

Wylder's taunt had me running faster than I had thought myself capable.

We rounded the corner intersecting the street my building was on. He slowed his pace and hung back to walk beside me, taking my hand as it swung at my side.

"I thought you'd run straight for the door. Can't you smell where it is?"

All of this was new to me but the scents around me where more potent than ever. Knowing if I'd closed my eyes, I could still find the bookshop on the corner or the bakery a street over.

My own scent was coming from just up ahead. *Weird.*

If I could smell it, Wylder definitely could.

"Of course, I can. I am just getting a feel for the area. The sounds, the smells..." He continued to glance at every shadow. "I don't like being caught unaware. And since I've never been in this part of town, I need to know the difference between what's normal and say, if a fae where to enter the area."

I hadn't even considered that a possibility.

Being back in the human world, letting all I knew of the supernatural fall away happened without a single thought.

This was my safe haven. *Well, isn't that thought a hot bottle of piss?*

"Do you think we were followed?" I asked. "I didn't smell anything out the norm."

He nodded once at my declaration. That was all he needed to continue to hear.

I'd never had someone who trusted me so completely. It was refreshing and yet, a little scary at the same time. As fallible as I could be, was that a good thing? *Get a grip, Negative Nancy.*

We walked hand in hand towards my building, up the stairs, and to the door. It was only when I needed both hands to find my keys that he'd let go.

It had been a comfortable, tender few moments of strolling through the moonlight.

Entering the dark apartment wasn't as problematic as it usually was.

For one thing, I could see. My eyes didn't need the light, but it was a habit that was hard to kick.

For another thing, I didn't have to be super quiet so as to not wake my roommate. Alayna was currently running around the Lupian Forest spying on the fae.

And most importantly, the last thing, I didn't have to worry about finding anyone hidden in the shadows, waiting to pounce on a single female in the city. *A gal could get use to this.*

Wylder took in the surroundings and his eyes landed on the bottle of whiskey still sitting on the coffee table.

"May I?" he asked.

"Have at it. I'm going to have some iced tea."

The kitchen was open to the living room so we could see each other while I added ice to the pitcher and asked if he'd like anything to eat.

"Well, if you're offering..." *Those damned waggling eyebrows of his.*

Setting the pitcher and a couple of glasses on the counter, I made my way towards the bedroom. "I'm going to look for that pendant. I'll be right back. Make yourself comfortable."

Entering my room with my new senses, the pungency of my unlaundered clothes hamper slapped me in the face. *Blehhhh.* The wash would have to come later.

Grams' pendant should be in the jewelry box she'd given me a few years ago.

Opening the top, the music tinkled its familiar song. A variation of Peter and the Wolf. *I get the irony now Grams. Thanks.*

Sitting to the side at the top of the box, was the stone pendant she'd sent months ago.

Picking it up, I held it to the light. The stone was odd, but pretty. It didn't look like anything special, definitely not my taste.

It was beautifully wrapped in an ornate wiring and hung from a simple chain. *Could this really be some magical stone?*

Swiping my robe from the back of the door, I sashayed out into the living room.

Wylder looked up and grinned at my exaggerated hip swings.

"Wanna join me in the shower big boy?" *Big boy? Gah... really Faelan?*

Jumping up like someone bit him on the ass, he was across the room in two long strides, making me giggle.

"I thought you'd never ask," he said. *Those dark caterpillars get me every time.*

I was beginning to think those little facial features he only showed to me would be my undoing.

We made it to the bathroom in three long strides. Leaning over and turning the water on full hot to heat up before we ventured in, I turned back around to find him already naked except for his socks and burst out laughing.

"What? You don't like my knee-high black socks?" he said in mocked disbelief. "My calves get achy from time to time."

I totally lost my composure at that point. "Okay, Grandpa."

Oops. I heard his growl and held my hands up in front of me in surrender.

Reaching across the short distance, he yanked me against his chest, bending slightly to snarl in my ear.

"I'm pretty sure you were told not to call me anything familial but Daddy." He tsked. "I suppose I'll have to figure out a decent punishment for your naughty behavior.

Swallowing the lump in my throat, I placed a hand on the underside of his balls and gave them a gentle squeeze.

Whimpering into the nape of his neck, I whispered "So, punish me, Daddy."

Chapter Twenty-Three

Wylder

Oh, this woman! Reaching for the nozzle, I turned off the running water. The feel of her purring into my neck, tongue flittering just behind my ear, made the hairs on my whole body stand up.

Quickly reaching down behind her knees, I knocked her legs out from under her as I scooped her up into my arms.

A little "Oof" escaped her lips and that one little sound brought all of the yearning I'd felt for her to the surface.

Luckily, the bedroom door was open, otherwise I'd have kicked it in and wouldn't have felt guilty in the least.

Plopping her onto the bed, something primal reared its ugly head from deep within. Without a conscious thought, my stance became a crouch. An electric current pass between us and her eyes widened. *Buckle up, cupcake.*

Hands up in prudent surrender, her whimper only excited me further. "Easy there, Wylder," she protested.

A coy smile donned my face for a fraction of a second before the beast was back in control.

Prowling towards the bed, I watched her scoot back like a cornered animal. *No where to go, sweetpea.*

Jumping from the end of the bed and landing with a hand on either side of her, she was caged in. My knee met her thighs, prying them open easily, rubbing her clit just below her panties with long, forceful intent.

Reaching down to cup her face, our lips met with elation. Parting them for me allowed my tongue access to wrestle with hers.

Leaning forward, Faelan ran her fingers through the hair on the back of my neck. A snarl resonated from deep within my throat. *Oh, no darlin. Not this time.*

Quick as lightening, I pinned her arms back down on the bed above her head.

"Ah ah ah, Red," I said with a devilish smirk. "As part of your punishment, you are not allowed to touch me without strict permission."

Her eyes widened and she chewed on the side of her mouth, holding back what I could only assume would be a sarcastic retort.

After a few long minutes as I held her gaze, I could see her resignation to the game I was presenting.

"Good girl." The momentary victory I'd won was short lived as she began to wriggle and push against my restraint after my condescending praise.

Her alpha side was rising in response to the challenge. *Well shit.*

"Easy there, Faelan. It's only a game, sweetpea." Sitting back on my heels for a moment. I gave her rational mind time to catch up to her primal instincts.

Taking a few breaths, I saw the moment awareness re-entered her eyes. With reverence and understanding, the mischievous grin I donned seemed to work in bringing us back to our initial intentions.

"Whatever am I going to do with you?" I tsked, running a gently placed finger down the side of her face.

"Whatever you want to do. I'll be good," she said, bringing her fingers up to make a criss cross over her heart. "That was... unexpected. I don't even know where it came from." *I do, my little Alpha*.

Brushing a stray hair from her eyes, I noticed the barely there smattering of freckles across her cheeks and nose. "You're still new to all of this. I should have been more careful."

"I don't want to be coddled, Wylder. I just need a bit of direction from time to time."

Shifting my weight, I settled fully between her legs.

"Okay, Red. I'll give you directions." Without warning, I yanked off her panties, ripping them in the process. "Lay that pretty little head of yours back and don't you dare lift it from that pillow until I say so."

I could feel the heat coming off of her sex and knew she'd be wet and ready for me.

She needed to learn control and to better control her mood shifts. If I could only teach myself to be more patient when it came to her, I'd benefit from the lessons as well. And with the added dilemma of the neighbors and thin walls, I wondered if I had it in me to hold back.

Being quiet or respectable to others around me wasn't my forte, but I was up for the challenge. One look in those eyes of hers and I knew I would do anything if she willed it.

"What are you waiting for?" she teased. "Did you forget what goes where?" *Smartass.*

That does it. She's toast. Quickly dipping my head between her legs and spreading her folds with two fingers like a peace sign, I used the other hand to lightly flick the erect bundle of nerves before me, eliciting a sudden intake of breath through her teeth.

"Do I have your attention now, witch?" I knew the dig would hit its mark. Sure enough...

"Hey!" she protested but I was already three moves ahead. With a firm hand, I pressed her abdomen to the bed to restrain her. Without another word, my mouth came crashing down on that lovely bean, sucking on it, hard.

The groan she made in response was worth the fallout from her irritation. *Mmmm. So sweet.*

Popping my head up to peer at her face, I said, "Is there a problem, Red? I can stop if you'd like."

Breathlessly, she replied, "If you stop, I will rip your throat out."

Chuckling at her frustration, I proceeded to make a meal of the feast laid before me. A few long passes of my tongue over every inch of her sex had her sweet honey dripping like a freshly tapped maple tree.

"Mmmmm. You're so fucking wet. Whatever shall I do with you?"

Before she had a chance to respond, my tongue plunged inside as I brought my thumb down, rubbing circles on her sensitive clit. With my eyes closed, I could hear every tiny moan even better.

Gyrating her hips and squeezing my head with every pass of pleasure, I couldn't get enough. My plan to prolong her torture was working against me.

Removing my tongue, I efficiently replaced it with two fingers, not giving her time to recover. Over and over those fingers curled in and up to that spot that dreams came from.

As her muscles began to tighten, I swiftly pulled out and she screamed her frustration. *Naughty girl.*

"Noooo! You bastard!" Trying to wiggle herself onto my fingers again, I tsked as her head lifted ever so slightly off the pillow.

"Oh no. Such a bad girl you are." With that, I grabbed her hips and flipped her over. Thwack!

The small whimper that she allowed to hiss through her teeth had my cock hard enough to chisel rock. A thrum low in my groin made it difficult to hold back the need to take her right here and now.

Gathering the last of my resolve, I put my desire in a box and closed it tight.

Gently caressing over the hot handprint on her delicate ass. Faelan lifted herself to her hand and knees.

"You don't listen very well, do you?" I said with a chuckle.

Pushing her head face first into the pillow, I leaned forward and whispered into her ear.

"Patience and control are important factors in learning to shift at will. Do you want to be at the mercy of the magics? ..."

I rubbed my hard cock along the length of her ass, down towards her wet opening, and forward towards that most sensitive bundle of nerves I knew would be aching from the near orgasm. She shuttered.

"Or do you want to be at my mercy when I could teach you to control it?"

I lifted her head with a firm, but gentle hand around her throat. Gliding myself back and forth across her sex, I knew her lack of sarcastic retort meant she was indeed at my mercy. *That cute little ass...mmmm.*

My tongue pushed through my lips. Releasing the hold on her throat, she let her head fall back down to the pillow, but I held her hips high as she remained on her knees.

Pressing the tip of my cock into her from behind, I let it sit there, tormenting us both. *Steady.* If keeping it motionless was what I needed to do to push more boundaries, then that was what I would do.

She began to wiggle her ass again, squirming, trying to force my hand. Chuckling once, I pulled out and yanked quickly on both of her ankles, so that she was flat on her belly.

My weight came down on top of her, but she seemed to welcome it. Pinning both her breast and shoulders to the mattress, I rubbed my cock in the crease of her bare backside.

"I think I should punish you by cumming all over your back and leaving you to suffer with no release." My balls danced playfully at her bottom.

"Oh no you will not!" she panted out. Her struggles beneath me only fueled the desire I had to release everything I had on her.

A tingling sensation came from just under her skin, making me sit up abruptly.

I wasn't prepared for the magics that flew from her hands.

Knocking me backwards, I landed flat on my ass.

Chapter Twenty-Four

Faelan

What the fuck was that? I looked down at my hands like they were a foreign object.

I'd never seen real magic before. It was unnerving but also exhilarating.

Wylder's face told me that he was as surprised as I was. He'd teased and tormented me so much that the untapped power within me rose to the surface.

A wicked smile played at my lips. *My turn.*

Thoroughly frustrated, I looked him up and down like he was now prey.

"Whoa, Red. Let's talk about this." His hands raised in surrender, a small grin at the corners of his lips turned downed a second later.

"What's wrong, big boy?" I said with a wicked smile. "Are ya scared?"

Watching him squirm, trying to sit up was titillating. The power coming from my hands holding him down was new and exciting. *Hot damn, this is amazing.*

Then I lost it. The magics dissipated as suddenly as they had come on. *Uh-oh.*

With my attention elsewhere, Wylder took his advantage, flipping me onto my back like a tackling dummy. The air rushed from my lungs, but he didn't give me any recovery time.

Wiggling himself into position between my legs, I only had half a second before he thrusted, fully inside of me.

"Ahhhh," I exclaimed. Breathlessly, I wrapped my arms around the back of his neck, drawing his mouth down to mine.

The kiss was as slow and anguished as the strokes he pumped inside of me. Agonizingly gentle strokes that were growing in speed.

He was inside of me and yet I couldn't get close enough. A moan of ecstasy escaped both of us as our kiss pulled apart.

"You. Are. Everything..." he growled with every glide in and out.

"You're not... half bad... yourself." Breathless, and with desire building all the while, I mustered a cry of glory as my muscles contracted around his length.

He brought his tempo up, climbing to the crescendo of the music we were playing together, until he fell over the side of the stage with me.

"By the gods! Faelan!" he cried out just as my own rapture broke me into a million little pieces.

"That's it. Right there," I moaned. "Oh, gods!"

We rode out the last of our pleasure until we were both completely spent. Panting as we pulled apart and laid back onto the sheets.

After a few minutes of catching our breath, he rolled to his side to look at me. *Stop staring weirdo.*

"I don't know about you but...," he hesitated, face scrunched up in doubt.

"But what?" I pushed. The nervous look he had made me sit up, dragging the sheets up to cover my chest.

"Well," he scrubbed at his chin, sliding a hand over his face, through his hair, and resting it on the back of his neck. "I just... I've never had such a tender moment like that before." *Awww. Sexy and sensitive wolf-man.* "Did you feel... I don't know." His words kept getting stuck.

"Yes. I felt it." *Swoony.* "It was sweet and dare I say..." I clammed up. It wasn't that I'd never been in a caring relationship before. *Just say it, Faelan!* "Well, lovingly tender." I quickly turned my head, embarrassment heating my cheeks.

His hand found my chin, turning it to look into his pearlescent silver-blue eyes. He was searching for something. I tried to pull out of his grip, but he held fast.

"Are you... are you upset by that?" The hurt in his tone made me blink back the sting of tears.

"No." The word was barely above a whisper. "I thought that maybe you would be."

My clarification brought a meek grin to his rugged face, and he pulled me into a tight hug against his chest.

"Good, because if you were, I don't know what I would do." Intertwining our fingers, he brought them to his lips. "I know

I told you that you wouldn't want to know my age yet, but I will tell you this. I am not young. And I only say this so that you are aware of the gravity of my next words." *Oh, by Luna. Sexy ancient grandpa?*

Turning to look at him again, the slight crinkle around his eyes was a road map to the twinkle I now saw there.

"O-kay. Tell me quick." *Rip it off like a bandage.*

Wylder's chuckle stirred deep in my lower belly. Longing took the place of my need for answers. That tug from the mating bond making my need to be with him insatiable.

I knew I would never get enough of him. And that thought alone made me brave my uneasiness over his age. *It's just a number.*

"I'm not telling you my age yet, silly. I said I have something that you should know the weight of in measure to my years." *Wonderful. Another mystery.*

Kissing our intertwined hands again, he took a breath and let his eyes rove over my face.

"I have never loved anyone but my parents. And they have been passed for many decades now." He brushed a chaste kiss to my temple. "I have never been attracted to anyone, other than just sexual trysts."

He kissed me on the forehead and my eyes fluttered shut. The heat coming from his chest was a balm to my nerves.

"I won't tell you that I love you yet either, Red. I barely even know you... but I can't deny that the mating bond is making me question whether all of my lonely years were because I was waiting for you." *No pressure.* "And I can feel good about that.

That my suffering and hardships were worth the wait. You, were worth the wait."

I hadn't expected a proclamation with the sex.

"I feel similarly, though I'm only a little over two and half decades old." I smiled up at him with all of my teeth on display. "We'll figure this out... Grandpa."

He pounced so fast it was a blur, and I giggled. *Sexy beefcake here is all Mine.*

Chapter Twenty-Five

Faelan

After another hour or so lost in the pleasure of each other, the last of which we'd broken the towel bar in the shower, we knew we were due back at the cottage in a few hours to meet up with the pack.

That was what made us finally decide to start getting dressed.

Wylder threw on his sweatpants and headed to the kitchen to get some of the tea I'd left on the counter. We were both dehydrated and could use the sugar rush to keep us going.

The pendant on the dresser caught my eye as I was buttoning up my jeans. Swiping it up to put it on, I noticed a crack along one side of the stone.

Running my finger down the crack, I snatched my hand back as a sliver of the stone imbedded in my thumb like a splinter.

Blood pulled to the surface and, instinctually, I sucked it clean, watching as the small wound closed over with the stone splinter still inside. *Well, shit.*

Fastening the pendant around my neck and heading to the bathroom to fetch the tweezers, a large thud sounded from out in the main room.

"Wylder?" No reply. A little more tentatively, I called again, "Everything okay out there?" Still no answer. *Shit.*

Cautiously. I walked down the hall towards where the sound had come from.

The room was unusually dark around the edges, and I quickly realized I couldn't smell the fragrant plants that along the wall like I had when we had first arrived.

With a quick look around the living room area toward the kitchen island, my eyes fell to Wylder lying statue still next to one of the barstools. A cup of spilled tea by his head.

Forgetting my concerns about the room's oddness, I ran to drop next to my mate. Finding his pulse, the beating of my own heart started up again.

"Wylder!" His eyes were open, but he was completely immobile. *No, no, no, no!* "What's happened? What do I do?"

He couldn't speak, blink, or move.

"Rather fitting, don't you think?" Loxias' voice floated to me from the shadows as he and two of the guards he had with him the last time stepped closer.

Standing quickly, instinct had me half crouched in front of him. "What did you do to him?!"

"I simply made the tea better... adding your grandmothers blend to it." His smile was wicked. "Oh, and freshened it up with a little wolfsbane." I growled. "Okay, a lot of wolfsbane."

He took a step towards us, and my fingernails grew into claws. Casually stepping back a pace or two, he put his hands up.

"I told you, Faelan, I need you. You're the only hope we have to break the curse." Using the fingertips of one hand, he brushed imaginary dust from his pristine jacket. *Ugh.* Prince douche-baggery here was a real piece of work.

Reaching his hand out for me to take it, I bared my teeth and the guttural sounds that bubbled from within my chest sounded truly menacing.

"Well, then, here is what you should know. If you do not come with us, I will instruct Quill here to shoot your friend with a bolt." He raised his hand to indicate the fae holding a crossbow. "And before you ask. Yes. The tip has been dipped in more wolfsbane. Any more of that in his system..." he lavished a hand in Wylder's direction, "and I am afraid that he may not make it."

Looking down at Wylder, his eyes open and alert, I knew he would come for me if I went with Loxias willingly. It gave me a small amount of comfort to know that, but it was hard to leave him here in this helpless state.

"I want your word. A promise from a fae is supposed to be unbreakable." Glancing down at Wylder again, I saw the fear in his eyes. Fear, I knew, was for me. Not himself.

Looking back to the prince and then his two lackies, I said, " Swear it. Swear that if I come with you willingly, he will live and that no harm shall come to him by anything you or your folk have done." Remembering how my Grams had told me that wording for the fae was more important than humans, I tacked on, "or will do."

An incredulous smile spread reluctantly across his face. I knew the promise I'd asked for was tied up nicely with no foreseeable loopholes.

His grin told me he was mildly impressed. Not that I cared what he thought. *Come on. Take the deal.*

After a moment of contemplation, reaching out his hand, he shook on it. "You have my word."

I took it, realizing a second too late that he was making contact with my skin.

Wylder's warning about Loxias' gifts sounded alarm bells through in my head.

Immediately leaning in, he whispered, "You feel sorrow at the loss of your mate, but you know that I have your best interests at heart."

Pulse quickening, I waited for the power of his gifts to overwhelm me.

The pendant at my neck was hidden by my shirt. It buzzed with a heating sensation and then cooled.

Nothing changed. My mind was still my own. The ritual stone must provide protection from his gifts.

Nice as that was, I knew I couldn't have it anywhere near me if he was escorting me to the Faery realm. It would be safer with Wylder and the pack until I got back and could use it against the fae.

I didn't know how to use my magics yet, so they would be no help to me right now.

Making a hasty decision, I turned to Loxias with, what I hoped, was the appropriate response to his statement. "Please," I begged, "let me say goodbye to my mate."

A twitch at the corner of his mouth was the only indication of his annoyance.

"If I've lost him, then I need the only closure that I can have. I need to kiss him goodbye and leave my tears on his chest."

I could tell that he didn't want me to go anywhere near Wylder, but he consented after a glance to Quill, who dipped his chin slightly. "Go. Say your goodbyes. You have two minutes."

He swept to the other side of the room and his two guards followed. The crossbow in Quill's hand still pointed directly at Wylder's chest.

Swallowing the fear that had crept in, I bent low to Wylder's ear. My body was blocking him from view.

As stealthily as I could manage, I ripped the chained pendant from around my neck.

Kissing his cheek and hiding the necklace in his closed fingers, I whispered, "Get this to the pack. Keep it safe. You'd better fight, Wylder! Live! Prepare for the ritual. I will return to you all as soon as I can manage to slip away."

"Thirty seconds," Loxias called over to us.

Placing another kiss on his cheek and a slightly longer one on his still lips, I whispered the only thing I could think in the moment, "I'm yours."

His eyes stared, emotions coursing just beneath the surface, but I wouldn't know what they were until we'd meet again.

Grabbing Alayna's jacket from the back of the barstool, I threw it over his bare upper half.

"Okay," I said. "I'm ready."

Loxias motioned the other two fae towards the door. With a hand to my lower back, he ushered me forward, grabbing my coat from the rack on the way out.

"Thank you."

The prince's eyes went wide. *Oops. Well, shit.*

A small grin brought out a dimple in his cheek that I hadn't noticed before. *Don't thank the sexy faery, you idiot.*

We'd both reached to close the door at the same time. The back of his hand made contact with mine and heat bloomed in my thumb that still held the stone splinter. *Ouch.*

A strange, barely there, electric sensation coursed through me. It was there and gone in a blink.

"Go ahead. You can lock up." Loxias' genuinely nice tone caught me off guard.

"That's kind of you." He inclined his head and stepped into the hallway.

With one last parting look to my mate, I crossed the threshold and closed the door behind me.

Chapter Twenty-Six

Faelan

We made it out of town rather quickly. I didn't even remember turning the corner that led to the outskirts of the forest.

As we entered the woods, Loxias motioned to the guard I hadn't learned the name of yet, and a dark shadow engulfed our party. It wasn't oppressive or hindering.

In fact, it seemed to help illuminate the whole area just outside of it.

"What is that?" I asked.

Loxias turned toward Quill and then the other guard. After a moment of hesitation, he answered. "Leif's gift is a shadow shield."

My face must have shown my confusion because he pressed on with a small smirk.

"He can create a shield with shadows, hiding us on the inside. It blocks us from sight, scent, and sound."

Leif stepped to my side and, instinctively, I took a step away. The fae male chuckled but didn't move any closer. "I can throw the shield out five to ten feet in all directions." *Cocky much?*

Impressed, but not wanting to give any of them kudos, I asked, "Is that all? I would have thought you could throw it farther."

That dimple appeared on Loxias' cheek again and Quill burst out laughing. Leif shuffled his feet and looked sheepishly towards the others.

"I can." he said, stumbling over his words. "I mean... I can't maintain it for long, but I have sent it out thirteen feet all the way around before."

"Sure, ya did, big boy," I replied.

Loxias joined in on Quill's laughing. *Yup.* Males were easy to steer.

Leif sputtered as his face turned red. Thrusting a finger in my direction, he stepped towards me once again. "It's your ancestor's fault!"

I felt uncharacteristically defensive. My snout elongated and nails grew into claws. A snarl ripped through my chest and out of my throat.

He stopped his advance immediately. Quill and Loxias stopped laughing at once.

Coming to rest a hand on mine, Loxias said, "Leif didn't mean anything by it. He's just sensitive to his gifts'... length."

The power of his suggestion coursed through me. He was trying to redirect me and subdue the Alpha wolf inside.

A mild heat from my thumb pulsed. I had known that I was upset but couldn't remember why. Another pulse from the splinter righted my thinking.

Before I could give away the only advantage in my favor, I took a deep breath and smiled.

"Okay. So, I take it that Quill and Leif are more than just your guards." It wasn't a question. Only true friends would be able to get away with the casualness of speaking freely around royalty.

"Quill here," Loxias motioned to the large male with the crossbow." "He's been my company since we first learned to pee outside our nappies." Quill rolled his eyes. "And Leif... well, if it wasn't for him and his gifts, I would have been dead a hundred times over by now. The last few centuries have been quite an adventurous ordeal." *Am I the only baby in all this mess?*

"I feel like I am missing so much." With a new tactic, I batted my eyes subtly, a small smile playing at my lips. "Is there anything you could possibly fill me in on? I'm just so new to this world."

If there was one thing that I knew, it was that males liked to feel needed. They liked to be the provider and protector.

Towards the end of any of my bartending shifts, I would note which males were not too drunk but inebriated just enough to flirt my way into a bigger tip when they cashed out.

He motioned for us to continue walking. Once we were on a trail headed in a direction I'd never taken, he finally spoke again.

"I won't pretend to know everything, but I will give you as much of an education as I can. Ask away?"

I thought about all of things I'd learned over the past week. Something had been bothering me with all the First Witch stuff.

I just couldn't make it make sense. Some of the blanks needed filling in and it occurred to me that he may have some answers. *Here goes nothing.*

"What do you know about the First Witch? Who was she and how did she come to being the First Witch?"

He shared a look with Quill. Voices and crunching leaves drew their attention to the right side of the trail.

Leif's hand splayed, then came in to make a fist. The shadows darkened, ever so slightly, and the area around us lit up more vividly.

I gasped and my hands came up to cover it. Zito, Piper, and Blaze were in wolf form, sniffing the surrounding area.

Realizing that they could not even smell me, much less see me, I had a sudden surge of gratitude for Leif's gifts.

I didn't want any of them to come to harm and, though I was reluctant to admit it, I wanted to see this through with the fae. I needed to understand the jumbled information that was my ancestry.

"I could have sworn I'd caught the scent of Faelan and Loxias heading in this direction," Zito said.

Shocked that I'd heard him inside of my mind in his wolf form, it only occurred to me after they'd left the area that I may have been able to communicate with them too. With practice.

The fae around me were stock still. Loxias eyed me with suspicion once the wolves had moved on.

"Interesting," he said. "I was prepared to silence you, but you didn't even seem to want them to find you."

If I told him a lie, and he didn't believe me, I'd lose whatever trust that I was trying to gain from him. I needed him to believe that his gifts affected me the way that they were supposed to.

And they did, it was only that sliver of stone embedded in my thumb that helped my mind burn off the effects each time. And that wasn't one hundred percent.

I knew that his power was meant to make me comply completely, without question.

As much as its presents annoyed me, I was grateful for the splinter. It provided, at least, some clarity.

Deciding that the truth was better than being caught in a lie, I offered them a half truth.

"I didn't want any altercations. I knew they wouldn't understand you having my best interests at heart. I couldn't let my presence be the cause of a fight." *Buy it, buy it, buy it.*

He took a step forward and put his hand under my chin. Fighting every instinct to swat it away, I allowed him to look into my eyes. *What in the name of Luna are you looking for?*

After a few more tense seconds, he dropped his hand, and the dimple appeared.

Brushing the side of my face...*Yuck...* "I do have your best interests at heart, my love."

The electric sensation that ran though my body at his magic didn't meet as much resistance as the last time. *Oh no, no, no, no, no!*

A feeling of warmth filled my chest and low in my belly. *What was I saying?*

I stared back at his beautiful face. Longing replaced the disgust. Leaning into his touch, I sighed.

The sharp pain snapped through me like a slap to the face. The splinter heated again, but this time the burn was taking longer to make its way around my body.

I still wanted to give in to his will, but my mind was fighting against it.

A tug from deep within my chest anchored me back to the reality of the situation. Wylder was rousing from his poisoned state. I could feel his rage and his... fear.

It would still be hours before he could move more completely, and he would never be able to get into Faery. I was on my own, for now.

Remembering my ruse, I smiled up at Loxias and batted my lashes, this time in a not-so-subtle way. His answering smile was adorable, and I couldn't help myself from feeling drawn to him.

Quill cleared his throat from behind us and Leif shook his head as he passed.

The forest was alive with the daytime animals skittering about and the birds singing in the trees.

A path just in front of us came into view when Quill flourished his hand out in front of him. The sparkling colors of tiny, iridescent particles danced in the dim light of the forest.

Magics.

An opening appeared in the tall overbrush.

With a wink, he waved his hand in front of an illuminated archway.

"Welcome to the land of Anavrin."

Chapter Twenty-Seven

Wylder

Watching Red leave with the very fae who had threatened her life when we'd first met was probably the worst thing I'd ever experienced in all of my long years.

Not being able to move or speak, or even scratch the itch on the tip of my nose as the pain from the wolfsbane burned throughout my entire body, was a special kind of torture.

It had been a couple of hours since they'd left. My system was slowly starting to become mobile again. The poisonous plant had no doubt slowed down the healing process and the more my body regained feeling, the more pain I experienced.

The hollowness in my chest was a direct response to the distance I was from my mate.

That bond had a different feel to it than the protector bond that Inara had enacted.

If Faelan were in trouble or hurt, I would feel it like a sharp knife to my gut. I was glad that that particular bond only worked one way.

The fact that I'd felt a flare of heartache in my chest could only mean that she was losing herself to Loxias' gifts.

Sending as much adoration along the mating bond as I could gather, I shoved out with all of my feelings towards her.

It was a long moment before I felt the adoration returned.

She was safe from physical harm so far, but I knew how Loxias craved power. And Faelan Was power, even if she didn't know how to use it yet.

If I could manage to shift, the healing process would speed up, but I was having difficulties making my body respond. *Shift. Shift, damn it!*

After what felt like at least another hour, feelings of fear and nervousness came down the bond.

That could mean anything, but I knew in my heart of hearts the only thing that would cause such a strong emotion to flow through Red.

They'd arrived at Anavrin. She'd passed the point of which I could go, or the pack would be able to help her. She was on her own.

Fear and rage coursed through me. My body shook and trembled with it. *Shift!*

The tang of red hot anger coated my tongue, and my fingers finally twitched. It took a few minutes but the ability to move my hands came back.

Loosely wrapping the pendant's chain around my middle finger, I clasped it like a lifeline. The action was labored and aggravatingly sluggish.

A roar of frustration finally slipped through my lips, waking more of my system and burning through the remainder of the wolfsbane. That familiar itch just under my skin set my annoyance to determination.

With a shake of my limbs, a burst of black fur and large paws stood where I'd been laying half naked on the floor. Faelan's jacket laid discarded, and my sweats were in tattered strips beside it.

The change caused the necklace wrapped around my finger to appear more like a ring high up on my knuckle. It wasn't going anywhere, but I was.

Gathering myself on wobbly legs, I hauled the weight of my wolves' body to all four limbs. A primal act to move, to be in action, to be doing something, helped remove the rest of the tea and wolfsbane from my system.

I couldn't reach Red now. There was no way into the faery-lands without fae assistance.

It was magically blocked. *Stupid, lousy faeries.*

So, as much as it killed me, I'd do what she'd asked and get the stone to the pack to prepare for the ritual.

Then, I'd call in a favor from an old friend.

Anavrin was no place for a shifter. The creatures of Faery were strong and deceptively beautiful. And all of them were deadly.

It didn't matter. If everything worked out the way I hoped, I'd be there sooner rather than later. Faelan could travel a million miles away and I would still search for her.

She was worth the danger.

Chapter Twenty-Eight

Faelan

*B*eautiful. I didn't want to be here, but I couldn't deny how awestruck I was at the sight of the faerylands.

Anavrin had lush landscapes and trees of every sort. The cobblestoned roads and the paths that led off in different directions implored you to follow them.

The sky was a beautiful shade of blue with big, puffy clouds floating like cotton candy. The sun shining throughout the land lit up every stream, tree, and sparse building I could see.

It wasn't too hot or too cold. Anavrin was magic itself in landscape form.

Trying to keep the wonderment off of my face, I turned to see Leif hold out his hands and felt the now familiar push of his gifts covering us.

"Why don't you want anyone to know we're here?" I asked Loxias.

A dark expression passed over his face and was gone in the next blink. If I hadn't been looking right at him, I would have missed it.

Maybe it was nothing, but the look shared between Quill and Leif confirmed what I saw. They were hiding.

Walking up behind me, Loxias reached out, offering his hand.

If I took it, he would push his will into me, and I didn't know how long the stone splinter would be able to fight against his gifts in Anavrin.

If I refused it, he would know I'd been able to fight off the effects so far.

Plastering a friendly smile upon my face, I took it. This was the land of faeries, and I had no allies. At least I knew he and his best friends would try to keep me safe amongst their kind. *The enemy you know.*

I sighed. It played nicely with my ruse because his returning smile lit up his dimple. *Arrogant, hunky idiot.*

At his touch, a gentle caress of energy flowed beneath the skin of my arm.

"You are safe with us. With me," he continued, "but there must be some protection surrounding a Prince of Anavrin."

The words made me feel stupid for even questioning his motives. *Why had I been so keen to not be here?*

My thumb heated, but this time only a mild warmth shifted inside of me. I couldn't remember what my previous objections to the fae had been.

I remembered Grams was missing and that I was a half witch and half werewolf. I remembered that I was the Alpha of her pack and that my mate had been a Sigma. *My mate!*

The splinter heated again and a tightness in my chest brought me up short. *Think, Faelan!*

I have a mate. He's not lost, like dead. He's lost, like I couldn't save him from... something.

The hollowness around my heart began to solidify with each detail I recalled. *Wylder!*

At the thought of his name, I remembered our bond. I remembered our bodies intertwined. I remembered the rawness of his emotions.

I dug my nails into the palms of my hands. The pain was my anchor against losing myself completely. *Hold on to that!*

"Faelan?" Loxias must have been calling my attention for a few moments because the dimple was gone. A stoic expression took up residence across his baby smooth face. "Have you been listening?"

Coming back to myself, I scrambled to make the adjustment of gratitude in the look I was wearing. "I haven't. I can't seem to take in the beauty of this place enough. I keep getting lost inside my own head."

Quill motioned to Loxias to have a sidebar with him and Leif. Their whispers couldn't be heard over the chirping of the birds and the babbling of the nearby stream.

After they conferred with one another, Loxias stepped back to my side.

"Excuse that interruption, love," he said. "It was a security issue that needed sorting out." *Doubtful.* "What was it you wanted to know before we'd crossed over the arch into Anavrin?"

Shit. I did want to know something, didn't I?

"I... I can't remember. Do you have any idea of what it might have been?" *The need to know about... what?* "This is really strange. I usually have a great memory."

"No worries." He waved away my concerns like they weren't the biggest thing consuming my mind right now.

No worries for you, jerk.

"We were discussing your ancestry, and you'd thought that I would have some more insight."

The details swam just out of reach. I could remember wanting to know more about... the First Witch. *That's right.*

"I remember now. How did the First witch come to be?"

Steepling his fingers, they came to rest on his lips as he thought. I wasn't sure if he was trying to edit the details in his mind ahead of time or not.

The fae couldn't lie, but that didn't mean they always spoke the truth into being.

Maybe he couldn't recall the details because of how long ago it was. Or maybe he wasn't sure if he should fill me in on all of the details.

Irrational frustration welled up inside of me the longer he took. "I came with you under the guise that you would give me answers to any question you have the knowledge to answer. Are you a male of honor, or not?"

A flash of anger crinkled at the corners of his eyes and along the curl of his lips. Stepping into my space quicker than I'd thought possible, he breathed a deadly warning.

"I will not be called dishonorable by a witch in my own homeland!" His face was contorted in a way that I could sense the hurt underneath the anger.

Quill cleared his throat and Loxias seemed to remember himself. Taking two full strides back from me, he bowed his head in apology.

"My regrets on my outburst. I do not lack honor, Faelan." He smiled but it didn't reach his eyes. "However, I do lack patience with some manner of things."

We all began to walk again. It had been many hours since we'd left my apartment in town. Blisters were beginning to form on my feet, and everything ached. Hunger and thirst also crept in. And who knew when the last time I had slept.

The weight of all those things brought my discomfort to the forefront of my thoughts.

"Are we nearly there? I don't know how much longer I can last." I hadn't gotten the answers to any of my questions yet and the anxiety of having to perform magics without knowing how was leaving me exhausted.

"It will be at least another day before we arrive at King Zyoden's castle," Leif answered.

I gaped at them. "You do remember that I am not a fae, don't you?"

Not missing the way that they all glanced at one another, I continued. "Look, I need to eat and rest. I don't know what your lives are like, but I can't just keep going for days on end."

"We can, but that leaves us vulnerable to attacks," Quill said. "We were planning on making camp at Max's tonight. It's only another fifteen miles or so from here."

Fifteen miles? Great Luna. These fae were a piece of work.

"Can I at least rest for a few hours? I'm extremely thirsty."

A few miles into Anavrin, we had passed a shimmering clear lake and had taken a worn trail to the left, off of the cobble-stoned road. I'd found myself in the shade of some of the most beautiful trees I'd ever seen.

There was a stream running along the path I assumed led to the lake because the water was just as crystal clear as it had been.

Loxias had been quiet since his little outburst and non-apology. That dimple in his cheek and twinkle in his eye hadn't made their way back yet.

He was somewhat of a mystery. Honor was important to him, but I had no idea about why it mattered so much.

His touchiness had to stem from something in his life, but it wasn't my mission to learn the inner workings of a fae prince's mind.

I was here to gather whatever information I could, return to the Lupian Forest and my pack, wait for the Full Blood Moon & perform the ritual that would ensure that the fae curse remained in place. Easy peasy... *yeah, right.*

"Let's take a few hours break so that the lovely Faelan here can shut her eyes for a bit." he announced to the group.

Whispering quickly into Quill's ear and then motioning me and Leif to the cool stones that lay on the banks of the stream, he took a deep breath and the brooding side of him vanished.

His adorable dimple lit up his face and he reached out his hand for me once more.

"Where is Quill off to?" I asked but, before he'd had time to answer, Quill was already coming back through the copse of trees with a couple of dead rabbits hanging from his hand.

Woah! That was fast.

"I thought that we could use something to eat, and Quill is an amazing shot with his crossbow. He obliged my request to scrounge something up." Loxias' eyes sparkled again now, and I found myself reaching for his outstretched hand without thinking. "You are hungry and thirsty, my love. After we rest and have refueled our bodies, the walk will seem all too quick and lovely."

We were farther into Anavrin and the warmth from the stone splinter did little to dispel what he'd projected to me.

Why would I want to? He was trying to take away the discomfort and that was a good thing. *Right?*

The stone splinter warmed again, and I could remember that it was his gifts making his will mine, but it didn't help me to push them away. *Shit. Shit. Shit.*

It was almost worse. The knowing and not being able to stop his wishes.

At least if I hadn't known, then it wouldn't feel like being held captive inside of my own body with a fuzzy mind.

Leif took the rabbits from Quill after he started a small cooking fire. It didn't take long for them to cook over the magically colored flames. Loxias went to the stream himself to bring back a skein of fresh water.

The mood around them had lightened with every bite.

Apparently the fae needed to eat more often than they thought. *Typical male arrogance.*

They were jovial and laughing as they passed around the refreshments. It was interesting to see my fae captors acting like any other group of friends.

I sat quietly as I ate, observing their comradery.

Quill was telling some sort of off-color joke and Leif laughed, bumping the side of his closed fist on his friend's arm. Loxias' smile was bright and unencumbered. They all appeared to be younger than their stoic, brooding side would lead you to believe them to be.

"Are we about ready to get a move on?" Loxias called over to me. "I would like to be there in the next few hours, before the sun sets."

I couldn't remember the last time I'd slept. Exhaustion wore on my limbs with every passing moment.

The pleasant weather helped stir feelings of contentment. With sweet smelling flowers and the babbling stream in the background, I wanted nothing more than to curl up in a ball on the lush grass and sleep for a few days.

That wasn't an option. They were taking me to their king, and I had a mission of my own to accomplish.

"Sure. I'm done," I said, hesitating on my next words. "I need to relieve myself, though." A small blush crept up my cheeks and Loxias returned it with a coy smile.

"No problem," he said.

Coming up beside me, he gently ran the back of his hand across the side of my face.

"Stick to the bushes just out of sight and come back to us right afterwards."

Again, the splinter warmed but didn't dispel the compulsion. I knew that I should be trying to get away. Knew it and couldn't make my body work against what he wanted.

"There are creatures in Anavrin that would consider you the same as we considered the rabbits." *Geesh.* Comforting thought there.

"Tha..." *Don't thank a faery, idiot.* "That's very thoughtful of you."

Amusement sparkled in his eyes.

"We'll leave upon your return." Trailing his fingers down the side of my neck, he made a pass along the top of my chest. I gave an involuntary shiver. "And you want to return to me quickly."

Damn it. Now I do.

Chapter Twenty-Nine

Wylder

I made a call before leaving her apartment to set a plan in motion.

The first few miles from town, my legs still shook with the aftereffects of the wolfsbane and Inara's tea burning out of my system slowly.

Thirsty after our tryst and downing a full glass in one long pull, my mind hadn't any time to catch up to the off taste. The floor came up to meet me fast and I'd had no time to shout out a warning to her before my entire body was immobilized.

Watching in horror as Loxias, Leif, and Quill stepped out of the shadows was new kind of fear that I had never experienced.

Never having cared for anyone the way that I did Red, it felt as if at any moment my chest would simply cave in. And watching her leave with them, while I could do nothing to stop it, tore out my heart, leaving a chasm of hollowness in its wake.

The walk through town and back into the forest took a lot longer than usual. Darkness was settling in as the trees whispered their disappointment through their leaves.

Often feeling that the Lupian Forest was somewhat sentient, the guilt weighed heavily upon my shoulders.

The snap of twigs and rustle of underbrush just off the trail alerted my attention to movement. *Shit.*

In between one breath and the next, a dark color feline emerged.

"Nixie! What on earth are you doing out here?"

Bending down to pick her up, that feeling of keen awareness that I often experienced around certain animals prickled along my neck.

"Did you... did you come out here to find me?"

It was a bizarre thought, but as her eyes fixed on my face, I was sure that she did, indeed, come in search of me.

Inara's cat was a familiar. And a witch's familiar was as good as a witch themselves.

They always had magical elements to them. They communicated with the forest and its critters. And they were intelligent creatures.

One would be remissed to ignore them.

"Alright, Nix. I'll shift and you jump on." The cat blinked her eyes once slowly and I took that to mean that she was in agreement to the situation.

Securing the pendant around my finger again, I shifted. Nixie immediately jumped up and settled herself between my shoulder blades, her nails digging in like she was preparing for the speed.

Hang on tight, little one. She gently bit the back of my neck, and I chuckled.

On the next breath, we were flying through the forest towards the cottage. The pack would be waiting. And without Faelan at my side, I was glad that I had Nixie for support.

Pack politics were my least favorite thing in the world. There was no time to argue or disagree.

They would know that Nixie finding me could mean only one thing; Inara willed it.

We had to do what was needed so that I could get to Anavrin, find Red, and make our way back to Ritual Rock by the height of the full moon to keep the curse in place.

No pressure.

Chapter Thirty

Faelan

We had walked on for over a mile already. No one spoke but it was a comfortable kind of silence. One that came with a full belly and the contentedness of a pleasant journey.

The birds chirped and sang their merry tunes. A gentle breeze was blowing through the trees as the sounds of the babbling stream floated towards our ears.

It was peaceful. I couldn't remember why I had felt anxiety before we had taken a break, only that I had felt it.

"You had some questions about the First Witch," Loxias said as he came up beside me. "What would you like to know? Mind you, I only have basic knowledge of the account. It was a few centuries before my time." *That damned dimple*!

"Yes. I was wondering how she'd come to be... well, the first witch in existence?" Another thought occurred to me, and I added, "Do you know who or what she was prior to becoming a witch? Or was she born that way?"

I didn't miss the silent conveyance between Quill and Loxias. They seemed to do that a lot. The smallest of chin dips after the smallest of glances.

Irrationally, my frustration at the pair flared. After all, I was their captive, but Loxias had made me feel important. He called me Love.

And the overly friendly way that he touched me and talked to me suggested that we were more to each other. *Why can't I remember*?

Taking my hand in his, he interlocked our fingers as we strolled casually down the trail. It dawned on me that the hollow ache in my chest had something to do with... someone.

The longer I stayed in Anavrin, the more blurred everything became.

"The First Witch was a fae," he said. "She was my father's mistress."

I stopped walking completely. If the First Witch was a fae, that meant that I was part fae myself.

Breathing in short, frantic breaths, I couldn't get enough air. Nausea roiled in my stomach as the edges of my vision grew dark. If this kept up, I'd pass out.

A strange sensation tugged at the core of my being. It was soothing and forceful. I concentrated on it.

Pulling my hand from Loxias' and placing both hands upon my knees, the slow breaths I now took helped to calm the anxiety.

After another few minutes, the tug at my core spread warmth around my chest. It cradled me like a hug.

Standing up and looking around at the fae males in my presence, an underlying warning bell in my mind dinged loudly. I needed to get away but as Loxias' hand came to rest on my lower back, that feeling subsided.

"You are fine, Faelan. You simply needed a minute to collect your thoughts and wrap your head around it, love."

The shadows that I came to associate with Leif's abilities spread over the lot of us. A shuffling noise just off the trail had Quill lifting his crossbow in that direction.

"Remain quiet for a moment," he said, brushing his fingers on the side of my hand.

The smell of fresh turned soil and stench of something foul crinkled my nose.

I didn't even dare to breathe again as a boar-like creature the size of a small pony came scrambling out from the underbrush.

It had golden bristles, and its tusks were every bit of two feet long and sharper than the sword Loxias had sheathed behind his back.

A few seconds later, two more of the creatures emerged. They were smaller, about the size of exceptionally large dogs. Babies, I'd realized. *Awww..cute little ugly things.*

The whisper that blew into my ear sent a thrill of shivers down my spine. "Stay still. The gullinbursti can be extremely dangerous when they have a farrow in tow."

His lips grazed my lobe as he spoke. Heat rose low in my stomach. Biting my bottom lip, I tried not to make a sound.

The gullinbursti passed through without every looking in our direction. Leif's gift was powerful to be sure. No scents even got through the barrier to the outside.

I turned to Leif after he dropped the blanket of shadows. "Your gifts are amazing... but they don't stop sound?"

A grimace played along his mouth. "They did... Actually, they still do. Only normal humans and regular woodland creatures can't hear what goes on inside the shadows now." My perplexed look forced him to elaborate. "Before the first curse took effect, I could block all sound. Even from fae hearing."

I understood now. The curse had taken something or dulled something for every fae apparently.

No wonder they were desperate to end it. *Well, fuck me sideways.*

Loxias drew my attention back to him and motioned that they all should start walking again. "As I was saying, the First Witch was a fae."

"What was her name?" I interrupted. Frustration appeared and disappeared in the blink of an eye from his face.

I was no stranger to narcissistic males. Working at a bar at night, I'd seen a fair many different types of characters. It was his acting nice while a beast lay just under the surface that gave me pause.

I could handle my own, but the fae were notoriously strong and pushing my luck here wouldn't serve me in the long run. *Reign it in, Faelan.*

"I'm sor... *Don't apologize to the faery!* ... "How rude of me. Do continue."

"No worries," he said. "Her name has been stricken from history. Only her surname is remembered, Isbith. Though I am fairly certain that my father and mother remember it."

His finger grazed the bottom of my back again as we walked.

"You are not just part faery, Faelan. Inara's line is a direct descendent of the First Witch's son, Tobias." When I didn't react to this news, his eyebrow arched. "That line has remained pure right down to you."

"I was made aware of this all recently. I don't understand it, but I know that Tobias killed his mother to take her magics and got his sisters' surface magics as well." *Wait, pure line*? "What do you mean by my line is pure?"

My heart beat faster and I couldn't stop the pounding in my ears.

"Ah, well... every female on your mother's side has had a child with a pureblooded faery." I could feel the color drain from my face entirely. "You didn't know?"

"That's not possible. I..." *I what?*

The fact was, I'd never met my grandfather. I'd never known about this world until recently even. How could I be sure?

Wait! "My dad wasn't a fae. He was all logic and statistics. He never believed in any of this stuff." *Right*?

"I assure you, he and all of the males in your line have been denizens of Anavrin at one point."

With a hand placed firmly on my shoulder, he bent his head to look straight into my eyes.

"You are more fae than you realize. My mother has ensured that a male with gifts of her choosing would search out the females of your line. Faeries are quite charming. They were instructed to not come back until they completed their tasks. If it's any comfort, not one of those male fae came home without falling head over heels for the female in their charge. Some of them never came home at all."

Dumbfounded. There was no other word to describe what I was feeling. The world was shifting on its axis, and it was all I could do not to tip off.

"Why would she do that? What would make her so vested in my heritage?"

"Ah, well, that is a very long and winding story." He walked a few paces more when he realized that I'd stopped altogether. "Love, we really must be going. We're nearly to our evenings encampment."

Quill and Leif forged ahead, looking into the bushes and around every turn as they went.

Somewhere in the back of my mind, the danger sign was flashing, but like I often did, I'd ignored it.

"So? If it is a long story, we have time for you to tell me!" Frustration seeped from my pores.

Anxiety, I was used to but this? It was anger and uncertainty and a suffocating weight.

Loxias shot forward faster than I'd thought possible. That inner Alpha wolf rose to the challenge without my permission.

Long claws and an elongated snout full of sharp pointed teeth met his quick approach. The snarl that tore through my chest and out my mouth didn't stop.

Smartly, he stayed out of arms reach, the mask of friendliness quickly replacing his rage at my perceived disrespectful tone.

"You're right," he said. "You are entitled to answers. And I am more than willing to fill in the details that I have knowledge of... AFTER we settle in for the night."

Taking calming breaths, I willed my features to go back to normal. And surprisingly quickly, they did.

Bringing my hand up in front of me, I swirled it in a circular pattern and watched as bits of light and sparkles danced in the surrounding air. The pull of magics in this land was an itch just under the skin.

I was parched and with my hand still moving, I thought of the water skein hanging from Leif's side as he came back into view.

It floated through the short space between them and into my waiting hand. *Oh, dear Luna!*

All eyes had followed its movement. A collective stillness blanketed our small group.

They had already thought me to be this Deliverer person and, while it meant nothing to me, the fear in their eyes showed that it truly meant something to them. *Good job, Faelan. Idiot.*

"Yes, well..." Loxias got us moving again. His fingers reached for mine and intertwined them before I could protest. "You're going to love the palace." The stone warmed. "I'm not so sure you'll like the king or some of my siblings when we finally make it to the Kingdom Seat. They can be rather infuriating, but you **will** try to be respectful with the tone you use."

"I will be respectful."

I will be respectful? What the actual fuck?

My head told me to rebel against his wishes, but my body and mouth submitted to his gifts without a fight.

Anavrin was their homeland and the farther into its depths they went, the more fortified the fae became.

I couldn't imagine what would happen if the curse was lifted. These beings were too strong already.

"Now then, the First Witch," he said. "She had been my father's mistress while he was married to his first wife."

"Noooo. Your father had a lover while he had a mate?"

Wylder had been a new link for me, but the bond wrapped around my very soul, I couldn't imagine taking a lover before he was... lost?

That doesn't feel right. That hollow feeling returned.

As we walked through the overgrowth, fallen leaves and tree branches littered the ground. The earthy smell of wooded areas permeated my nose.

"Queen Ombriana was not his mate. She was simply his wife. She was The Queen. He was from a noble house, and they fell in love. And then out of love. It was Her throne."

Could Zito have gotten it wrong? If it had been the queen's throne, was the king banning females from taking up the mantle?

"I was told that only one of King Zyoden's sons would take up the throne. Do you have no sisters?"

Leif held a long branch aside so that we could all walk by it. I gave him a smile but offered no thanks. He nodded back with a knowing grin of his own.

"I have three. In fact, the twins are Queen Ombriana's daughters." He said it all matter-of-factly but, I could tell that he wasn't comfortable talking about it.

"And you and your other sister are not?"

His eyelids drifted closed, and a grimace took up residence on his face. Pain and torment plagued his features.

Quill came and whispered something in his ear and walked off again.

"We're nearly there. The way is mostly clear." After I didn't respond to the new information, he pushed forward with his story. "My mother, Queen Leyashna, is not my father's mate either. He treats her well enough, I suppose. She is his second wife. He still pines after his lost mistress."

Dear gods. The fae royalty were proving to be as bad as a daytime soap opera.

"Why did he take another wife if he didn't love her? Is that commonplace here?" *So not cool.*

"The First Witch killed Queen Ombriana. And ever since, King Zyoden has been a cruel ruler with no heart." Rubbing his temples raw, he sighed with frustration.

Maybe he was tired or losing patience with my line of questioning. My memory wasn't the best at the moment.

"Your, however many greats, grandmother was the First Witch. It was she who broke the magics of this land."

Chapter Thirty-One

Wylder

I slowed about a quarter mile from the cottage. Nixie hopped down from my back, and I shifted back to two legs.

Inara usually kept some extra clothes around for me, so I didn't bother trying to keep any tied to my person. Being buck naked around others was normal for all shifters.

Though now, having Faelan on display for all of them to see, made my skin tight at the very thought.

Me and Nixie approached the door quickly. Inside, we could hear a cacophony of voices trying to talk over one another. *Yeah, this is gonna suck.*

Taking a deep breath, I turned the knob and shouldered through the door.

All voices silenced and eyes moved to me. *Great.*

Alayna smirked as my junk swung like a tree when I walked past them to the cabinet that held extra sweatpants.

"Did ya get a good look, Laynie? I'm sure Faelan would appreciate you eye fucking me."

Her smirk fell instantly. *Good.*

"Speaking of which, where is our baby Alpha?" Reed's voice grated my nerves.

I'd like nothing more than to rip out his vocal cords, but that wouldn't solve anything right now.

"She was taken by Loxias, Quill, And Leif." *Three. Two. One...*

"What?" .. "When?... "Oh, no".. "Serves her right"... They all spoke in unison. The last one hit a spot I'd been dying to scratch.

Grabbing Blaze by the throat and sailing him across the room felt good. I'd have to pay to replace Inara's table, but it'd been worth it.

Reed was in my face in an instant, but I was ready for the wannabe Alpha. A growl ripped through my chest as I shoved the Beta, hard. *Oops. I owe Inara a chair too.*

Zito and Piper put themselves between us, the Sigma and the Beta. This wasn't a pack challenge. It was simply male testosterone needing a place to go.

"If you're through destroying Inara's things, can we please focus?" Zito was no meek pup.

In fact, if I had to place bets, I'd bet on Zito to take Reed every time. He was, however, gentle, intelligent, and logical.

There was a reason that they turned to him when in need of calculations or information.

Piper so rarely spoke that it caught me off guard to hear her voice come out so strong.

"Wylder, report what you know. Faelan put you in charge in her absence and we are **All** going to adhere to her wishes." *Damn, woman! Way to step up.*

After a few seconds of stunned silence, without saying a word, they took seats around the room.

Waiting for the first bit of a report, Zito turned to me. "What happened in town? Do we know where the ritual stone is?"

Unwrapping it from my finger, I held up the pendant so that they could all see it before latching the chain around my neck.

The weight of it settled there, just under my Adam's apple. I felt it warm for a moment and then cool back to its usual temperature.

An owl hooted from somewhere around the forest. A cool evening breeze carried through the half opened window.

"Maybe I should hold onto it... for safe keepings." Reed reached out a hand and I didn't hesitate to smack it away.

For years I had fought every instinct to pummel the arrogant asshole. Inara's friendship being the only thing keeping me from beating his ass.

"You reach for it, or my throat again, and you'll lose that arm." *Damn Putz.*

I knew Reed wanted to control the situation, but Faelyn put me in charge, and I wouldn't disrespect her wishes.

"How about we start with Faelan? How did they get her?" Alayna asked. Red was her roommate, but she didn't get to set the pace of this meeting either.

Pouring a glass of whiskey from Inara's stash... *Keep on racking up that debt...* I swigged it down before pouring another and facing the pack.

"We were ambushed. We went to her apartment in town looking for the stone, had some fun, and when we were done... Leif had them all hidden there in the living room." Shamed gripped my core.

"They overpowered the both of you?" Zito's tone suggested that he couldn't understand a situation like that happening.

Guilt rocked me again.

"See, there was this pitcher of iced tea Red put on the counter, and I was thirsty... and I didn't think about it before chugging down a full glass..." *Flounder much*?

"Let me get this straight. You were defeated and let your mate be taken by faeries... because of some iced tea?"

The condescending prick that Reed was, I couldn't fault him for the assessment.

"It had Inara's blend of immobilizing tea and a whole shit ton of wolfsbane in it... Did I mention that I was really thirsty?" *Gods, I'm lame.*

Zito came closer, sniffed and walked back to where he'd been standing.

"Okay. So, what do we do now. We need Faelan for the ritual. And they need the stone if Faelan is to help them." Watching the male ponder all kinds of scenarios was rather awe inspiring.

He would make a great Alpha someday if he chose to lead a pack.

"I felt a tug of fear and anxiety that crept along the spell bond earlier. I figured that must mean that they entered Anavrin already. I pushed as much ... love... down the mating bond towards her as I could. It seemed to help ease that ache in my gut."

Taking another swig of the whiskey, a thought popped into my head.

"I haven't felt anything in a few hours from her. Zito, do you think that Anavrin is interfering with the connection?"

He pondered it for a brief moment. "It's a possibility. I say we concentrate on what she wanted for us to do before you lost contact."

A thought occurred to me. "Hold on. Why were Loxias and his goons able to slip passed you lot? You were supposed to be watching them."

"Yes, well," it was Zito's turn to have shame color his cheeks. "Leif saw us and, within seconds, they all quite literally disappeared. No sight of them. Not a single sound. And the scent was just... gone."

I chuckled darkly. "Yeah, I know how you feel... I mean, I should have been more aware of my surroundings, but honestly, I could have turned over every piece of furniture in her apartment and still never known they were there."

Zito bumped his fist against my shoulder. A sense of camaraderie washed over me. I didn't have a pack, but I realized that I did have a few friends.

"Alright then. Alayna and Blaze, I'm going to need you to gather Inara's book from my cabin. Zito, you're going to need to study the passage about the ritual."

"I'll try my best but remember what I told Faelan. That script can only be read by one of her bloodline. It may be slow going."

Piper spoke up for a second time in less than half an hour. "I'll help Zito. Inara showed me a bunch of stuff during our luncheons."

Weird, but okay. I didn't know she and Inara were that close.

"Sounds great... Now, Reed. I'm going to ask you this. Not tell you. I'd like to show you some respect as the Beta of this pack."

Unhitching the pendant from around my neck, I held it out to the asshole wolf.

"I am asking that you keep this safe. We will need it when it comes time for the ritual, and I can't afford it falling into the wrong hands."

Setting the empty whiskey glass on the counter, I took a steadying breath. I knew he wouldn't be able to control his smart mouth.

"Why can't you keep it? Are you bailing on us?" *Snarky mother fucker.* "I mean, I know you have no allegiances to anyone, but I didn't think you'd shirk your life's debt to Inara."

The corners of his mouth curled up into an unsightly grin as I turned to face him.

Thwack! I open hand slapped him so hard, it stung. Blood trickled down his lip from the blow as his head snapped back. The most incredulous look was plastered across his face.

"I'm gonna say this once. And once only. Inara is my friend above all else. I will always cherish her more than you could ever fathom. Red is my mate. I will protect her to my very last breath."

I was close enough to Reed's face that the spit flying from my mouth glistened on the Beta's cheeks.

"And I am a Sigma. A lone wolf by Choice! That means, if you fuck around, you find out! Got it?"

A moment of intense silence fell throughout the wolves present. Reed dipped his chin slightly but didn't utter a single word.

Heading for the door, I turn as Zito called my name. "What are You going to do?"

"I'm going to get Faelan back. Any questions?"

It was Blaze who spoke up, though not with his usual bravado. "Um, yeah. How? Only a fae can get you into Anavrin."

With an arch to my brow and quick tip of my head, I replied.

"Then I guess it's lucky one owes **Me** a life debt."

Chapter Thirty-Two

Faelan

"Broke the magics?" Loxias hadn't elaborated on Queen Ombriana's death or on how the First Witch had broken the magics, but he said that he would fill me in on everything once we settled in for the evening.

He left with Quill shortly after we'd arrived at a dilapidated castle.

The land was so overgrown that it crept through the open stone windows and meandered down hallways.

I could imagine the beauty it had been before its ruin, but the way that the plants and flowers claimed the building was a beauty unto itself.

Leif had brought us to a great room that housed a single throne. The ceiling high above had many open spots that had deteriorated and showed the clear blue sky, lighting the chamber nicely.

It was an hour or so before dusk when we'd arrived. Firewood was plentiful and the pit in the middle of the room was ready for its offering.

Leif cleared away the greenery and set up the bedrolls that he pulled out of some pocket.

My eyes went wide when the four little flat squares expanded, then quadrupled. After they'd become the size of an overlarge sleeping bag, they puffed up like an air mattress.

Only, it wasn't air that filled them as I placed a hand down, testing the comfort level. The mattresses were filled with, what felt like, down feathers.

"Hey! If you had these, why did we have to rest on the leaves earlier?" My hand went to the hip that I'd rested wrong on, rubbing it soothingly.

His mouth curled up and I noticed, not for the first time, the twinkle in his eyes. He had a boyish face, though that didn't convey anything about the age of the fae.

"They're kind of a pain in the ass to get closed back up." Sheepishly, he fluffed his on bedroll. "And I was just too exhausted to let my magics flow freely if it was only going to be a few hours."

I thought about that for a minute. "So, it's your magics that are keeping these," I motioned to the beds, "fluffed and comfy?"

"In a way. As you know by now, all fae have different gifts." I nodded. "Well, what you maybe don't know, is that there are four types of magic here in Anavrin. Water magics. Earth magics. Fire magics. And Air magics."

"Every fae only houses one of these?" It seemed appropriate.

From what I'd understood about nature my whole life, it was about balance. And if the balance went unchecked, then chaos was the result.

"Yes, and no. The First Witch housed all four, but before you ask, I will let Loxias fill you in on all of those details when he returns." Leif turned back to tend the fire before he spoke again. "Our gifts, as well as our lesser gifts, are derivatives of those baser magics."

He waved his hand over the fire and the flames burned brighter, reaching higher.

"So, yours are fire? That doesn't make sense with your cloaking abilities."

He smiled broadly. "Mine are air. I can fan the flames, not ignite them. My cloaking gifts, as you put it, flow the air around in ways that block sight, scent, and sound."

Something dawned on me then. "Quill is air too, isn't he? He pushes his shot to always hit its target."

"Very good, Faelan." Gathering some additional wood from a nearby pile he'd placed close to our makeshift camp, he tossed another log in the pit. "This should be hot enough to cook by the time the guys get back."

The smell of burning wood brought back fond memories of sitting around a bon fire toasting marshmallows with Grams. My heart gave a small pang of heartache.

We sat quietly for a while. Dusk settled in around the castle and the others had yet to return. Worry crept into my bones, but Leif seemed perfectly contented.

"Do you think they're alright?" *Who cares, Faelan. Stop worrying about the sexy fae douche canoes.*

"I'm sure they're fine." He took the water skein from his side and a couple of apples from a knapsack, passing them across to me. "I'm surprised you haven't asked me about Loxias' magical element."

I'd thought about it. I'd went back and forth in my brain about the possibilities. No clear answer had presented itself and I didn't want to appear any more ignorant than necessary.

"I suppose I didn't" I waited, but he didn't say any more. *The bastard's gonna make me ask.* "Okay, Leif, what elemental house does Loxias' magics hail from?"

A twisted smile spread from one ear to the other. He was awfully happy with himself.

That, or maybe he was glad that Loxias could still hold some secrets without analysis. "You're a smart female. Take a guess?"

His nonchalant attitude began to wear thin on my over sensitive nerves. *Seriously*?

"You don't even know me. How would you know if I was smart or not?"

"I'm more observant than anybody ever gives me credit for." There was an edge to his tone. "I've been watching you fight off Loxias' push gifts since before we left your apartment."

That was news. I hadn't thought that any of them had caught on.

"I've also observed that it appears harder for you to do so the farther we get into Anavrin."

He took a bite of the fruit in his hand and peered over at my incredulous face. The irrational emotion to throw the apple at his smug head took a few seconds to fade.

With the knowledge that he knew I wasn't totally enthralled to the prince's will, I wondered why he hadn't told the others yet.

Taking a bite of my own, I pondered the possibility that I may have overplayed my hand. Giving information freely had never been my strong suit.

Every time anyone had tried to get close to me, a wall erected that either they had to climb, or they gave up and left because of it.

That wouldn't help my situation here. I needed to give Leif something that would ensure that he'd want to stay this course.

"I would have thought that your friends would value your insights." I chewed on my bottom lip. "I just assumed that you were their go-to guy for intel."

Color actually rose high on his cheeks. I had laid it on thick, but it appeared to have worked.

"I mean, anyone could tell that you're the brains of this little operation." *Too thick, too thick. Pull back.*

He didn't call me on the overage. Grams' stories had always told tales of how the fae craved flattery. It had worked and I wasn't about to look a gift horse in the mouth.

"Well, I'm not as old as they are." I could tell that he was debating how much to let me in on. "They do, sometimes, treat me like a faeling. I've only been alive for a little over two and a half centuries and..."

"Wait! What? You're over two hundred years old and they think that that is still young?" *Yup. I'm a baby to them.* "How old are they?"

The blush color graced the big apples of his cheeks again. I didn't know where to look.

His feelings could be hurt if I stared at his embarrassment, but in all of the stories of the fae, it was clear that you didn't want to break eye contact if they were angry, emotional, or embarrassed. That was when they would strike.

So, I held his gaze, smiling at him in a way that felt like comradery. *Come on. Take the friend bait.*

Leif smiled. It wasn't a big one, but it let that knot in my chest ease just a tad.

"They're old. That's not my story to tell though... They should be back any time now." He took another bite of his apple and then asked me again. "Are ya gonna venture a guess, or not?"

It'd be rude, now, not to. *Think.*

"Okay. Let's see. He touches people and they bend to his will." Tapping a finger to my lips, a thought popped into my head. "When people die, eventually, they become ash... and ash goes back to the earth. That's it, isn't it?" I clapped my hands once. "His gifts stem from the earth element?"

Whoo-hoo. Not such a dummy after all.

"I knew you could do it." His adorable young face lit up. "I said you were smart," he winked at me. "And look at you, proving me right."

Crunching branches towards the throne dais drew our attention.

"Don't just sit there. Give us a hand." Quill had a deer over one shoulder and his crossbow over the other.

Loxias stepped out from behind him with his arms full of an array of fruits, vegetables, and leafy greens.

Leif jumped up to help like he'd been bitten, but I stayed where I was.

The bounty that they'd brought in was enough to feed ten people. If only we'd have had some wine, it would be a great feast.

As if on cue... "Looky what we have here." Loxias held up two glass bottles with some form of liquid in them. "Honey mead from Maximus' own cellar."

I had no idea who Maximus was but thank the gods he had liquor.

Praise Sol and Luna for small miracles.

Chapter Thirty-Three

Faelan

They got the deer cleaned and hung over the fire. Everyone, including me, set about preparing the vegetables.

There were purple carrots, some sort of tubers, and string beans. Onions had been brought back as well, but they, along with a portion of carrots and some of the leafy greens, had been stuffed inside of the deer for flavoring as it cooked.

Mead was passed around and around until one full bottle was empty.

"Leif, how about you go and fetch us another couple of bottles before we start eating?" Loxias posed it as a question, but it was clearly an order.

After Leif had vanished around the corner, Loxias turned his full attention to me.

Handing me another tuber to peel, he maintained contact. "Did you have a pleasant time while I was away? I know you want to tell me everything."

That pull of his will tugged against my mind, shuttering through me. The stone splinter warmed. A slight tingling running its course under the skin.

For just a millisecond, my brain shouted no!

He wanted me to submit. An Alpha doesn't submit. They fight.

It wasn't the stone now, it was me. I forced myself to concentrate on that tingling. *My magics.*

I held on to that feeling, letting it build and build.

Looking down at my hands, the sparkly particles drifted between my fingertips.

Clenching my fists, I forced the light to be stifled but the magics were still flowing. *Play the long game.*

Forcing a smile to my face, I picked up the mead again and took a long swig.

Leif had been kind to me, nice even. He was clearly Loxias' guard, but he was also his friend. And yet... he tried to convey to me information that I didn't think Prince Handsome Pants would want me to have at the ready.

"Leif was just telling me about how fae magics stem from the four elements. I'd thought the flames might have grown from his magics when they were going down, but he explained that he used air to fan the flames. Not fire itself." I forced even more saccharine sweetness into my upturned lips.

I didn't miss, yet another, look that he shared with Quill.

"He was correct. Have you had any dealings with magics before?" It was a loaded question.

Answering half-truths would be the only way to keep him from figuring out everything I wanted to stay hidden for now.

"Does the magics of potions count?" Brushing a rogue hair from in front of my eyes and sweeping it behind my ear, I batted my eyelashes slowly.

It was how I got bigger tips from arrogant males at the bar. Never let them think that the door was closed to possibilities. Flirting was an art form and I had learned to be DaVinci.

"Yes. I suppose they do." Loxias studied my face for signs of lies but I knew that he wouldn't find any. "You must be hungry. All of this walking has built up my own appetite. I can't imagine what it's done to yours."

Leif returned with two more bottles of mead and a large skein of water that he hadn't had before.

Quill pulled out a curved dagger and sliced hunks of meat from the roasting deer.

The tubers, carrots, and string beans, which had been wrapped in some sort of large leaves and placed under the dripping deer, were now tender when he'd opened one of the leaves to test its doneness.

The smell of herbs and onions and roasting meat filled the area and made my mouth water.

"I'm starving. It all smells wonderful." Now that the hunger had been brought to the forefront of my mind, it was all that I could think about.

That first bite of venison melted on my tongue, drawing a hushed moan from my lips. I didn't miss the lingering lust in Loxias' eyes. *Hook, line, and sinker.*

"This is amazing. You males did a great job. Hunters, gatherers, and chefs too." *Thick. Too thick.*

Quill gave me the first true smile I'd seen from him. *Okay. Maybe not too thick.*

A glance in Leif's direction told me that he hadn't bought it though.

"So, you had questions about the First Witch," he said.

Loxias and Quill stared at him like he had lost all his senses, but he went on anyway.

"We have time now. Maximus's castle is secure. And it's probably a good idea to have you filled in on whatever you might need to know about the past before we get to King Zyoden's palace."

With the incredulous look on Quill's face, he added, "Ya know, to make sure that you can break the curse, an all."

Sheepishly, he grabbed for a piece of meat and shoved it in his mouth before he could say anymore.

I found him truly endearing. He was one of my captors. A fae. Most importantly, he was one of Loxias' inner circle, and yet, he had been nothing but helpful to me.

"Yes. I would like to know how the First Witch became... well, the very first witch in existence."

The carrot that I'd just popped into my mouth exploded with the flavoring of the fat drippings. My moan of pleasure was nearly sexual in nature.

They all glanced at my glistening fingers as I brought them away from my mouth.

"Sor"... *Do Not Apologize To The Faeries!* ..."So, who was she? How did she obtain her powers?"

Loxias' lustful eyes shimmered as he licked his lips. Quill tried to kick him with his foot, not wanting the attention drawn his way, but I saw it.

The prince snapped out of his longing long enough to stare daggers at his friend. Leif and Quill both snickered at the arrogant male but hid their mouths behind a face full of food.

"As I said, the First Witch was a fae once. She was my father's mistress." He took a long pull from the bottle of mead. "She had more... elements, than any other fae."

Seeing my eyes grow wide, he explained.

"At most, we have two that can be dominant. One from our mother and one from our father if they are not from the same elemental housing. And usually, one of those is much more dominant than the other. The fae can have a small amount in our lines from all four elements, depending on how the lines have combined."

Dripping fat caused one of the embers to pop and my scaredy cat ass jumped. Quill snickered again. I shot him a sneer which made him laugh harder.

Sticking my tongue out, they all three busted out laughing. *Stupid, magical, male douche canoes!*

"You were saying?" My temper was beginning to flare. It felt like they had dragged out telling me about the First Witch until we were so far into Anavrin that I had lost who I was and what my goals were. "Stop laughing!"

Taking a deep breath in through my nose and slowly out through my mouth, calmness settled back into my chest.

"Okay. I assume the reason for that is it's a magics 101 lesson. Let's hear it."

Wiping the tears from his eyes, Loxias turned to face me again. Even Leif had cracked up at my Oh So Big and Bad Alpha-ness jumping at the sounds of a crackling fire.

"Well, the First Witch..." he said but I interrupted him. Again.

"This is crazy, Surely, you know her name. Why can you not tell me?" Leif looked to me and pleaded with his eyes.

I was definitely missing something but maybe it was something that they couldn't say. They physically couldn't speak the name perhaps.

"Can you not call the First Witch by name?"

Loxias and Quill said nothing, but Leif's finger grazed his nose quickly and was back at his side before the other two noticed. *File under later information.*

"The First Witch," Loxias continued like I hadn't even asked a question... "had all four elements of magic. Earth. Air. Fire. And Water. The difference was... ALL of them were dominant in her. She called forth any element and therefore had more gifts than any other fae. Ever."

He took another draught of mead, and his eyes glazed over.

"Word had reached my father about her abilities from one of the villages around Maximus's," he gestured to the building around them, "court. My brother had known for a decade or so and never told the King. And when he found out, he was most unpleased by my brother's lack of forthcoming."

Darkness washed over his face. I could tell that he was thinking about things far off, another time.

"My father made Maximus bring the four element commoner fae to the palace. He wished to assess her himself. And after meeting her, he found that he was enthralled with not only her magics, but the female herself."

Another swig of mead and his tone became lighter. Whatever the past held, he didn't like to dwell there for long.

"I guess that I shouldn't be upset by that. If it weren't for their falling for each other, the demise of Queen Ombriana wouldn't have happened, and I never would have been born."

Holding up the bottle in a toast to no one, he smiled into the ether and brought it back down to his lips.

"How did Queen Ombriana die? What did the First Witch do?"

This was my ancestor. Nausea roiled in my stomach at the thoughts scattering around in my mind.

"The Queen was a powerful fire element fae. And, as I told you before, she was the monarch. She married my father and retained full control of the crown. After she'd learned of King Zyoden's affair, with a commoner at that, she called the First Witch into the throne room, in front of a full court of courtiers. Legend has it that her gaze never drifted to her husband. Her eyes never left his mistress. She accused her of ensorcelling the King. Using her elemental magics to wrap around his mind and enslave him to her will. It is also said that he never looked upon the First Witch during the whole ordeal. Not once while the Queen charged her with behavior unbecoming of a fae. Not once while she banished all of her line from Anavrin. And not even a glance as she sentenced her to the final death."

My breath caught on the last part. Queen Ombriana hadn't blamed her cheating husband at all. She'd look down her nose and saw only a commoner and couldn't fathom a reason that a noble would lower themselves that way.

Could she really blame the First Witch for retaliating?

"The Queen decreed that the First Witch's name would be stricken from all records and that the fae were to never speak of the four-element abomination again, under penalty of treason... but it backfired on her. As was required by long standing fae law, the King's mistress was given the right to speak final words. Drawing on all of her combined magics, she spoke the first curse into existence. Her intent was to kill the king... but the powerful queen stood to counter the First Witch's magics. Her fire element hummed through the air, an undercurrent to her gift of flame manipulation. She had no idea that the First Witch's gift was that of ... I think you would call it... particle manipulation. She could shape and reshape anything. She could bring it to her or push it away. She could reshape the very air in your lungs. Her abilities were not as powerful as that of a noble line. While she held all four elements dominant, it still hadn't been but a third of the power that was suppressed by her commoners' blood."

I had bitten my nails to the quick. The air was thick with the tension of the story. A glance in my direction and he continued with more animation to his features.

"The Queen sent her magics racing for my father's mistress. He still didn't turn to look. Not as the magics collided. Not as the Queens fire opened up a channel to the First Witch's well of magics and bound itself to her glowing hands. And not even when Queen Ombriana fell, dead to the floor. Drained of her very life's essence."

A quick intake of breath was all that I managed to let slip passed my lips. There were no words to convey the awful feelings that stirred in my blood.

A wronged queen. A powerful commoner who had an affair with a king. A spoken curse. And a force of magics that became the ultimate demise of a royal. It was the stuff of fairytales. *Oh, dear gods.*

I couldn't help the slow laughter that escaped.

It was surreal. I was in Anavrin. A land of faeries. And they were sitting around a campfire... telling fairytale stories.

All three males looked at me like I'd lost my mind. I was beyond tired and probably a little punch drunk.

"I don't mean to poke fun of your histories. Honestly. I was a bit overwhelmed by the whole tale." I had eaten my fill and then some, but I took an unnecessary bite of meat to have something else to do. "What did she say?"

"What's that, love?" Loxias said as he poked the dying flames with a long stick. The crackling fire popped again, but I'd grown use to its lull and pull.

"The First Witch. You said that she spoke the first curse into existence. What did she say?"

Leveling me with a puzzling stare, after a few seconds, he must have decided that I was worthy of his trust.

Glancing sideways at Leif, he was astutely looking at his feet, but I could see the upturned corners of his mouth.

"She said... "**May the ruin of Anavrin plague its people until our lines meet again.**"

Loxias must have assumed that I would understand what that meant, but I had absolutely no clue.

"What happen next? Did Anavrin's people suffer?" I didn't want to know but I needed to hear it. To understand what I was dealing with.

Quill picked up a rock and skipped it across the open chamber.

His voice solemn, "After the Queen fell, the courtier lords and ladies demanded her banishment. He still had not looked at her, even after his wife lay dead three feet away from him."

Seeing my mouth hanging open, he continued, and I was glad I didn't have to press.

"You see, he loved the First Witch. He also knew that if he wanted the support of the nobles around him in order to retain the crown, he would have to banish her from the lands and never see her again."

Leif chimed in. "The First Witch was now imbued with her full magics, all four elements, bound by the dead queens hand. Her hate for the king and nobles around her grew fierce in those moments after the queen fell. By all rights, the First Witch could seiz..."

"That's enough, Leif." Loxias said. "We don't want to overwhelm her with minutiae."

Quill cleared his throat, the smallest of chin dips from the prince.

"All that she needs to know is that my father banished her, and her curse remained in place until around two-hundred years ago. A curse that, for all intent and purpose, decreased our magics the farther we are from King Zyoden's palace, where her heart remained."

"What happened two hundred years ago?"

I thought it odd that the First Witch's line was over eight-hundred years old and the curse that she was expected to break was only roughly two hundred. *I'm lost.*

"My brother, Maximus..." he again gestured to the castle in which we sat. "He fell in love... with a witch-shifter. From what we have gathered over the years, it seems that the First Witch's curse has come to full fruition."

Chapter Thirty-Four

Wylder

As I headed out the door, howls went up behind me. The urge to howl right along with them was intense.

I wasn't part of their pack, but with my mate's link, it was driving me to do just that.

Fighting all of my instincts, I turned onto the trail, stripped, and placed my clothes in the satchel strapped to the top of my leg.

I was going into Anavrin and I didn't want to have to walk around naked in front of all those fae.

Besides, I knew that shifting was much more difficult in the land of faery. It had something to do with the First Witch, but I didn't know the particulars.

Shifting into my powerful wolf form, I took off at top speed. Imus might owe me a debt but that didn't mean that he'd stick around long after the time I told him to meet up.

Taking off at a full run, the trees flew by. Their scent and the feel of them as they brushed my legs was comforting in a way that spoke to my primal side.

The moon was less than a week from full and that pull was growing stronger with every passing hour.

Coming up to about a quarter mile from where we were scheduled to meet, I slowed my pace.

If I were to run up on Imus, I might catch him off guard and it would be an instant instinctual fight.

Sometimes, the wolf thing overriding the thinking human thing was a pain in the ass. I was grateful for it in other times though. Like when it kept me alive.

There were several different types of shifters in the Lupian Forest... Wolves, bears, deer and the now extinct panthers. I'd even heard others talk of some form of beast shifter.

Hoping to never encounter one, I moved with calculated steps.

The padded paws of my feet crunched the twigs and leaves around me to alert Imus to my approach. I stayed in my wolf form to allow that scent to permeate the air for several moments before switching to my human form.

After I changed, I shook out my clothes and threw them on quickly.

"It's fine, Wylder," a male voice called over from the fork I was approaching on the trail. "I know it's you."

Coming into view now, the male was leaning against a large tree. He pushed off of it with the ease and grace of his species... Fae.

"Imus. My gratitude for you meeting me." I watched as the fae took in the sight of me.

Imus radiated power. In the nearly two centuries that I'd known him, not once had the fae before me wielded his abilities outside of Anavrin. At least, not that I knew of.

"I need to get in, old friend. My mate..."

"What? You can't have a mate!" Imus's attention darted to my chest.

Listening, he realized. Scenting the air around him.

"By the gods... how?"

Carefully, I took a step back. *Do it swift and quickly.*

"Eowyn's heir. Her line survived. The Deliver is my mate, Imus."

The fae male shook his head in disbelief, but he knew I'd never lie to him.

"It's your great granddaughter. She's been born to right the wrongs."

Chapter Thirty-Five

Faelan

"I guess I'm a little slow today. How do you mean that it came to fruition?" I shifted on the hard seat.

I wasn't sure whether it was the position I'd been sitting in or the information dumped in my lap that had made me suddenly uncomfortable.

"The curse came fully to light?"

Darkness filled Loxias' eyes. I could tell that his thoughts were far away, reminiscing at some unseen event.

Leif cleared his throat, and the prince reeled himself back.

The darkness I'd witnessed dropped from the fae's face instantly. He took another swig of the mead. *Drink much*?

"My eldest brother, Maximus, was next in line to inherit the throne. He was a fair and just male. The villagers of his lands adored him." He took an even longer pull of the golden liquid.

"Was? He's not... around anymore?"

Fae were not easy to kill. I'd learned rather quickly that they heal super-fast.

"No. He is not." I couldn't help squirming in my seat. The air itself had become thick with sorrow. "He was my favorite sibling. He never cared that I wasn't of his mother's blood. Or that I was the youngest of all eight of us. He still saw me as a prince, as an equal. Never once did he talk down to me or dismiss whatever I had to say."

Unshed tears in his eyes had me averting my gaze to give him some semblance of privacy.

"If I may ask, what happened to him? To fulfill the curse?" I still needed to know, even if was slightly callous to ask.

Quill poked at the dying embers in the pit. It wasn't cold enough that we'd need it to keep warm, but the glow gave the castle a bit of light.

Giving Loxias time to gather his thoughts, Quill said, "The curse says that the First Witch's line must meet again to stop the ruination of Anavrin. Well, most assumed that meant someone from her kin's line. She had left the land and crossed the arch into the Lupian Forest. If you'll remember, her kin were banished with her. So, that made sense."

Finding his voice, the prince looked

"My father still loved her, but he'd chosen the crown over that love. He's never loved my mother. She knew that it would be a hollow marriage, but she was from a noble line and the king needed a queen to maintain the balance and respect of the fae. They married only three months after Queen Ombriana's death."

The tension in the air became thick with challenge. If I could assume one thing, it would be that the past haunted him more than he was saying.

Leaning forward to level me with a look, he said, "Queen Leyashna is kindhearted but no fool. She began sending fae to the First Witch's daughters and their female heirs every time one came of courting age. The First Witch herself made sure that she bedded three different fae to have three powerful daughters, each with different abilities. Queen Leyashna believed that the curse could be satisfied if anyone from the land of Anavrin crossed the witch's line."

"They never knew they were fae?" I shook my head. "How in the world did a bunch of witches not even realize that they were bedding faeries?" *Stupid, charming, sexy faeries!*

To my chagrin, he chuckled at me. It was the first bit of true lightness from him I'd seen since we had encountered that gullinbursti.

Gold flecks in his irises shined brighter, like miniature suns. It made his whole face more handsome, boyish even.

I didn't know the story of his life, but I could feel the strife ridden undercurrent of it whenever his eyes went dark.

Wylder, I miss you.

The thought hit me out of nowhere. The chasm in my chest expanded, its hollowness a sucking black hole of despair.

Loxias must have noticed me rubbing the spot in the center of my chest because he reached over, interlocking our hands.

"Your mate was a good male. The pain of his loss, I'm sure, is still unbearable. It will grow easier with every passing minute."

That push of his will only came from the last sentence. He was trying to make me speed up the healing process and my magics rushed to the surface in protest.

"Thank you, Loxias. Wylder **is** my mate. Not **was**. As long as my heart beats and my mind remembers him, he will always live..." I pointed to my heart." Here. He is part of my soul."

A quick shadow passed over his face and was gone just as quickly.

Leif spoke for the first time since the prince began telling the First Witch's tale.

"So, her line is pure fae? The First Witch had three children by three different fae. And each of those daughters bedded fae to conceive their daughters, and so on..."

"Four," I interjected.

"I beg your pardon?" Loxias had a bemused look on his face. A look that spoke volumes as to what he'd already known, but apparently, Leif and Quill were not privy to all of the information.

"There were four children. Tobias Isbith, her only son. The one who took her life."

While they were looking at me like I'd grown three heads, Loxias was smiling sheepishly. The look made him just that much more adorable. *That stupid dimple.*

"Ah, well. That isn't common knowledge here in Anavrin. Queen Leyashna has kept it quiet for centuries."

A noise from the overgrowth surrounding the chamber caught our attention for a moment. It was merely an owl, taking flight for its nighttime hunt.

"But why would she do that? Wouldn't the king want to know how his love, his mistress died?" It was Leif who'd voiced the concern.

"Yes. He would." A wicked smile spread broadly over Loxias' face. "She may have accepted that he would never love her... but she could deny him closure. And it seemed a fitting vengeance for a husband who had gotten his first wife killed. Had taken a throne that was never his. And that required a young, naive noble to become queen to a cursed kingdom."

This twisted psycho thinks his mommy is the bee's knees.

"Okay. So, let's brush past the fact that a whole line of witches never knew that they were conceiving the next generations with fae. That even my father was a fae. And the fact that, I am some sort of witch- werewolf- fae combo." *Mind boggling understatement alert!* "How does Prince Maximus play into all of this?"

A few more sounds came from somewhere in the castle but if it didn't concern them, I wasn't going to be bothered by noises either.

"Well, after several centuries with no luck breaking the ruination curse, the queen asked Maximus to go to the Lupian Forest and find out whatever he could about the First Witch's line. She wanted to understand how the lines of the Anavrin fae had crossed with the lines of her husband's former mistress."

I found myself leaning in, biting my non-existent nails. "And... what did he find?" *Out with it already. Geesh!*

"He found that her line had lost some of its strength. When her son had killed her, he'd also taken the surface magics of his sisters."

Loxias glanced at Quill and Leif whose mouths hung open in disbelief. Best friends or not, the royals kept some secrets close to the vest it appeared.

"He found that, depending on the original daughter's gift, each of their line, in turn, shifted slightly more with the next generation. The more it shifted from its fae origins, the shifters... werewolves, panthers, and bears... couldn't shift into anything other than the one shifter state. And most of them didn't even attempt witchcraft. And the more each of those shifters crossed, the more types of shifter species the magics produced."

Now I really needed a white board and some different colored dry erase markers. *Just need some sleep.*

"So, what about Tobias's line. How did Maximus find out about the male and what had happened?" I didn't even know if I wanted to know anymore but pushed forward anyway. "Why did those females keep the witch's grimoire going?"

"Maximus hadn't gone to sire anyone. He'd gone to find out information to help his people break a curse that had held them hostage for nearly five centuries at that point."

Pouring another glass of mead, he sipped it like it consumed his every longing.

"What he had found instead..." Another sip. "... was the other half of his soul."

Chapter Thirty-Six

Wylder

"How's that possible?" Imus's hand scrubbed at his face and back through his hair. "Eowyn never spoke of being with child."

I felt bad for him.

Me and Inara had speculated about who her father might be, but it had never crossed my mind that Imus could be the M that she'd mentioned time and again in her family's grimoire.

Inara had been researching the matter of the curse and the First Witch's heritage for a long time.

She would tell me over our weekly tea all about her wonky magics and the power that felt raw and untapped barely under the surface.

Inara was glad that Red's mother had chosen a different path but had a sneaking suspicion that her granddaughter was meant to have a grand purpose. She still didn't know what that destiny was the last time I'd seen her before she'd gone missing.

"I owe your daughter a life debt." *Gods, that sounds lame.*

Imus glared at me. "You know my daughter?" He advanced a step towards me, power exuding from every pore. "You know my daughter and have never mentioned it to me?"

Shit. This isn't going well at all.

"It's not like that, old friend. I never knew she was your daughter... neither did she. I've only pieced it together in the last twenty-four hours."

The fae finally took a breath I hadn't realized that he'd been holding.

"Inara had been looking into who her sire might have been for a long time."

Chancing a step towards him, I took a steadying breath. I could feel the heat coming off his skin, the power itching to get out, but my friend deserved the truth.

Clamping a reassuring hand on his shoulder, I said, "Had I known it was you, I would have told her... and you. I have no reason to keep anything from you."

Imus backed away from my touch. Not from anger. More from needing space to wrap his head around the situation.

"I have a daughter." *Gods. I have to be the one to tell him she's missing.* "And my great-granddaughter is your mate, you say?"

Light sparks danced in his eyes. It was like fireflies dancing in the dark. *Whoa. Interesting.*

"Yeah, there's something that I need to tell you now though." I motioned for us to take a seat on a nearby log.

After the long couple of days, it was a relief to get off of my feet for a moment.

"Your daughter, Inara... she's missing. Her cottage had been ransacked and there was blood... it wasn't a pretty sight."

An immediate charge filled the air. The surrounding trees stopped swaying. The animals scurried quickly from the area.

"My daughter is dead." Imus stated it like an emotionless robot, but I saw it for what it hid... pain.

"We don't know that" I quickly interjected. "There was blood... but no body. And she had forewarning of what was going to happen."

He looked up at me with understanding written all over his face. I hadn't known Eowyn, but maybe she had visions too.

"She left me a note. A binding spell actually." I took the bloodied piece of paper and handed it to Imus. "I'm bound by its spell to protect your great granddaughter... It is what pulled me to her in the first place."

Hope reigned in his eyes. The life debt he owed me was because of his loss of that particular emotion. I'd never thought I'd get to see it in his eyes.

"If she had foreknowledge, then she could have possibly gotten away." The fae male was lost in thought and I decided to give him a few minutes to process everything.

There was one more bomb to drop in my friend's lap. *Rip it off quick.*

"There's something else you need to know. Faelan has been captured by Loxias and taken to Anavrin." *Time to detonate.* "He's taking her to face the king and queen to be the hero and break the curse completely." *3...2...1.*

Ducking to the ground just a second before the trees around us broke, exploded and flew in all different directions, fire burning all around, I evaded any damage.

Imus, on the other hand, was covered in splinters and shallow cuts which were already instantaneously healing.

I had never seen the male even use magic before. It must have been pent up for years. *Great Grand Daddio is bad ass.*

"How could you let this happen?" He'd turn his attention and rage at me. "If you are bound to protect her... and she's your mate to boot, how could you allow this to happen?"

Raising my hands in surrender, I took a tentative step towards him.

"The fae still have gifts, Imus. I was paralyzed before I even knew that they were there." *How to explain Red*? "And that great-granddaughter of yours? She's a Take No Shit kind of girl."

A small bit light gleamed in the male's eyes.

There was no denying it. "I couldn't have stopped her from doing her thing if I wanted to."

Imus snickered. It was just as small moment of levity but that was a start. "That was how Eowyn was."

The longing in his voice when he spoke her name brought a hollowness to my own chest.

"She was a force of nature, that one."

Holding out my hand for help up, he pulled me to my feet. "What do ya say we go get Faelan back?"

With a faraway look in his eyes, he huffed out some of the pent-up feelings he'd held in for so long.

"I haven't been back in Anavrin in two hundred years. I've never wanted to step foot in there since Eowyn's ..." His words drifted off.

After two centuries, the male in front of me still hadn't gotten over the loss of his mate.

It was all that I could do to keep myself from unraveling with Faelan being held captive. I had no idea how I'd survive if anything happened to her.

I hadn't known that Eowyn was Imus's mate during all of those afternoon teas with Inara. All that I'd known about Imus was that he was a noble fae.

I'd happened upon him just after something major had happened. Imus was bloodied and the wounds he'd sustained were life threatening.

He was a closed lip sort of male, so it was nearly a quarter of a century before he'd even revealed that he'd lost his mate.

I remembered being in awe of the male. It had been just that long since mated couples had existed.

He had mentioned Wyn one night only about fifteen years back, during one of our get togethers. Every few weeks, we'd watch Netflix and have a few drinks.

Imus had drank quite a bit more that night than usual. It was the one and only time he'd mentioned his mates name, and I still didn't put it together that Wyn was short for Eowyn.

Had I realized that at the time, I could have saved Inara so much time and energy looking for her father.

It was only after Red had been taken and I'd had hours, paralyzed, to think about it all. On what Zito had told us and the tidbits that Faelan had filled me in on from what she'd read in the family grimoire. Everything started to fit together like the edges of a puzzle.

The middle was still missing a lot of pieces but the links to hold the picture in place fell in one by one.

"It's time, old friend." I clapped him on the back. "Let's go claim what is ours."

Chapter Thirty-Seven

Faelan

My hands came up to cover my mouth. The thought of my line intersecting with Loxias' line was too much.

He'd known that his half-brother was related to me and yet I'd felt his desire to covet me for his own.

Every time he would touch me or whisper close enough to feel his breath on my skin had given me reason to suspect his lechery. The fact that these fae didn't seem to mind incest made me want to vomit.

"You knew!" I shouted, standing in my haste. "You knew that Maximus was my blood relation and still..." My thoughts were jumbled in my head and stuck in my throat. "You tried to draw me closer. You tried to make me feel things for you!" *Stupid fae bastard*!

He'd apparently bought my acting skills from before. One look at his incredulous face told me as much. Loxias had fully believed that his gifts were what brought us to this point.

"How? I mean... How?"

Lost in his failure, I rounded on Quill.

"Aren't you at all concerned by this depravity? Your prince is a twisted piece of work!" Heaving heavily from my outburst, exhaustion threatened to overtake me as the adrenaline died away.

Quill just grinned. *Well, that's not disconcerting or anything.*

I sat back down. Leif picked up a rock and skipped it across the palace floor towards the crumbling throne.

He wasn't smiling. A forlorn expression enveloped his face.

"The fae live a millennia. The lines cross in many places but it does not affect our kind as it does humankind." His tone wasn't solemn, but it wasn't boastful either. I appreciated that.

Zito's factual voice popped into my head and my thoughts strayed to how the pack might be coping in my absence.

The sorrow in Loxias' voice resonated in my chest as he spoke.

"Those who can conceive are truly blessed. Most fae have only one, maybe two heirs, in a hundred-year span. Like in your world, females only have a finite number of reproductive years. If they miss their window, they will have no heirs. Their line will stop with them. And a lot of pregnancies are extremely difficult. We lose just as many babes... mothers even, that the process is ventured into as carefully as possible."

Loxias looked at his guard, his friend. "It wasn't your fault, Leif." I didn't know what he meant but Leif gave him a weak smile.

"My siblings are a blessing and a curse. Two females. Four children each. If we weren't royals, that would never have come to pass. No one knows why royals have more power... or more protection."

Quill came to sit next to me. "Look," he said. "I get it. You grew up with humans. You don't understand our ways." He bumped my shoulder with his in a playful way. "He wasn't creeping on you because your, like, his great- grand niece or something." He looked at Loxias then. "He thinks you're alluring. You have this way about you, kiddo."

Kiddo? Geesh. These fae were incorrigibles.

"What I am, is taken." My patience had just about run out.

I glanced over to the prince who was studiously not meeting my glare.

"My mate is not dead. I feel his loss, but only because of lack of proximity."

Picking up the almost empty bottle of mead, I chugged the rest like it was water after a long run.

"Your gifts **Tried** to work their magics through me. My magics, however, were having none of that."

I opened and closed my hands, waggling my fingers as I did so. Glittering light blossomed all around them, clinging to my skin.

Turning my head to the side, I saw a pile of stones stacked at the back of the room. *Please work.*

Taking a deep breath, I forced the coursing power out of my chest, down my arms, and into my hands.

I'd barely had time to aim before a blast of power shot from my fingertips, smashing the rocks into pebbles.

Loxias, Quill, and even Leif all jumped to their feet.

Quill drew his sword in one hand and had a bolt nocked in his crossbow in the other.

Leif's hands flew out to the sides, gathering the shadows from every corner.

Even Loxias, who hadn't showed me any other power than that of his touch and wishes, had lifted other rocks in the room with a mere thought.

They were all looking at me as a threat now. I knew that I shouldn't have shown my hand this early but per usual, my emotions took charge over my common sense.

Damn it! Now what do I do?

A crashing noise reached our ears just as a creature the size of a small SUV came barreling into the chamber. It skidded to a halt when it saw us.

Hanging from its teeth was a smaller animal, maybe the size of a large dog, that I didn't recognize.

Blood dripped from the creature's claws which were the size of chef's knives.

It had two sharp horns on its head; one appeared to have been snapped off midway down. The fur covering its bottom half was course while the feathered down that ran around its chest and arms looked soft.

My eyes met with the beast's, and I felt the terror in its gaze.

There was another crashing sound, louder this time, from the same direction that this beast had appeared.

The beast approached me, but I was frozen in place.

I couldn't figure out why I wasn't more afraid of the creature... until I realized that it was scared.

Oh, dear Luna. It's just a baby.

Quill pointed his crossbow at the thing at the same time Leif and Loxias made to aim their gifts at it.

"STOP!" I screamed, jumping to put myself between the creature and their fire. "Can't you see that he's just a terrified child?"

Again, the loud crunching and crashing sounds met our ears from the distance.

"Move, Faelan," Loxias commanded. "The beast is a Halfien! It will grow enormous and cannot be left to terrorize all of Anavrin. Step aside."

I would do no such thing. Giving it one more long, pleading look, I turned my back on the beast. *Don't kill me. Don't kill me. Don't kill me.*

Raising my hands back in front of me, my magics came readily to the surface.

"I don't want to hurt you, but I will not let you hurt a child just because you are scared." A glance behind me to the baby beast fortified my resolve.

I felt the beast come to stand at my shoulder and tensed. The carcass it was holding dropped to the floor beside me.

Nausea turned my stomach, but I held my ground, not daring to take my eyes off of the fae in front of me.

The halfien huffed its hot breath, just over my head, towards the males in front of us.

Out of the corner of my eye, Quill loosed a bolt from his crossbow but it wasn't aimed for me or the creature beside me.

In what felt like slow motion, I turned and watched the forementioned bolt land true. Right into the eye of another beastly creature the size of a school bus.

The halfien wrapped around my middle and it rolled us both safely to the other side of the fire pit. I didn't feel anything but its large body cradling mine as we rolled.

Coming to a stop beside Leif, he took a step away from the creature but threw me a smile.

Quill continued to pummel the larger beast with bolt after bolt.

Its cries rang through the stone building, bringing tears to my eyes. It's song of loss and vengeance stinging my throat.

Loxias threw large boulders, and Leif used his gifts to shelter me and the halfien behind his shadows.

The fight continued but I turned my attention back to the halfien.

I was sad and tired. The Halfien rested its paw on my shoulder and huffed again. My neck craned to look it in the eyes. Hunger and remorse were what I saw.

"I know," I said softly. "The circle of life can be hard."

The creature tried to nuzzle it's too large head into my neck. I sighed. "Come on."

Motioning for it to follow me, I led it back to the carcass. "Eat."

I patted the beast on the side of the face. "It would be a waste of its sacrifice not to."

When I realized that the larger beast, obviously the mother of the dog-sized carcass, was no longer making any noise...

I turned to find the incredulous gazes of *five* males looking back at me.

Chapter Thirty-Eight

Wylder

We hadn't had to run all evening like I thought we would.

Imus used his dormant magics. He teleported us only a few miles at a time at first.

The farther that we traveled into Anavrin it seemed that his magics awoke.

I couldn't deny Anavrin's beauty. Even at night, this land held wonderous magic that oozed from every blade of grass to the endless sparkle of each body of water.

The climate here was much milder than that of the Lupian Forest. It wasn't too hot, nor too cold. The breeze was gentle enough to stir the air without being windy enough to tussle our hair.

I never asked Imus where we were or where we were going.

Once this fae had learned that his mate bore his child and that his great-granddaughter had been taken, it was all that I could do to keep a hold of his arm during teleporting.

We approached a castle that looked as if it had fallen into ruin and he slowed, not magicking us right to it.

Halting about a dozen yards from the entrance, he held out his hands and gestured to the building in front of us.

"Well, it's still standing at least." *No... he can't be.* "Welcome to my humble abode."

"By the gods! How have you kept the fact that you are a prince of faery from me all of these years?" Shaking my head, my thoughts stayed muddled.

"I am not. Maybe at one time I was..." His feet seemed to be taking him forward without a conscious thought. "But the loss of Eowyn and the curse she placed upon mated pairs."

It was now the fae prince's turn to shake his head.

"I couldn't stay here, Wylder. How could I be responsible for my people when my soul wasn't whole any longer?"

We walked a few feet in silence. "I'm sorry... about your mate." Imus grinned up at me for half a second.

Shit. Faery trap.

"None of that crap now, Imus. I wouldn't say sorry to a real faery. Asshole."

His grin turned into a full-face consuming smile.

"A real faery, huh?" he chuckled. The sound was like wind-chimes in a light breeze.

"You know what I mean. Two hundred years outside of Anavrin is a long time." I chuckled now myself. "Hel, I'm probably more faery than you are now. At least I live in the forest. You, Mr.-I'm-A-Big-Shot-Broker... you live in a plush high-rise condo on the upscale side of town."

We walked a hundred steps more before Imus reached over and grabbed my arm, stopping our progress.

"Listen, I have a lot of wealth and holdings. If something should happen to me..." I started to interrupt but, raising a hand to silence my protests, he pushed forward. "If anything should happen to me, there is a code on the bottom of an Athenian bust in my condo to all of my accounts. Take it and take care of her. Get Faelan and get out of here as quickly as possible. The doorman will let you in. Just tell him **Mr. Maximus requires the long night**. He'll understand."

"Who the Hel is Maxim..." *Well, damn.* "Imus? Prince Maximus? The first in line to the Anavrin throne?"

This just keeps getting better and better.

"The one and the same. Though my castle is in as much disrepair as my name, don't ya think?" He winked then took off running again.

Asshole.

Chapter Thirty-Nine

Wylder

When we entered the castle, we had heard terrifying wails of some sort of beast. The unmistakable shouts of an attack filled our ears.

I didn't wait for Imus as I darted through the entrance to the castle and fought my way through all of the overgrowth.

It was no surprise to see the former prince only a few steps behind me when we turned the corner into the throne room.

The first thing I noticed was an exceptionally large, very dead beastly creature that lay a mere twenty-five feet in front of the three fae that had taken Red hostage.

Imus stood shoulder to shoulder with me, taking in the scene. He and I must have spotted Faelan at the same time because as I went to take a step forward, the fae's hand came up to stop me.

There was a different kind of beast of faery standing just a foot away from my mate. Eating something dead and bloody, its long, sharp teeth dripping with viscera.

At first, I was cautious because I thought that the creature might turn on Red... but after a few seconds, I stood in disbelief as her hand came up to pet the thing as it ate.

Her voice was a soft coo. She was soothing the beast.

I wasn't the only one locked in place with incredulity. Her three captors and Imus all stared at her like she had lost her mind.

It was dark in the throne room except for the dying embers that lit the fire pit. Shifters had great night vision but the fae vision, I knew was superior.

Imus's eyes never left his great-granddaughter. I could almost see the calculations running through his head.

Leaning over to whisper, Imus asked, "Can she speak with animals?"

It was a fair question I wished I knew. Before she'd been taken, her magics were expanding quickly but I had no idea of what she might be capable of.

"I can't say. We should..." I motioned for the former prince and I to split up, take it from both sides.

Faelan's eyes had landed on all five of us. Her stance became defensive instinctually.

Through the dark shadows in which I'd stood, I could see her nails grow into claws. Her mouth elongated into a snout full of bone crushing teeth and sparkling light that ringed each of her hands.

The magics that had tossed me around in her bedroom were now responding to her willingly.

The sounds of crunching bones and flesh being torn from the carcass were the only sounds now.

Imus took a step in one direction, and I took one in the other.

An arrow whizzed by Imus's ear and my cheek simultaneously. *How the fuck?*

"Not another step. Announce yourself?" Loxias demanded.

Faelan gasped and the beast immediately looked up from its meal.

The wind changed direction, blowing towards her. Her eyes lit up and it took every ounce of self-control that I possessed to not close the distance and draw her into my arms.

Imus sneered at the demand, then snickered. "What's the matter little brother? Do you not recognize your own kin?"

Whatever the youngest prince had expected, it wasn't this. His face went slack for a fraction of a moment but the arrogance that I'd come to know from this fae was back in the next breath.

"Roxalus? What are you doing here?" Loxias' outward demeanor gave little away, but I knew him well enough to see the nervousness under the surface. "It is my charge to find the last Blood Red Heir and break the curse. You will not take her!"

Imus laughed. "Oh, you poor fool. Is Roxalus making your life difficult?" He shook his head. "No, dear brother. It is I, Maximus. And you would do well to not disrespect me in my own home."

I couldn't help myself. I took a few more steps towards Faelan and she stepped away from the creature, towards me. Only fifteen feet separated us now.

"Max? It can't be." The sadness in Loxias' voice had both Faelan and me turning in his direction. "My brother hasn't been seen in over two hundred years. Why would you claim such a thing!?" he demanded.

Stale air mixed with leftover campfire meal permeated the air. Hunger gnawed at me, but I pushed it aside.

"You took my great-granddaughter, you fool!" Imus's words hung there, heavy in the air.

Faelan sucked in an uneasy breath, and I rushed to her side... but the beast was faster.

"Nooooo!" she shouted. Too late.

One of its forearm length tusks gashed a hole in my side. Blood spurted everywhere. Pain seared my vision.

"Bad halfien!" She smacked the creature lightly on the nose like it was a naughty puppy. *Gods, this woman!*

Rushing over, she pressed her hand to my side to apply pressure and leaned into my chest.

She was warm, and safe, and still mine. Her hair still smelled of strawberries.

Whether that was shampoo or her, I didn't know. Nor did I care. She was here, with me.

The others came rushing at the beast. *A halfien?*

I'd admired her speed before, but this new speed was unnerving. She was up and in front of the creature before I'd even blinked.

"Do Not Touch Him!" she exclaimed.

Power rolled off her. The hairs on my body stood on end. *By Luna, I've missed that fire.*

Both princes raised their hands in surrender. The other two fae were a little less quick on the uptake and Red's whole body shimmered in that light, not just her hands.

All of them took a step back from her threatening magics and she relaxed. The light disappeared with her next breath.

I'd never felt so proud... or so powerless.

When the halfien came to stand beside her, I didn't feel anything from the protector's bond. That had to mean that she wasn't in any danger from the thing. *Right?*

"No one is going to hurt you," she cooed again to the thing. "You're safe here."

All four males stood staring at her with open mouths. When she rounded on them, they'd at least had the sense not to contradict her.

"None of you are going to hurt this precious baby. Do you understand me?"

The hands that had landed on her hips were too much. I couldn't help myself. I laughed and my side hurt more.

It was mending quickly but the laugh split it open again. I couldn't stop.

She was the most ridiculous female I'd ever met, and she was all that more amazing because of it.

Faelan dropped down beside me. "Are you alright? He didn't know any better. He was just trying to protect me," she said. "Don't be angry with him. He's just a bab..."

I had cut her off with a kiss. My hand snaked around the back of her neck and drew her closer as the kiss intensified.

I wanted it to last forever, but we were in the middle of a ruined castle, surrounded by fae and creatures of faery, heading into the heart of Anavrin.

Now was not the time for our passion's, though the strain of my jeans said otherwise.

Gradually, the kiss ended. Awareness of voices whispering from across the room brought me back to the reality at hand.

"I've missed you, Red. You have no idea."

"Oh, I think I have a pretty good idea." A blush crept up her cheeks as her hand grazed my hardened length.

A chest rumbling lustful growl erupted from within me and the halfien looked to her for reassurance.

"Um, Wylder?" called the former fae prince. "I'd really like to meet my great granddaughter now."

The half smile was a reminder that she was his family but that he also understood the mating bond. And I was grateful for that.

Slowly getting to my feet, assisted by Faelan, we walked over to the pit.

"Red, I'd like you to meet Maximus Suilari, Formerly Crowned Prince of Anavrin. Your great-grandfather."

Chapter Forty

Faelan

Great-grandfather? Of all the things I had learned since my grandmother's disappearance, this one tugged at something sharp in my mind.

Grams had wanted to know who her father was for as long as I could remember.

If Wylder and Maximus had known all along...? *What in the actual fuck?*

Maximus extended his hand to me, but I stared at it like it was a snake.

Letting go of Wylder's side, I turned to face him full on. "Did you know? Grams spent hours in search of her father! Did. You. Know?"

Sparks flew with every word. *Get a grip.*

"NO. I swear it," he said. "After you were taken, I had hours on that floor to think through so many different things that we'd learned. Something clicked into place about an hour before I was able to move."

He took a step into my personal space, and I took a step back.

"Red, listen to me. If I had known anything that could have been of help to Inara, I would have offered it up freely. She'd saved my life. I would have given her anything that I could."

The anxiety that had been building in my chest was slowly leaking away. I could hear the earnestness in his voice. I could feel the truth of his words in my soul.

Closing the gapped between us, I let the world fall away as my lips pressed gently to his. "I believe you."

Then I rounded on Maximus. "What about you? Were you just another siring fae, come to bed one of the women of my line in hopes to break the curse?" My voice huffed out in a snarl. "Did you not care enough to stick around after fathering a child?"

Maximus's face crumbled. The pain and hurt that I saw there made my feet move towards him of their own accord.

"No," he said. "I had no idea that my mate was with child." A bitter note hung in the air at his words. *Mate?* "I never wanted to leave her side. If I had known she was carrying your grandmother, not even her desire for me to go to my father and ask his blessing of our union would have pushed me to leave her unattended."

Wylder squeezed me around the waist. A silent plea for me to be gentle with his friend.

"I don't understand. Explain it to me?" I didn't want to be angry.

It wasn't an emotion that I'd thought to have when meeting my newly found great granddad, but it leaked from me all the same.

The halfien gave a contented sigh as it came up behind me. Its belly full, it laid down, wanting my hand to stroke its down feathers.

Sitting down at its side, I leaned against the beast. Wylder motioned for them all to sit down with us.

Prince Loxias was still quiet. He hadn't said another word since first encountering his eldest brother.

Maximus blew out a breath. I wasn't the only one anxious at this meeting. That realization gave me an odd sense of comfort.

Wylder sat down gingerly. His side was closed over but the pain that remained was evident upon his face. Reaching out, I took his hand, interlocking our fingers.

"Eowyn was my world." Maximus's eyes glazed over in that way people had when remembering the past.

The crackling of the dying fire brought a soft, lullaby tone to his story.

"The queen and I saw things differently than my father. And I believed in her methods. She'd sent fae after fae to father a child with those of the First Witch's line, but never any fae from the royal line. She came to me one afternoon and asked if I would travel to the other side and gather as much information that I could about how the four lines split and what the results had been. Loxias' mother is smart."

He winked over to the prince who still looked like he was entertaining a ghost.

"She concluded that, because the First Witch's line had never been to Anavrin, the magics that they held were diminishing, even though they were sired by pureblooded fae."

"So, where does Eowyn come into all of this?" *Eowyn. My Grams mom.* "What happened?"

A quiet snore came from the beast. The poor baby had had a big day. My heart went out to him.

"I was there, hiding in the forest." A blush colored his cheeks, and he smiled. "Arrogant male that I am, I never thought for even a second that I would be discovered." He shook his head. "Eowyn called out... **You can come out. I know you're there**. I didn't have a second to consider before she ran up on me. Her eyes were bright and alluring and I lost all my thoughts as the pull in my chest drew me to her lips. She giggled. Actually giggled. And then we both felt the zinging electric bond course through us."

"She was your mate." Loxias found his voice at last. "The witch that cursed us to have half a soul? A mateless existence?" His anger was written all over his face. Darkness crept behind those golden eyes.

Ignorance isn't so funny now, huh, Captain Moody McMagic Touch?

"Yes, brother," Max said. "She was my mate... and father stopped us from being together by making me believe he'd had her killed. That while I left her behind in the Lupian Forest and came to his castle to beg his blessing for her to be my wife, he had sent forces to, as he put it... *Eradicate the problem of the First Witch's line.* I was held in the dungeons for thirty-seven years on the charge of treason. Yet, my siblings all failed to notice."

Maximus held Loxias' glare, a stand-off of wills. Loxias looked away first.

"Queen Leyashna would visit and give me hope for the first decade or so. She told me that King Zyoden had ordered my castle abandoned and that trespassers upon it would be given the final death. She also told me that the people of all nine kingdoms believed that I'd simply disappeared. No one knew whether I was a deserter or dead by some unknown beast's hand or where I had ended up. I thought that surely one of my brothers or sisters would come hunting for me. That they would seek answers to my absence."

It was quiet for a few moments. The only sounds, the popping of logs in the fire and the snores of the halfien.

"You were in the dungeons for all that time?" My voice quavered as I asked.

Wylder tried to sooth the growing anxiousness, rubbing circles on my arm with his thumb.

"I was. I had lived in near darkness and amongst the rats. I caught a sickness every other week from the dampness. Mold. mildew, and rot were my only friends. The stench lived inside of me by the end of the first decade. The queen visited less frequently, maybe once a month. And as time went on, I was lucky to see her once a year. There were only four guards that knew of me. Two daytime, and two nighttime. They worked in twelve-hour shifts. By the time the thirty-fifth year came around, only one day guard and one night guard stood as my vigil."

Running a hand over his face, he sighed. It was the most hopeless sound I'd ever heard.

"The evening that I made my escape, I waited for the changing of the guards. They were both unpleasant fae who delighted in my torment. I threw a coughing fit, pretended that I was choking. After all of those years, they thought that I had given up. That I was no threat to them at all." He huffed. "Their mistake. I would never have given up getting back to Eowyn. Never. Even if it was simply to mourn my mate properly."

A fierce protectiveness took up residence behind my ribcage for a past I could never correct.

"I take it you killed them?" It was Leif who asked the question.

I had nearly forgotten that he was there. His lips were tightly pursed, and I noticed the glances that he stole at Max's face every few minutes.

Something in his eyes gave me pause but I didn't ask Leif any questions about it.

"I did. Then I made my way back to the Lupian Forest under the cover of darkness. I could see better than most in the dark after all of that time in the dungeons. The journey, that normally took even the swiftest of fae two and a half to three days took me only one. I wasn't recovered enough to teleport directly, but I did not stop to rest or to eat or to sleep. My sole goal was to find her."

Maximus stared silently into the dying fire. "I found her grave instead."

Tears welled in my eyes as Max's slipped down his cheeks.

"Someone paid their respects with a cluster of gems set around a stone marker. Her name and the date of her death etched there. I missed seeing her alive one last time by mere weeks."

Shaking his head and wiping his face, he looked to me. "You look very much like her."

I didn't know what to say to that. I knew how I'd felt after only a few days of separation from Wylder. I couldn't imagine the heartache that Maximus still felt.

"It wasn't father," Loxias sniffed, and I realized that he'd been crying.

Maximus took in his brother's wet face.

"It wasn't father. He never ordered anyone to harm any of the First Witch's heirs. I don't know why he told you that, but after your disappearance, he made an official decree that no fae may cross over to the other realm without permission from the King or Queen."

He picked up a stick and poked at a rock just to the outside of the pit.

"He didn't know that my mother was sending fae to father the children of every generation of the witch's line... until all three daughter's lines stopped producing witches. The queen suspects that it was due to the distance from our lands over the years."

I had more questions than I knew what to do with.

"What am I missing?" Wylder asked before I had the chance. We were on the same page more and more.

"Tobias Isbith had children from three different fae females. With the magics he inherited from his mother, the magics he gathered from her passing, and the magics that he had stolen from his sisters, his first order of business after killing her was to spread his seed to three females that had gifts that he wanted to pass down. After he bedded them, he whisked them away to the Lupian Forest and cloaked them in magics. None were royals, so their lesser gifts were no match to his powers."

Loxias took a swig of mead. "I don't think that they had been willing participants."

I fidgeted at Wylder's side. Not only was my ancestor a murderer, but now, come to find out he was possibly a depraved rapist.

My stomach roiled. Jumping to my feet, I sprinted several feet away from the group and emptied my latest meal into the brush.

A hand was in my hair, and I didn't need to look to know that it was Wylder who held it back from my face.

Hearing the growls of the halfien, I turned to see Maximus trying to approach with a skein of water.

"Shhh shhh shhh," I cooed to the baby beast. "He won't hurt me."

Maximus took a tentative step forward. Then another. The halfien settled at my feet but made no move to attack and he closed the distance.

"Much obliged." I said, reaching out for the skein.

The corners of Maximus' mouth twitch in amusement.

Swishing the water around and spitting it to the ground, exhaustion threatened to pull me under.

We'd walked at least fifteen miles since yesterday. Hiking in nature always made me feel invigorated, but I'd never in my life walked for more than ten miles in a day.

"I need to sleep." The ground was looking good to me at this point.

Without another word, Wylder scooped me up into his arms. The scent of him did funny things to me.

Leaning in to whisper in his ear, I let my fingers trail along the scruff at his jawline. "Or maybe we could find a spot away from the others and reunite properly."

The growl from low in his chest had heat building between my legs. A chaste kiss brushed my lips, but he pulled back too quickly for my liking.

"You need sleep. The long hike and all of what you've learned today need rest to process."

He kissed the top of my head as he laid me on the bedroll that Leif had set up earlier.

"Besides that, magics take a lot of energy, Red. And I want to claim you 'til you can't walk straight."

A flutter low in my belly had me squirming in his arms, but he didn't give in. "Sleep, sweetpea. After you've rested, I will give you anything that you ask of me."

"Mmmm." It was a contented sound.

I didn't need to say anything else. I knew that he would keep me safe while I rested and that he would be there when I woke up.

Darkness overtook me as I drifted into a peaceful slumber.

Chapter Forty-One

Wylder

Faelan drifted off much quicker than I'd expected. I wanted to hold her. And take her there and now.

The exhaustion that I knew came from new magics is something that I'd talked long hours into the night about with Inara.

Fate was a crazy thing. It was as if it had been preparing me for all of this my whole life.

Had I still been a part of my old pack, I'd have never met my mate.

If it hadn't been for Inara saving my life, I would have never known much about magics.

If I had met Imus when I was with my old pack, I'd have probably left the fae to die.

As it were, fate had lined up all of my ducks in a row to bring me to this intersection. Everything that needs to play out in a lifetime will do just that.

Well, damn. A case of the heeby jeebies ran down my spine.

Imus huffed a long breath out that stoked the fire with his gifts. His eyes held a full array of emotions as he watched Faelan sleep.

"I had no idea that Eowyn was with child when I left for Anavrin." His eyes filled with unshed tears. "I would never have left her side if I'd known."

Quill shifted on the bedroll to face him. "Are you certain that her line is yours? Perhaps she..."

At the look on Imus's face, he trailed the thought into nothingness,

"It would only be his child," I spoke up for my friend. "I haven't been with Faelan long, but I know that neither of us would bed another. Even if one of us were to pass on."

I rubbed at the spot over my heart. With her this near, it was no longer an ache, but a longing.

"I knew about mated pairs. I'd seen my great grandparent's bond... but I never believed in how strong the connection was until mine snapped into place with Red."

Loxias shuffled his feet in the dried leaves that laid by his bedroll.

Leif remained quiet but I could sense an unseen torrent of emotions.

For a fae, Leif was young, the youngest in this group by far, other than Faelan. If he had a story to tell, it wouldn't be one of any length.

It would have to be something of depth, but I wouldn't be the one to push him for it.

"What did you have planned for my great granddaughter, Prince Loxias?" Imus's tone was stoic, but the undercurrent was seen more readily, if you knew what to look for.

I had met him just after he'd found Eowyn's grave. There had been blood everywhere.

Faeries heal quickly and he'd been trying to take his own life for hours.

Recalling the different ways he'd attempted it brought unwanted memories to the surface. I had never been squeamish, but some of the things that Imus had done made my stomach churn.

It had been all I could do to stop his attempts, patch him up, and keep him subdued for the following days.

After I was certain that we had talked through the worst parts, I untied him. The first thing that Imus did was smack me across the face as hard as he could.

The pain of the hit wasn't nearly as bad as watching Imus drop to his knees and sob. He did so for hours... until his throat was dry, and his tears had long since stopped flowing.

After I'd gotten him into a chair and settled down, that same look that he'd had then now shown through his eyes.

It was one of fierce determination. I admired that about my friend.

"I had a plan," Loxias started in a low voice. "My regrets, Max. I had no idea she was your heir until very recently. Mere hours ago."

His eyes grew frantic. His hands rung over and over.

"I had no idea that you'd been in those dungeons." The more he spoke, the wilder he became. "I would never have..." Loxias trailed off, standing and pacing now. "I just wanted to prove to father that..."

"King Zyoden has Inara in the dungeons," Quill interjected on his prince's behalf. "When we couldn't find the stone, we took her to the palace for safe keeping. Her line is needed to break the curse. Eowyn's curse, Max. She fortified the First Witch's curse to dampen our power when she made the mateless curse to keep our souls from connecting with our other halves."

The warmth in the air had nothing to do with the weather.

I got to my feet to stop Imus from doing something that he'd regret later but Imus didn't move. He wasn't speaking or blinking or breathing.

This can't be good.

Quill must have come to the same conclusion because he lifted his crossbow and directed it at Imus's head. Leif brought his shadows to surround the young prince from view.

Loxias begged from the darkness, "Please brother, you must understand."

Imus took a step towards the shadows. The halfien lifted its head and growled in our direction but didn't leave Faelan's side.

"I would never have touched a hair on your line's head had I known. I would have given my court, my castle, to know that you still lived!"

I was angry enough at him on Inara and Faelan's account, but his eyes spoke the truth of his sadness.

Imus took two deep breaths, blowing warmth across my own skin. The air gradually slipped back into the normal weather pattern, taking the stifling heat with it.

"My daughter is in the dungeons," he said. "And you were walking my great granddaughter to the same fate?"

"No! No, I was trying to break the curse." He looked to his friends for help. Not physical help, but for the words that he couldn't find. "I needed to prove myself."

Leif dropped the shadows around them.

"The king's health is failing. He is in his last century." He looked to Quill before proceeding.

The other fae gave him the slightest of nods but I didn't miss it, nor did Imus.

"Roxalus is set to inherit the throne. He is not kind to Prince Loxias, nor to any of Queen Leyashna's children. He feels them to be unworthy of a royal title." *That's harsh.* "He is also not kind to the subjects of Anavrin that fall under their rule."

Leif rubbed the back of his neck and looked at the eldest prince.

"Prince Ayxian tries to stand up for Noxian, Elodie, and Loxias but Roxalus feels that Queen Leyashna heirs have no claim to their court's land. That the fact that his mother was Queen Ruler, not King Zyoden, means that his blood and that of the twin princesses, Embla and Emenda, are all that should be able to claim royal privileges. Your absence has emboldened Prince Roxalus to confront his siblings time and time again. He has even gone as far as to throw snippets of flippancy at the queen herself."

With a humorless laugh, Imus plopped back down on the ground where we'd been sitting earlier.

"That's ridiculous!" Imus muttered. "My brother had lofty ambitions before I left and met Eowyn. I never thought them to be tyrannical."

He brought a hand up to scrub at his face and I felt as exhausted as he looked.

"So, here's the thing. I'm going to ask you this just once. I'd choose my words carefully if I were you," I said. "What was your plan for my mate?"

Loxias stopped pacing and looked at his brother before turning to me.

"I wanted to prove myself worthy to the king in hopes that he could temper Roxalus before his passing." A shadow passed over his eyes, there and gone in a blink. "I'd hoped Faelan could use the stone and break the mate curse. I thought that if she could stir some magics enough, it would remind King Zyoden of his love for the First Witch."

I hadn't realized that I was moving until I was on top of the fae, fists punching wildly at his face, his neck, the side of his head.

To Loxias' credit, he didn't fight back. He knew that he deserved this beating.

The prince's hand brushed the side of my arm and with a word, "stop," my hands fell to my sides. Loxias's fingers wrapped around my wrist. "Stand and be at peace with me."

... And just like that, I did.

Stepping back to Imus's side, my friend asked, "Feel better?"

"Actually... yeah." I knew that I'd been mad and that fighting Loxias had been what I'd wanted to do, but now... *Shit, this is weird.*

From behind them, Faelan giggled. "Are we allowed to beat up Prince's of Faery now?"

My heart raced. She was all that mattered. The sound of her laughter was the sweetest music.

"I'm sorry we woke you. Go back to sleep, sweetpea."

Her mouth curled up on one side.

"And miss all of the fun? Not a chance."

Gods, This woman.

Chapter Forty-Two

Faelan

My fingers pulled through the down fur on the halfien, and I realized that it needed a name. Calling it beast or creature was cruel when I knew it personally.

"I think I will call you Odie." I scratched behind the halfien's ears, and he whimpered into my hand. "You like your new name, don't you Odie?"

"Odie?" Wyder asked from beside me.

"Yes. Odie. I've always loved the Garfield comics and Odie was so adorable."

The halfien flopped to his side, exposing its belly for me to pet.

"You're really going to call a vicious beast of faery Odie?" He shook his head, but a smile played at his lips. "Gods, I love you, Red."

He went still and so did I. We were still new to this mating bond. We hadn't known each other that long.

It was way too early in normal circumstances for the declarations of love yet. *Right?*

... But these weren't normal circumstances. We were in another realm. I was a pure blooded fae that turned into a werewolf. And magics flowed through my body as easy as breathing.

If I were being honest with myself, the thought of being with anyone else now physically repulsed me. And the thought of Wylder being with anyone else tortured my mind and heart.

Where did that leave us? We were the other half to each other's soul. *Hmmm, I do love myself.*

That only left me with one option.

Grinning like the cat who ate the canary, I bit my bottom lip and the bullet. "I love you right back."

His returning smile beamed so bright that it knocked the breath out of me.

Before I realized what was happening, Wylder scooped me up into his arms and was rushing us to the shadowed foyer of the castle.

"Stay, Odie," I hollered. "We'll be back."

The halfien whimpered again but stayed with the others.

The corridor was dark and smelled of the overgrown foliage. He'd found a soft flowerbed and laid me back gently upon the pedals.

In one quick move, Wylder yanked my shirt open, exposing my bare breast. I hadn't thrown on any undergarments before we'd been ambushed back at my apartment.

"By Luna, you are so damn beautiful, Faelan." His lips came crushing down on mine. Opening up for him, our tongues brushed tenderly against one another.

After pulling apart, his mouth found purchase on my neck, meandering down to my nipples.

The travel had been long. Sweat and dirt crusted my skin, and I suddenly became self-conscious of my need to bathe.

Putting my fingers through his hair, I roughly pulled his head back to look at me. "Enough of that, Wylder."

His resounding growl was predatorial. He was going to make a meal of me and that made my pulse quicken.

"I want to feel you inside me. No foreplay... my love." I teased him, but it meant something too.

Wylder's purr as my words vibrated in his chest. Nestling in between my legs, he stroked the side of my face gently.

"How would you like me to take you?"... he said with a wicked smile. "Because I am going to take you." A kiss to my forehead. "I mean to claim you." Suckling my earlobe. "I can take you gently."

A kiss at the base of my neck. His hand came up to wrap around my throat.

"Or I can take you roughly." *Oh, fuck.*

A gentle squeeze and I gulped in anticipation.

"But no matter how I claim you, Red... you're going to forget your own name."

My hands found their way to his hardened length.

Leaning forward, I whispered in his ear, "Do your worse, big boy."

He chuckled. His voice a rugged song only my heart would ever know.

"My name is Faelan Waverly Lupa-Callileach, and I too, aim to take what's mine."

Chapter Forty-Three

Wylder

After She'd been taken captive, I hadn't known what to expect for our reunion.

The fae were not known for being kind. I knew that Loxias had the gift of pushing his will into others, but I didn't know what gifts the other fae might possess.

Fear that she wouldn't want to be near me anymore had my heart in a vice from the moment she'd left the apartment.

When I'd come into the throne room and she was all but cooing at that creature, I knew that instant that I loved her.

The feeling overwhelmed me and yet, I didn't rush to pull her into my arms.

When we'd sat around the fire discussing all of the important things that needed to be learned, she sat snuggled up next to me, her scent hitting me like an arrow to my heart.

She was warm, and soft, and smelled of all of the things that made my pulse race. I wanted to sweep her into an embrace and nestle into her hair.

I'd contented myself with sitting by her side instead.

When her stomach couldn't hold its contents because her heart couldn't hold the knowledge of ancestorial depravity, I simply held her hair.

Drawing her against my chest, she whispered of sleep and then of arousal. The mere mention of her longing nearly brought me to my knees... but I put her need for rest above my need of her.

If that's not love, I don't know what is.

But now... Faelan put forth a different challenge. I wanted to take her both gently and roughly at the same time. The confliction warring on my ability to act.

Faelan pulled me down to her mouth by my shirt. She must have exhausted all of her patience waiting to be away from the rest of the group because her hands were everywhere.

I chuckled, "Slow down there, Kemo Sloppy."

The way that her nose scrunched up at my words had to be the cutest thing ever.

"Kemo Sloppy? Is that some kind of crack at my messy room or my messy nature?" Her eyes lit with indignation.

Maybe she didn't realize I was winding her up on purpose but that was even cuter still.

"Neither actually. It's just something that used to get my hackles in a huff when Inara would say it to me. My limbs often got ahead of my thought processes. It was her way of telling me to be in the moment. I guess it stuck."

Hmmm. Inara knew what she was doing. She'd been a great mentor.

"Grams would say that?" I couldn't understand her sudden distress. "I've never heard her say it. I swear, I don't think she and I were as close as I thought we were."

Tears filled her eyes. Illogically, I wanted to irradicate whatever the cause was for them.

"Oh, honey. Shh shh shh. I didn't mean to upset you."

Wrapping my arms around her and kissing the top of her head, I waited for her to quiet before pulling back.

"Your grams is one of the strongest people I know. By the time we get there to retrieve her, she'll likely be having tea with the queen. Inara always has such a way about her. Charming and wise, while still calculating and cunning. I'm sure she's fine."

She pulled from my arms slightly, but I couldn't let her suffer alone. I held on like a lifeline. For her or me, I wasn't sure.

"You can't know that." It was barely a whisper, but I heard it. "Who knows if they dressed her wounds or how much blood she's lost. Infection could set in easily in the dark damp dungeons and maybe no one would know until it was too late."

"Ah, I see." While the placating tone I used was meant to comfort her, it had the opposite effect.

"What do you see?" she demanded. Pulling back to glare at me, her arms came up to cross her bare chest.

That pout of hers was almost comical. *Awww. Silly wolf.*

"I think that you've forgotten two important things." She made to interrupt me, but I pushed on. "First, your grandmother is a very formidable magical faery. And second, that her werewolf is an Alpha. If she was bleeding, not only would it have healed rather quickly, but she most likely took some pretty big chunks from those around her... Did you see any blood or chunks taken out of Loxias and the others?"

"Well, no... but..." her words were stunted. "I heard him say that he took her, and we'd found all of that blood."

I raised an eyebrow at her. She was clearly missing my point. "Faelan, if they are already healed, then more than likely, so has she."

I watched as she thought it through. *Get there, Ace.*

"Oh... OH." A smile lit up her face and her arms fell away, exposing her bare nipples to the night air.

Nipples that were flat and saucer like and when the breeze hit them just right, they pebbled to hard points. I wanted to drink them in.

A deep growl started in my chest and ripped from my throat.

The returning smile that donned her plump lips brought the attention back to where it should have been all along.

I could probably chisel granite right now. My cock was painfully hard.

"Would you like me to take the lead, Red? Or were you planning to ravage me with your big bad Alpha strength?" I was only half joking.

It would always be her choice. I didn't find her strength threatening to my male ego one bit.

On the contrary, she was even more bad ass because of her **take no shit** attitude.

"How about I take what's mine without using either?"

The wicked curl to her lips was my only warning before she attacked.

Luna, have mercy.

Chapter Forty-Four

Faelan

The magics that slithered and wriggled just under my skin now came quick and easily to the surface. It reacted to my intent rather than my thoughts.

It was intoxicating and I could see how that kind of power could be abused.

Taking a hold of Wylder with it, however, was not what I'd consider an abuse of power. It was more like a playful weapon against a worthy opponent.

As his eyes lit with the challenge, mine steeled themselves for his retaliation.

"I'm going to fuck you until you're screaming **my** name," I said. "If there ever comes a time that I don't remember it, at least it'll be etched in your mind."

A snarl ripped from him. Playful and wild and all the things that made my nerve endings stand at attention.

Wetness pooled between my legs again and the Alpha in me longed for the fight.

His lips met mine with bruising force once again. Using my magics to pull him closer, his audible gasp sent my hormones into overdrive.

"I can use that unfair advantage to my benefit, Red." Sliding me down the length of his cock with only the leggings I'd thrown on in haste between us, it was my turn to gasp. "Mmmmm. I think I should start calling you Puddin."

I bit my lip and reached for the waistband of his sweats.

"So impatient." The sound of his chuckle set me on fire.

Every fiber of my being called out to him. He was truly mine and I was truly his.

"I love you, Wylder... "

"My heart's yours, Red..."

We'd both spoken at the same time.

I could feel the blush in my cheeks just as vividly as I could see it on his face.

Our lips met again, only this time the kiss was slow. Tender and yearning.

There were no words needed. A conveyance of emotions traveled along the kiss and in every touch.

He struggled to get my leggings off and I giggled into his mouth. *He is so freaking adorable.*

"I could just rip them," he growled.

"Oh, sure. I bet the males we're traveling with would enjoy seeing me naked from the waist down for the rest of this trip. Especially my gg-dad."

The coyness in my smile got the better of him. I could tell that he wasn't pleased with that thought.

This time his snarl was anything but friendly. "I somehow don't think that me gouging the eyes out of two princes of faery and their subjects would go over so well."

His hands worked quickly now but the carefulness at not ripping my pants was almost comical.

Once off, the crisp night air nipped at my throbbing nerve endings. Wylder's hand clamped down on my swollen mound.

Need welled up inside of me like a shaken bottle of soda. Desire for release was a growing beast with no chance of being tamed.

"Wylllderrr..." I cried. "Now. I want you now."

His need must have rivaled my own because the sudden slam of his cock filled me to the brim. A pleasurable intake of breath from both of us gave new meaning to **Mine**.

"Gods, Red. I can't believe that you're all mine."

He pumped into me with agonizingly slow repetition. It was sweet and intimate and everything that I'd never had from any other encounter my whole life.

A tear rolled down my cheek and his thumb came down to wipe it away. When I looked at his face, unshed tears rimmed his eyes, taking my breath away.

He was just as emotional as I was in this moment. Love and adoration shown through every touch, every thrust.

My mate was a manly male. I knew that he could be a vicious werewolf.

But here... in this moment... just for me, he allowed his sensitive side to show on his face.

He didn't turn to look away. He held my stare like his life depended on it.

Thrust after thrust. Kiss after gentle kiss. We made love like the troubles in the world outside of our little bubble didn't exist.

Harder, faster... chasing our bliss, my velvety walls cradled him in their grips and began to spasm. A cry of elation left me just as his own climax took him.

Exhaustion had my body shaking but his was doing the same.

Maybe it wasn't all exhaustion. Maybe the love that we'd shared was the culprit.

Never had anyone brought tears to my eyes in such a beautiful way.

Laying down beside me, he pulled me over to rest my head on his chest. Neither of us spoke but it was a contented silence.

The others would come searching for us soon enough, but for right now, only me and my mate existed.

Chapter Forty-Five

Wylder

Faelan fell asleep in my arms twenty minutes ago. There was a twig sticking in my thigh, but I didn't want to disturb her much needed rest.

If I could, I would freeze this moment forever. Love wasn't something that I'd ever thought about.

Maybe the universe had planned it that way. Fate had a funny way of making all of the puzzle pieces line up.

She wasn't the first girl to catch my fancy. I'd had other relationships. None of them lasted long. Maybe this was the reason.

All of the hardships with my former pack. All of the times that I'd ranted to Inara about being lonely. All of the struggles to become a calmer, more patient male.

She was the reason... and I was suddenly glad for all of it.

Faelan stirred when I kissed the top of her head. She looked up at me from the circle of my arms, a satisfied grin on her face.

"Hey there, sleepy head," I said. "Go back to sleep."

A head poked around the corner, and I growled a warning. Red was still naked and my instinct to keep her all to myself was in the running for asshole of the year.

Rationally, I knew that she was a strong, capable woman.

Not so rationally, I wanted to be her knight. Never let anyone within a ten-foot radius of her.

Reign it in, Captain Dick-holio.

"It's just about time to go," Imus said as he averted his eyes. *Smart male.* "I wanted to give you guys a twenty-minute heads up." With a quick wink, he was gone.

The blush on Faelan's cheeks was endearing. Leaving this perfect moment in time was proving harder than it should be, but she stood to dress, and I followed suit.

"So, I have a question," her meekness surprised me. "You saved Maximus from himself after he found out Eowyn had died."

I waited for her to continue but she didn't. "That's not a question."

"Eowyn was pregnant with Grams when Maximus had disappeared in Anavrin."

She was leading somewhere but the dancing around it brought a smile to my face.

"That's also not a question." Taking her hand in mine and using the other to lift her chin, heat erupted from those two small points of contact. "Ask your question, Red."

Trying to turn her head away, I held tighter. "Grams... she's two-hundred years old."

Not giving an inch, I waited until she found her voice.

"How old are you, Wylder?"

Ahh, now comes the creepy to human's part.

Drawing her back into the circle of my arms, I placed another kiss upon the top of her head.

She'd lived a mortal life until recently. Her thoughts ranged only so far right now.

"I had been ousted from my pack for over three years. Inara was still a fairly new Alpha when she'd found me."

Thinking about how to tell her everything without freaking her out, I paused a moment, but she was a clever girl.

"Max said that he'd been stuck in the dungeons for over thirty-seven years. Are you and Grams the same age?"

There it is. That horrified look.

"I was a young pup at that time. Basically, the same age as Blaze is now. I had much of the same temperament too."

I wasn't sure what confidences of Inara's I should keep and what I should divulge, but the mating bond trumped any other bonds or relationship.

"I knew your great grandmother. Inara tried so hard to get her to tell her who her father was. Eowyn would always have tears in her eyes and pursed lips at the mention of it, but Inara would try to sneak it into conversation to trip her up."

Thinking back, I gave a huff of a laugh at the way Inara would be talking about nothing over noon tea and casually slip it into the mix.

"You knew Eowyn?" she asked. "Do you know who my grandfather was? Grams has always said that she loved him, but she'd never give me any details, not even his name."

Faelan's mood soured and I lifted her chin again. My lips pressed to her forehead.

"You were there when she was pregnant with my mom? And when my mom met my dad and had me?"

Yup, here comes the creepy aspect.

"Inara and I have been friends since before she'd taken over as pack leader. And no, before you ask, we were never love interests. Just childhood friends."

"Hold up." She leaned away to look at my face. "Why does Grams look so much older than you?"

I laughed. "I've always found the glamour she uses hilariously funny. She looks like an old bitty." Brushing a stray piece of hair away from her face, my tone turned more serious. "When you do see her without the glamour for the first time, it may be quite the shock."

Odie huffed loudly from around the corner, and I was grateful for the little distraction, but when Faelan turned back, she was all seriousness.

"And why is that? Is she all freckle faced and rosy cheeked?"

The words were said in gest but the undercurrent to them held a hint of unease.

"Red, if I tell you, you have to promise not to get all wigged out on me." Taking both of her hands in mine, I waited for her to nod in agreement. "She looks almost the same age as you do. Maybe a decade older. Your hair, nose, and your build are different, but your resemblance to her is unmistakable if you look past that."

Firecrackers ignite. Here we go.

"Let me get this straight. I look like your childhood BFF and you think that I'm beautiful but have never had any desire to be with my grandmother. Am I missing something here?"

She pulled her hands from my grasp and through them up in the air in frustration.

I guess we're doing this.

"That's just great. Freaking great!" she exclaimed.

Leif came into view and stopped when he saw her agitated state. I was very aware that the male was only looking at Faelan.

Whether or not it was rational, I didn't want him to concern himself with her well-being. That was my job.

Get a grip, asshole.

Reaching out to take her hand, she pulled away. Leif took another step in her direction.

"Is everything okay here?" His question was directed towards her only and it set my teeth grinding.

"We're fine," I answered before Faelan could reply. She leveled me with a look that said **Do Not Speak for Me**, but I ignored it. "We'll be over in a minute."

Leif looked to her for confirmation, and I didn't miss the small dip of her chin in response.

I liked Leif. The male was the youngest fae in the group. His allegiance to Loxias was as a friend, not just a guard.

From what I'd observed of him the few encounters we'd had over the years; he was smart and considerate. He didn't follow blindly but he also didn't generally speak out either.

Right now, however, I wanted to shake him and tell him that Faelan was no concern of his. The urge to toss him, bodily, from the room was overwhelming. *Damn Bond.*

Clenching and unclenching my fist, I gritted my teeth and shook the thoughts from my head.

"We're coming." She said to him.

Turning to glare at me, "We have more important things to do than waste time with the semantics of familial acquaintances."

Without another glance in my direction, she turned and strode off towards the others.

Well, isn't this just a ball of sunshine and a hot bag of peanuts?! Luna, help me.

Chapter Forty-Six

Faelan

I was more confused about the mating bond than ever.

On one hand, the attraction and love that I felt for Wylder was undeniable.

On the other hand, he was so much older than me and best friends with my grandmother. *Gram's age. Ugh.*

And the realization that I was nearly an immortal hit me right in the feels. It was exciting and terrifying all at the same time.

What was a couple hundred years age difference when you lived for over a millennia?

The nonsensical way I'd gotten upset and the irrational irritation that I'd felt wasn't anything that I'd been used to in the past.

Calm detachedness was my wheelhouse. The bond was new and foreign and made no logical sense. It was all consuming.

The sexy asshole didn't do anything wrong, weirdo.

Taking a deep breath, I walked over to Odie. The baby halfien huffed against my palm.

Another deep breath. The frequency in which my normal panic attacks would occur had decreased substantially.

Whether that was due to Wylder's presents in my life or the fact that my magics were becoming in tune with me more with every step into Anavrin, I didn't know.

Wylder entered the area and glanced at Odie before looking to my face. His hands were fidgeting at his sides. *Interesting.*

Beckoning him over, I raised my hand to take his.

"I'm not mad at you, Wylder. You've done nothing wrong," I said. "I just needed a few minutes to wrap my head around the whole situation. I mean, I love you. And I love my Grams. It's weird for me, is all. You can understand that, right?"

"I can. I didn't want to keep anything from you. I 've interacted with humans for quite a long time, and I know how differently they perceive age gaps." Dropping his hand, his arms came around my waist as he placed a kiss on top of my hair.

Smiling broadly, my feelings of disquiet settled into ones of being content here in his arms.

A growl issued from Odie's throat. Maximus had both hands up in surrender as he approached our trio.

"Easy there, little friend," he said. "I won't hurt her... or you." He stuck out his hand for the halfien to sniff.

If Odie bit him, he'd surely lose his whole hand.

Odie may be a baby halfien, but he was every bit of ten feet tall. I cooed encouraging words to the beast, and he allowed Maximus to pet him behind the ear.

"See? I'm not so bad." Max was easily likable.

"Have you given any thought as to what you're going to do with him when we leave?" Wylder asked.

Tension gripped my body for a brief second. The thought of leaving him alone, to fend for himself, had anxiety rising in my chest.

"If I may make a suggestion?" Max said. "I'll go check out my private rooms. Give me a moment."

Before I could register what he'd meant, he was gone. A blur of color and then... nothing.

"What in the hell was that? Where did he go?" Shock surely was written all over my face. "How did he do that?"

"He teleported. I didn't know he could do that until we crossed over the border into Anavrin and he grabbed hold of my hand. Then... boom. We were a mile farther in." He shook his head. "That's how we caught up to you so fast. His abilities must be back to full power now."

Loxias and Quill were chuckling. They clearly knew that it was one of Maximus's gifts.

The attention now squarely placed on them, an uneasy quiet settled over the group.

"What's the plan now?" I asked. "You have to know by now that I'm not going to lift the curse."

Loxias' eyes widened to the size of golf balls.

"You have to do whatever the king commands!" he shouted. "We need access to our full abilities if we're to survive the changing of the houses once father dies."

There was something else there in the set of his lips.

With his chin turned down, the words left him in a whisper.

"I need the ability to find my other half."

Wylder growled beside me but pressing a hand upon his chest, he stilled.

"Your king is not **my** king. I am under no obligation to help you or any of the fae."

Raising his fist, Quill grabbed his arm, and Wylder took a half step in front of me just as Maximus reappeared.

"Good news... What the hell is going on?"

"Your brother thinks it a good idea to threaten Faelan for not wanting to break the curse." Wylder's expression was murderous, but he hadn't made a move to harm him.

I understood the overprotectiveness of my mate, but I also saw that he respected my wishes. It was empowering to know that he thought me capable of handling myself.

Power shimmered at the ends of my fingers. Maximus grabbed his brother by the arm, swinging him to face the others.

"Look around, Loxias. This is what has become of my kingdom. It doesn't matter what you think of King Zyoden or Prince Roxalus. This is the price of having all that power. This is the price that I paid for having a mate that didn't suit the royal decrees."

Letting go of Loxias' arm, he placed his hand on his shoulder.

"Do you really think that finding your mate, only to have them stripped from you because of royal impertinence is better? I can tell you from experience that it's worse than not knowing them at all."

"Well Brother. That may be. I, however, think of the subjects of my court before I think of myself." He shook off Maximus's touch. "I will do what I must to help the fae of Anavrin."

He pointed a finger at me. "And she is the key to it all."

Ahh, damn it. Handsome Uncle Loxi for the win.

"Don't you see? If Roxalus, or father for that matter, know that a person has a mate, they will use that against them to get whatever they want?" Maximus hung his head. "I, too, would like to help the people who had once called me their prince, but doing that... it puts the power right back into the King's hands."

Odie was becoming more agitated by the conflict with every passing minute.

"None of this has any bearing on what I'm going to do." I looked to Loxias. "Trying to convince me to give you more power and access to your other half by threatening violence is not going to win me over. I need to see that you can be fair and just. I need to see how you react in situations when you don't get your own way. That is the only true measure of what you'll do with unfiltered power."

I took a step closer to him. Odie whimpered behind me.

"And so far, you've failed."

Chapter Forty-Seven

Wylder

*B*y the gods, I love this woman. I laced my fingers through hers in solidarity. "So, what's the plan, Red?"

"I need to meet with the king. If I truly am the Deliverer, then I am the only one who can break the curse. That's leverage," she said.

Leif smiled at her. I didn't mind it so much from this male. He wasn't forceful or cruel like those he hung out with.

There was something under the surface that he never spoke of but that wasn't any of my business unless he wanted to tell me.

"Okay, so listen," Imus said. "My rooms are on the upper level of the castle in the west wing. There's plenty of natural light through many windows. The overgrowth of vegetation is giving off forest vibes. There are many smaller critters living in there right now and the fountain in the center of the room still flows with water from the spring. If we close the doors, it will be secure enough until we can make it back here."

Quill took a step towards the foyer and Imus snagged his arm. "I was just going to hunt us some breakfast. If there's rabbit and other things this close, I don't want to waste the opportunity."

The former prince shook his head. His castle, his call.

"Not from there. I scouted it out so that Faelan could lead the Halfien..."

"Odie. I've named him Odie," she said with a curl to her lips. "I've always liked the Garfield comics."

He smiled in return. "Alright. I scouted it out so that Odie would be safe to leave there until she could come back for him... if she wants to. Or he can stay in the castle if I reclaim my throne, and she returns to the Lupian Forest."

He reached out and took her hand, speaking directly to her. "He'll be safe. I promise to give him a good home. It's the least that I can do seeing as how I've missed every birthday you've ever had."

After a few seconds of awkwardness, I cleared my throat. "We're going to the palace. If that's the goal, then what's the plan?"

"Well, I was thinking. Would you be opposed to being tied up?" Loxias said this as if discussing the weather. "The Sanguine Luna feast is the day after tomorrow. All of Anavrin's royals will already be gathered for the event."

I didn't miss the look that was shared between the two princes.

Before I could speak up, Faelan had already made up her mind. "On one condition... My bindings are for show only. I will have the ability to get out of them at any time."

"Done." His answer was too quick. I could tell that the prince was hiding something, but this wasn't my call to make.

I trusted Red and Imus. They were both smart. If they didn't pick up on it, I'd mention it, but I didn't think I'd have to.

"We still need a plan. Walking in with Faelan tied up isn't a plan. How are we going to get an audience with the king and queen?" Imus asked.

"The feast is the perfect time." Leif was full of optimism.

Something lit in his eyes that I hadn't seen there before. *Interesting.*

"All of the royals will be seated at long tables on either side of the throne room. We can walk in, Faelan between us, and go straight up the middle to the king and queen." Turning to speak to Red, he said, "All eyes will be on us, so we'll have to make whatever you plan to do count."

I didn't like the idea of any of it. I'd only gotten her back a few hours ago. Now, they wanted to risk her life to what? Have more power?

Loxias was put out mostly about the mating bond. That much was clear. His access to his full powers never entered the conversation in a meaningful way. And that made me more suspicious of him than ever.

"Do you really think that an exiled prince and a wolf shifter can just prance down the center aisle of royals and not be detained?" Quill's words were harsh, but rational.

Leif flinched like he'd been hit. I'd never really paid attention to how they treated the younger male before, but now that I did, I could see the lack of respect Loxias and Quill gave him.

"Perhaps Wylder and I could be glamoured," Imus winked at Faelan. "We'd just be another two nobody guards in Prince Loxias' entourage."

Faelan blanched. I knew that her magics were powerful, but she was unpracticed. As much as she was advancing, I doubted that she put a lot of faith in herself for the purpose of keeping us safe from prying eyes.

My hand found her waist and I pulled her closer. "You can do it. You're stronger than you think," I said.

She began worrying at her bottom lip. Lifting her chin, the fear in her eyes knocked me back.

"I'll be right there with you. You're not alone in this."

"I know that the power is inside of me... but if anything happened to you, I don't know that I could stop myself from going full on postal."

That's what she was worrying about?

Leaning down to let my breath mingle in her hair, I snarled playfully.

"I don't know that I'd be opposed to watching you defend me." Nuzzling into the nape of her neck, I lightly bit just below her ear. Her gasp of pleasure fueled me on. "I understand the need to protect what's mine..."

Now purring, my mouth was a breadth away. "But I know that you don't think me weak." She gasped at the proclamation and tried to shift in my arms, but I held tight. "I've got you, Red."

She stopped squirming when she felt me harden. I wanted to take her right there, in front of everyone. *Damn it, get a grip.*

Clearing his throat, Imus smirked.

Right. Her great-grandfather would definitely not appreciate that.

"Odie will be safe. And we really need to get going if we're to make the feast."

Everything was already packed up. They'd been waiting on us to rejoin the group.

When we walked out of here, everything would change. I knew Faelan as a shifter, an Alpha werewolf.

That wasn't the truth though. She was a fae. A pure blooded fae. A princess of Anavrin if Maximus reclaimed his throne.

Once they left here and the king found out that little fact, he could try to force his great- great- granddaughter to abandon me.

Imus would have never been allowed to stay with Eowyn. Even though she was his mate, she was not royalty, and he found a way to keep them apart.

King Zyoden would be even less inclined to allow his bloodline to be soiled by a plain, run of the mill, werewolf.

Whatever Faelan decided, I would give it to her. If she wanted to live her life as a princess here in Anavrin without me, for her happiness, I would have to let her go.

As if she could read my mind, she stepped away from the circle of my arms.

"Mine," she said, turning and wrapping me in a tight hug. "No matter what, Wylder, you are mine!"

Always.

Chapter Forty-Eight

Faelan

O die had been sitting off to the side, eating a few rabbits that Quill had thought to bring him back along with the rest of our breakfasts.

He purred a contented sound as I approached. His down feathers were beginning to fall out and be replaced with adult feathers.

Maximus had filled me in on all of the different things about halfiens.

They weren't mean or aggressive by nature. Their circumstances tended to dictate their temperament as adults.

It reminded me of the way it was back in the human world with pit bulls.

I'd known some of the sweetest, most loving pits ever, but the stray one that I encountered in an alley around the corner from my apartment building had growled and charged and bared its teeth wanting to bite me.

I could see the blood on the side of its head and paws. It limped back after charging didn't work because I remained planted to the spot. It was hurt, afraid, and all alone.

After reassuring it in that way of mine, the poor thing whimpered and wagged its tail tentatively. It took nearly twenty minutes before I could get close enough to let it sniff me and another ten before it allowed me to pet it.

Fear was often at the root of animal aggression. Once they got over their fear, if they ever did, then they became more acceptable to love.

Odie was no different. Max had told me that their mothers stayed with them until they were two to three years old.

Around a year old, they taught their young to hunt and hide and all of the things that helped them survive.

By Maximus' estimation, this halfien was only about a year and a half since he still had down. And that could only mean that something had happened to its mother.

From the way I'd met Odie, that something must have happened before he'd been taught how to flourish.

"I have to go away for a bit," I said as I rubbed behind his ears. "I don't want to leave you but it's too dangerous for you to come with me."

Odie dropped the rabbit from his mouth and whimpered.

"I'm coming back. I promise. I don't know when, but I will come back to see you. You'll be safe. Maximus will show you to the rooms that will be your haven for the time being. There's plenty of small things for food and a fountain for water." Tears brimmed in my eyes. "Don't eat just to eat. You'll need to make the most of what's there. And do not try to leave once Maximus locks the doors. It's for your own safety."

Odie nudged me with his head. Though animals didn't speak to me, I'd understood them my whole life.

Max came over, gave me a nod and placed his hand on Odie's side. Within the span of a breath, they both disappeared.

"I hope he'll be alright." Worry for my new furry friend colored my mood.

"I'm sure that Imus wouldn't lead you astray, love." Wylder wrapped his arms around my waist once again. "I've known him for... a long time."

I could tell that he'd censored himself from saying centuries and I appreciated that he was taking my feelings into consideration about the whole creepy old age thing.

He really is a good guy.

"Why do you call him Imus?" A sheepish grin curled the corners of my mouth. "Did you really never know that he was Prince Maximus Sulilari of Anavrin, first in line to the throne? That seems to throw a huge wrench into the nature of your friendship, huh?"

Baring his teeth, he took a playful nip at my neck.

"To me, he will always be Imus. A fae who lost his mate. A simple guy that likes to live in town and blend in with the humans. The heartbroken male who always made time to hang out at the cabin, have a few drinks and watch Gilmore Girls with me."

I spun around in his arms, huffing out a laugh.

"Gilmore Girls? You two powerful beasts hung out and watched a show about a mother and daughter best friends instead of ... oh, I don't know, football maybe?"

I love the show but wow.

Pictures filled my mind as I imagined lying about the cabin. My Great G-dad and Grams having a few cocktails with Wylder. Arguing about whether Dean or Jesse was the better boyfriend...

...And suddenly, I was there with them. And Max was laughing as I scrunched up my nose because Grams thought Logan was the best guy for Rory and that Lorelai and Digger were great together.

It was just a flash of images, but it was everything.

Aww, Grams. Melancholy rocketed through me. If we could rescue Grams, and balance the fae curse, then just maybe the scene that played in my mind could come true.

"Hey! Do Not Mock the G-girls," he said just as Max reappeared. "That is sacrilege. Tell her, Imus."

"Lorelai's coffee addiction and ADHD are not things up for making fun of in our presence," he said with a wink. "Have you never watched the show?"

It was one of my comfort shows. Even if I only had it playing in the background while I did other things, it was a comfort zone.

"Oh, I don't know. I think I could use a coffee, coffee, coffee though." The smiles that lit both Wylder and Max's faces were priceless.

Reaching over and squeezing his hand, a grin split my lips.

"Of course I love all things Stars Hollow."

Wylder kissed the top of my head. Again. *I'm going to go bald there.*

"Good. I'd hate to have to kick you out of the cabin during our marathons, Red."

"Welcome to the club, girlfriend," Max said with a hand on his hips and two snaps for good measure.

I giggled. *He's just so... human.*

Breaking up our lighthearted moment, Quill, Loxias, and Leif approached our small group carrying all of the hiking gear with us.

"It's time we head out. We'll need to camp for a few hours tonight. We've got to get going before first light, though, if we're going to make the feast just after they've all been seated for the first course," Loxias said.

Leif handed me a skein of water and an apple.

Wylder processing his emotions made his face scrunch up. He wasn't overly fond of other males when it came to me, but I'd noticed that he was less intense with Leif and wondered why.

Before I had the chance to ask, a loud horn blared. It sounded all around us.

Me and Wylder were the only ones to cringe and look for danger.

Max and Loxias said in unison, "The Sanguine Luna festival has begun."

Chapter Forty-Nine

Wylder

The horn was loud and resonated deep into my bones.

Luna was my deity of choice whenever I did throw up a prayer, but I'd never realized that the fae took the Blood Moon seriously enough to hold a festival in her honor.

Maybe that's why it's the key to the First Witch's curse.

Getting to my feet and reaching out to Faelan, I pulled her up and into a tight embrace.

"If the time comes and you need to get away, do not wait for me." She began to protest but I continued. "We have to keep the fae power binding part of the curse from breaking, Red. If we can't, then the human world won't stand a chance."

"Let's hope that I can keep you and Max concealed until we can make our escape. Oh, and rescue Grams in the process. You know, no pressure at all."

I laughed into her hair. The world was on her shoulders and all I could do was be a pillar to support her wherever I could.

"I'll be right there with you. I know you can do this, Princess." *Now there's a thought.* "Ouch."

Her fist had connected with my side. She didn't even know her own strength. *Beautiful bully.*

"Don't call me that! I am not any kind of royalty." Her mood leaked off of her in waves.

"I beg to differ, Your Highness," Imus said from behind us. "You are the great granddaughter of a High Prince of Faery. And as such, the title fits."

Watching her scrunch up her nose at Imus was becoming one of my new favorite things. With a gentle squeeze, I let her go and picked up one of the packs that Leif left in front of us.

"Right. Now, if you'll all follow Quill here, we can get this caravan moving."

Loxias reached out and placed a hand on my arm while my attention was diverted. "Faelan breaking the curse is the most important thing on this mission."

Resolve for that purpose filled my mind, even as I pushed against it. The protector bond flared. *Fucking bastard!*

Before I could process everything that was happening, Loxias went flying across the room. Faelan's hands were still raised, magics shimmering in the new light of morning.

Quill raised his bow and aimed it straight for her head while Leif's shadows surrounded the downed prince, obscuring him from sight.

Imus rushed forward and placed himself between Quill and Faelan, her face twisted in rage.

A feral growl rumbled in a steady stream from her throat. She began to crouch. Her fangs elongated, her claws grew, and the shape of her head became more wolf. Magics still danced at her fingertips.

Several arrows whipped through the air. Imus caught three out of four of them, but the last one was quickly slipping by the fae prince's grasp.

Snapping out of the stupor that Loxias' power had put me in, I dove for my mate, crushing her to the ground.

The last arrow embedded itself in my back, just under my ribcage. *Son of a bitch*!

If I'd been able to react like I'd intended to, I would have let her blast it away. The protector bond that Inara had placed on me overrode my own instincts. It made my actions to protect Red from harm take the forefront of everything else.

"Wylder!" she screamed out my name, numb in my ears.

Blood oozed from my wound and wouldn't close. Quill's arrows were dipped in fae venom.

Imus teleported to Quill, ripped the bow out of his hand, and smashed it into the side of his head. The surprised look on the arrogant fae's face was priceless.

Nice. That's almost worth the pain.

Leif rushed forward, dropping his shadows as he ran.

Loxias had recovered from being tossed into the stone wall and was striding towards the fray. The murderous look upon his face had Faelan snarling louder.

Imus lifted a hand to keep his brother from approaching Faelan or myself. "Stay where you are brother. I would hate to have to end this myself."

The young prince halted in his tracks. I felt the powerful energy roiling off of Imus and knew that it wasn't an empty threat.

Loxias scrubbed at the back of his neck, mouth gaping open with incredulity.

"You would do well to remember that that is my great granddaughter there. Eowyn's blood flows through her veins and I will not allow you to live if you harm her." Flames swirled around Imus's hands like a mini tornado, waiting for the command to be unleashed.

Pain shot through me in waves as Leif broke the arrowhead off and pushed the shaft through. It clanged to the ground.

The venom began working its way through my system. I could feel it pushing towards my heart, fogging my mind. The venom must become more potent the farther into Anavrin were.

Darkness closed in, pulling my eyes shut. I could hear Red's anguished sobs, but no tears leaked onto my skin.

Be strong, sweetpea.

I tried to use my tongue to make words of comfort, but it wouldn't co-operate.

Heaviness pressed in on me from every side and the last thing I heard was a maelstrom of whooshing air and crackling power before I lost consciousness.

Chapter Fifty

Faelan

"I need a bottle of water to flush the wound," Leif said.

I didn't move, didn't breathe. He reached over and grabbed my wrist and was met with a zap.

Raising his hands in surrender, he took a step back.

"Easy there, friend. I only want to help. Can you get a bottle of water from that pack over there so that I can keep pressure to the wound?"

The red I was seeing faded a little and rational thought was beginning to return to me.

Running over to the pack, I grabbed a bottle of water, taking steadying breaths as I walked back.

"The venom is spreading fast. I don't know what we can do. All of the antidotes are in the main castles, but your castle was gutted of everything years ago." Leif had tried to whisper to Max, but I heard every word.

Fear crept into my heart. I couldn't lose him. It was too much. Faltering in my steps, I let the bottle crash to the floor with a thud.

Max turned to see me drop to my knees. "I did this. I over-reacted and now..." my voice trailed off.

Bringing my hands to my face, I let the tears finally fall.

A firm hand fell on my shoulder. The comfort warmed me from the inside out.

"No. You didn't. I would have reacted the same way if my mate were threatened." Max's hand fell away from my shoulder, and he stood straight.

Offering me that hand, I just stared.

"Now, get up! Your mate is not yet lost, and I will not lose my friend."

"I don't have Grams' book here. I don't remember all of the herbs that go into making the remedy."

I should never have parted with the damn thing!

"I said get to your feet, Princess. You will not give up hope."

His command was firm but not callous. There was warmth and caring embedded into each one. That gave me the resolve to rise.

"You are the Deliverer. You are a descendant of the First Witch. Your gifts are of particle manipulation. Do you under-stand what that means?"

I nodded. Tenth grade science class was quite a while ago, but I remembered the gist. And Sci-fi movies helped fill in the gaps, though they couldn't be relied on as fact.

"It means that I can makes thing into other things."

The scent of blood threatened to push me over the edge. There was so much of it. He was bleeding and the poison was making too fast for his healing abilities to slow the process.

"Yes. And not only that, if you are as gifted as the First Witch, then you will be able to sense every cell of every single thing, living or inanimate. You can dismantle anything. And you can reassemble them anyway or anywhere you want."

His eyes crinkled with admiration, and I felt emboldened by his declaration.

"You are more powerful than the First Witch, Faelan. You have royal blood. That means that your gifts will be augmented."

He placed both hands on my shoulders and gazed directly into my eyes. "You have the power within you to remove the venom and heal him. So, let's get to saving your mate."

"Okay. I can do this." Wylder hadn't moved since he'd passed out. His breathing was becoming more erratic with every passing moment.

Getting onto my knees by the wound, I glanced over towards Loxias and Quill.

"Stay back while I work. I won't hesitate to rip you apart cell by cell if you approach. We aren't done yet."

I turned back to Wylder's still form. "Max, what do I do?"

"When I knew the First Witch, she would tell me of how she'd concentrate on the outcome of what she wanted. Don't focus too much on the details." His words made sense, but all I could think about was how that venom was racing towards my mate's heart.

Laying my hands on the wound, I concentrated on the venom. I saw it as a green glowing light in my mind's eye. Saw all of the particles rushing around his system.

My hands began to tingle. I imagined the green glow trying to get away, but I pulled it back towards the wound. Blood leaked heavily under my hands, but I didn't dare look down at it.

Concentrating on the venom and calling it back to me, I felt the surge of it fill my cupped palm. It pooled there, looking toxic to my eyes. "What now?" I asked Max.

"Do you have all of it?"

"Can you not see it in my hands?" *Weird. It looks like a nuclear sludge.*

"No, Faelan. Only you can see particle trails. So, if you're sure that you have it all, toss it. Then close the wound." Max's reassuring smile felt familiar.

It spoke of family, and it was inspiriting. He believed in me so I would believe in myself.

"You only need to concentrate on closing the holes on the front and in the back. You don't want to heal him completely." Whipping my head to his face, he smiled encouragingly. "He's a werewolf, honey. He'll heal very quickly. If you heal him completely, it won't help his system adjust to the sudden shift."

I raised an eyebrow at him. It sort of made sense but I wished he be more plain about it.

"He'll wolf out and lose himself for a few minutes before his mind recognizes any of us. We don't want that," he said with a wink.

I grinned weakly but my worry over Wylder didn't allow for pleasantries at the moment.

Sparkling light crackled at my fingertips as I placed them against his front and back wounds. The skin under my hands stitched itself up and just like that, the wounds were gone. *I did it*!

Taking another moment of concentration, the blood coating everything evaporated with just a thought. It wasn't something that I wanted a reminder of on our journey.

Wylder stirred under my touch. "Hi there sleepy head."

Bending to brush a light kiss to his lips, my hair fell onto his face.

His breathing became steadier. Winces of pain rode his face as his body mended itself on the inside.

"How long was I out this time?" he said with a raspy voice. Lifting his head slightly, he looked around. "Couldn't have been that long."

A laugh of relief fell from my lips.

"Everyone's still alive," Max called over my shoulder to my lap where Wylder's head rested. "Faelan healed you. Ya know..." he wiggled his fingers. "Magics. Ohhh... ahhh."

Smart ass.

Reaching down to press another kiss to his lips, the ache in my heart receded. "You've got to stop doing this to me. Three times is too many."

A sheepish grin donned his face. "I'll try, love. Can't make any promises though."

Trying to stand, he swayed for a moment, and I grabbed him under the arms.

"Well, if you're not going to kill the huntsman, can I at least kick his and Quill's asses?"

Max stepped forward and clapped him on the back. "A sparring match can be arranged but right now, we have a mission to complete."

He looked back at me with a question in his eyes and I nodded my agreement. It felt nice to have another person looking out for what I wanted.

Being forced into doing things was not something I'd ever responded well to.

Max didn't treat me like he was in control of my decisions or action. He was there to walk a path with me by his side, as equals.

And the way that he, a High Prince, had just subtly asked for my conformation of the plan, it gave me confidence. He wouldn't act like a misogynistic prick.

The realization that both Wylder and Maximus valued my input and weren't threatened by my strengths gave me hope that our plans just might succeed. *My guys.*

Warmth bubbled up from a deep well inside of my chest. Love seeped into every crevice, making me feel buoyant. For the first time in weeks, I felt optimistic of our success.

Slinging his bow and quiver over his shoulder and bending down to retrieve his crossbow from the ground, Quill huffed in disappointment.

"No hard feelings, Wolf. Just protecting my own." He shouldered into Wylder as he passed and the growl that ushered from deep in my chest was one of possession.

Get a grip. He's quite capable of fighting his own battles, psycho.

Wylder chuckled. "Understandable," he said but he grabbed his arm before he could get too far. His fist collided with the side of Quill's jaw before anyone could bat an eye. "So, now ya know. Try to hurt her again and a broken jaw will be the least of your problems, Fae."

Quill rubbed at his jaw, snapping it back into place. I watched as it healed right before my eyes. All of four seconds passed and his face was perfect again.

Leif picked up his pack from the ground and motioned for us all to do the same. "We really should get going. We're already running way behind."

Loxias looked on at the group like he was seeing all of us in a different light.

"I had an idea," Max scrubbed at the stubble on his chin while he spoke. "I was thinking, maybe Faelan and I could teleport all of us to the border of my lands. We can't risk being seen doing so after we leave them yet, but it would cut half a day of walking off our trip."

"I don't know that I can teleport me, let alone anyone else. What if I fuck it up and put our arms and legs back together wrong." Anxiety gripped me so tight that I'd stopped breathing.

Wylder reached over and wrapped his arms around my waist.

"I'm sure you can do it. You just need to concentrate."

One minute Max was in front of me, the next he and all of the packs were gone. He popped back into existence in the next breath.

"See? Easy peasy. You don't know where to concentrate on, so you'll have to concentrate on me. Usually, you'd think of the place you want to go. Imagine it in the center of your mind, and Poof. You're there. Since you've never seen the borders of my lands, though, you'll need to think about me. Imagine me and only me, not what's surrounding me. Then, will yourself to be in front of me."

He reached over and took Leif by the arm. "I'm going to take these guys first but when I've taken the last one, I want you to take Wylder by the arm and concentrate on me. Got it?"

I nodded but didn't feel the least bit of confidence in myself. "Can't you take him with you too? I don't want to accidentally hurt him."

Biting on my bottom lip, the blood drained from my face at the thought.

Wylder placed a finger under my chin. "Hey, I believe in you. You've got this."

"Faelan," Max said. "If I didn't think you could do it, I wouldn't blow smoke up your ass."

I snorted loudly. *Nice.*

"Wylder is someone that I know you will protect at all costs. That's why it only makes sense for him to be the one you bring with you. You'll concentrate harder without even meaning too. He's right. You've got this."

Without another word, Max grabbed Loxias and Quill and was gone. It was time to go. *Stupid faery gg-dad. Ugh.*

Placing my arms around Wylder's neck while he held fast to my waist, I closed my eyes and imagined Maximus. The color of his hair, the cadence of his voice, the smell of his skin.

He was of my blood. It almost sung to me. Maybe that was why he knew I could do it. It gave me a boost of confidence.

"Are you ready?"

Wylder kissed that spot on the top of my head again, bringing a smile to my lips.

Shutting out my lust, Max's face stood out in the center of my mind's eye. I thought of him and only him.

A tingling sensation lit up my very being.

With a light shimmer, we were off.

Chapter Fifty-One

Wyder

The strangest sensation ever lit my body from the inside out. I couldn't, exactly, feel every particle rearrange, but I could swear that for a brief second, I could feel every individual cell in my body separately.

The way that Imus's teleporting felt had been different. His was more like being under water for brief spurts.

Red's was better. *That's my girl.*

Just as quickly as it begun, it was over.

We were staring at a stone structure on the outskirts of a copse of trees. There were a few small houses scattered this far out from the castle.

The smell of petrichor was heavy in the air. Rain must have fallen over night.

The main road in Anavrin that led to the Kingdom's Seat castle was about a hundred meters away. Imus and the others were mere inches from us. A foot at most. *Woah.*

"I did it." Her exuberant smile made my heart swell with pride. "I actually teleported. Look out Harry Potter. I'm on the trail of becoming a wizard."

The sparkle that beamed from her eyes did funny things to me.

Scooping her into my arms and nuzzling into her neck, my cock swelled. She noticed the moment my affection became lust.

"Eww. Please don't encourage him, Faelan." Loxias said as he noticed the bulge barely contained beneath my jeans. "I don't want to witness you having that thing on display while you defile my great niece."

"I second that." Imus looked pointedly toward Wylder with a raised eyebrow. "I mean, I get it, but just... no."

Well, that's an erection killer.

Faelan took a step back, realizing that we had an audience. The pink that colored her cheeks only made her more irresistible and it frustrated that need I felt deep within.

"Let's get going. We still have half a day's walk from here." Loxias picked up his pack and we followed suit.

The sound of swift feet had us all turning defensively towards the source of the sound. Quill's crossbow raised, Leif's shadows swam around his feet, and even Red's magics sparkled at her fingertips.

Only Imus remained calm... smiling even.

"Your Highness! You have returned." An older looking fae ran at us but stopped short once she noticed that we were all posed to fight. Her enthusiasm faltered.

"I am here on a quest, dear Zelda." Imus took a few steps in her direction, and she dropped to her knees, forehead nearly touching the ground. "Please, rise. The ground still holds chill, and it would do me no good to have you suffer for your loyalty."

Raising her head slowly, and even slower to get to her feet, she gazed in awe at Prince Maximus.

"My Lord, your faithful subjects have never lost hope of your return. Please," she pleaded. "You must stay. We need you."

I watched, just like the rest of them, as Imus walked over and embraced her.

It wasn't lost on us that he knew the names of those in his court, even here in the outmost reaches of his lands.

"I am sorry for my long absence. You may tell whomever you wish that I have returned, but only after three day's time." He gave her a pointed look, waiting for her to register understanding. "My quest is of the utmost importance, and I must remain undetected."

"Of course, Your Highness." She stole a glance at Loxias before lowering her voice and continuing. "The royal houses are said to be divided, sire. Are you sure you should be in the company of this brother?"

With all of them having superior hearing, no one missed her warning. Loxias rolled his eyes and Quill growled.

"Trust is not something that I do lightly, Zelda. You and those of my court know this." He placed a hand on her shoulder. "I want you to know this and spread the word once the time has passed... Queen Leyashna's children are my blood.

And there will be no animosity or ill will towards any of them. Roxalus, Embla, and Emenda will be reminded of that swiftly."

Zelda looked at him like a wilting flower longing for the rain. Admiration donned every feature of her wrinkled face.

She must have been incredibly old to be aged that way, and it gave me a sense of unease to remember that true immorality did not exist.

With another stolen glance towards Prince Loxias, she smiled. Looking back to Imus, her voice rose for us all to hear even though it wasn't necessary.

"You are still the honorable man I remember, Your Highness." With a dip of her chin to Loxias, she said "I will spread the word far and wide in three day's time."

With that, she turned on her heels and was off.

"So, Imus. You're back?" If Faelan was upset by this news, she didn't let on.

I imagined that my old friend wanted to meet his daughter and hang out with his great granddaughter, but if he was going to take over his lands once again, how was that going to be possible?

Well, isn't this just a gag of sweat and a full bottle of spit?

"Really? You'll stay?" The longing in Loxias voice for his brother's return wasn't hidden. "Roxalus won't take this news well, but me and mine will wholly back you."

I couldn't be sure if the young prince actually meant what he said or not. I noticed that he didn't promise or swear it. A fae's word was a magical binding. And as much as I wanted to believe him, something didn't sit right without it.

"I will, but I will also be going to the Lupian Forest to visit Inara and Faelan as regularly as I can." I cleared my throat loudly. "And, of course, I could never leave my best tv watching buddy hanging, either."

"Thanks for the afterthought there, asshole," I said with a smirk. "Faelan, your thoughts?"

She'd been quiet since we'd first arrived and now that I could see the anxiousness on her face, it had all of my attention.

"You're staying." It wasn't a question. "You're staying and reclaiming your court and eventually the throne." Her hands twisted in knots in front of her. "Grams and I deserve to know you, Max. Are you sure that you can balance the weight of Anavrin and visits to the Lupian Forest?"

Pulling her against him, he wrapped his arms around her in a big hug, and I felt a twinge of irrational male jealousy but quickly shook it out of my mind.

"Nothing and no one could stop me, sunshine." It struck me that this was the first time that Red had allowed him to touch her, to fully acknowledge her as his kin. "I swear it on our blood."

A shimmer lit the small space between her chest and his. It was the magics of a fae binding. He would have to follow through with that vow no matter what.

A bit of the peace Faelan felt through the promise made its way down the mating bond and settled around my heart as well.

It was Leif who voiced his concerns about the future of Anavrin in the wake of his statement.

"If you become king, Inara or Faelan would need to rule your court. The people of it would accept no one else but your blood."

I couldn't put my finger on it, but something about Lief's declaration prickled at the back of my mind.

"That would be their call. I could speak to my people if they don't wish to take up the throne." A grin that didn't quite reach his eyes fell upon his lips. "I'm sure we'll be able to figure something out if it comes to that."

After a few minutes, Quill's patience with all of the touchy feely emotions came to an end. "This shit can wait. We need to get going. Right now!"

Both princes turned to him with incredulity clearly written upon their faces. And the princess that Red was, like it or not, still glared at him as if he were a fly caught in the sights of a toad.

By Luna, I love this woman.

Picking up my pack to break the tension and get us moving, I took her by the elbow and started walking.

Over my shoulder, I threw out a retort. "Ya might want to remember your place among the royalty," I said smugly.

Wrapping my arm around Faelan's waist, we took the lead.

I called back without turning. Disrespect coloring my tone...

"And Quill... talk to my girl like that again, it'll take you awhile to grow back your tongue."

Chapter Fifty-Two

Wylder

We'd walked for hours now, and the outskirts of the festival were coming into view.

The smell of cooked meats and fried dough reached us from here. Balloons and flags of varying colors brought a sense of excitement in the air.

Sounds of merriment reaching to the outskirts of the closest village that we'd passed.

The castle was still roughly five miles from where we were. More and more festival goers passed us along the main road, heading towards all of the activities as the afternoon stretched its way into evening.

With the first group to pass us, everyone took on a defensive stance. It was Leif who hid us in shadows before realizing what we were seeing.

Two more groups, a small family and a group of younger fae, were the next to pass. The main road into the kingdom wasn't narrow but it was the only road to travel from our direction.

It became congested with festival goers making their way to the castle grounds with every step that we took.

Along the way, Red had proceeded in front of him to talk to Leif. I didn't feel irritation with him the way that I did with every other male that made for Faelan's attention.

As much as I thought on it, I couldn't reason out why.

I watched as they shared light conversation and whispered things back and forth.

At first, they had laughed. Then their conversation appeared more serious.

I did my best not to listen, but I couldn't hear them anyway. Whatever it was that Leif was telling her, he used his shadow gifts to stop the sound from traveling to the rest of us.

Loxias and Imus hung back. It had been a long time since the brothers had a chance to catch up. There was a comradery between them. Loxias being the youngest sibling and Imus being the oldest, they had an undeniable bond as I glanced their way.

If I didn't know them separately before I'd seen them talking like this, I would never have believed any time had passed.

The fact was, I did know them separately.

Imus had been a good friend. He had never been a cruel male. We'd hung out, had drinks, watched television. It hadn't even been a thought in my head that Imus could be as trick-stery as any of the other fae I'd ever met.

And Loxias was all of that. Cruel and a trickster with his words. He used his gifts regularly. He saw himself as kind and better than others so it wasn't an issue if he took away their will and replaced it with his own.

Quill was just as typical of a faery. His gifts came in the way of marksmanship. Showing off that marksmanship came naturally.

It wasn't a boast. It was simply superiority. Arrogant and unfeeling.

Leif was different. He used his gifts, but it was never in the fae way. He had always displayed empathy whenever our paths crossed.

Most fae didn't seem to possess empathy at all.

With the others engaged in their own little conversations, it left Quill to walk with me. *Yay me.*

The fae's bow and quiver were slung lazily over his shoulder. His crossbow rested in a holster on his hip.

As we walked, he would shoot a watchful eye around the periphery. His gaze landed on Loxias half a dozen times.

I thought that I saw a twinge of longing in the male's eyes with every pass, but it wasn't my business. If Quill wanted the young prince, it could interfere with guarding him, but that was between them.

It could have just been that Imus had been gone for so long and with him back, that meant that Loxias would be looking to his favorite brother again as his confidant rather than his bodyguard and friend.

"What will you do now that you're not his go-to guy any-more?" I teased. He was owed some torment. "The princes seem to be getting back into their familial stride rather quickly."

"What makes you think that I care? If Prince Loxias wants to throw his lot in with the lost heir, I will stand at his side. Just as I have for centuries."

His upper lip quivered slightly, like he was trying to contain more emotions than he was capable of holding on to.

"Besides, their castles are a day's journey apart. They won't be able to confer as often as I will be able to hold Loxias's confidences." *Oh, really?*

Rubbing the stubble on my chin in mock thought, I smirked. "I'm sure you're right," I said. "Prince Maximus wouldn't dream of teleporting to his brother's side at a moment's thought."

Quill stopped walking and it gave me satisfaction to leave him standing there as I caught up to Red.

Check and mate. Payback's a bitch.

Chapter Fifty-Three

Faelan

Wylder's smile at Quill's backwards retreat to Loxias' side made me grin. I'd come to recognize when he was being mischievous or ornery.

My heart sang at the thought of him in a happy space. As strange as it was to be so aware of another person so quickly, it also brought a sense of comfort.

Catching his hand as I approached, he smiled more fully. "Are you over here causing trouble?" I said playfully.

"Me? Never." All waggling brows, a smirk for miles.

Yeah, and if the Cheshire cat could grin that wide, he'd swallow all of Wonderland.

He sighed as I patiently waited. "I was just pointing out some things that the arrogant fae overlooked."

"Hey! You'd do well to remember that I am one of those arrogant fae." It was the first time I'd admitted it to myself, much less, out loud.

"Fae, yes... but Red, I don't think that anyone who's ever met you would call you arrogant." Wrapping me into his arms, he went to kiss that spot on my head again and I turned last second.

My eye caught the full wetness of Wyder's lips, and he laughed, letting me go.

"It's the third eye that you're supposed to kiss, Wolf," Max said as he caught me by the elbow.

The unexpected contact made me snarl and snap my teeth in his direction.

"Sorry, sorry." *Don't apologize to the faeries, dumbass.* Luckily, gg-dad didn't press the issue. "I didn't mean to nearly bite you."

Looking around at the others, he leaned in. "No worries, sunshine."

I didn't understand the look he was giving me, and it must have shown on my face.

"You remind me greatly of Eowyn. She was a force of nature."

"She'd have to have been to raise Grams. Just wait until you meet her. You'll see." I couldn't wait for them to meet. I couldn't wait to see her, safe and sound, again either.

Wylder shifted beside me. "What?" I said.

"Inara might not react well to the news that we're mated. I might get my ass kicked when she finds out." The seriousness to his words made both me and Max laugh. "I'm not joking. Inara might take my balls for sullying her precious granddaughter." That only made us laugh harder.

Two children ran by us as one of them hollered about getting to eat some sort of pastry before the other one.

"Your balls will be safe. I can handle Grams," I said. "Besides, with everything else going on, it may take a bit for that to take a priority."

Leif called out to us from the scouting point fifty yards out. "It's time."

Coming back to join our little group, he cast shadows around us so that we wouldn't be seen or heard.

"There are eight guards on the high wall, four at the door, and two more in the dual towers."

Loxias clapped his hands together. Excitement and worry etched in the lines around his eyes.

"Alright. Faelan, you're going to need to concentrate at first, but it should become a little easier the longer you hold the glamours on Max and Wylder. When we get in front of the king and queen, do try not to be flippant. We need them to bring Inara up from the dungeons before the last course is served. If all goes to plan, you can grab her and shield her. I'm counting on you to hold up your end of the deal."

"Know this brother" Max said... "if my father tries to harm my daughter or my great granddaughter, I won't hold back."

Well, there's a death glare I'd never want to be on the receiving end of.

He leaned in towards Loxias without hesitation. "Make peace with that fact now. I will send him to his final rest if I must."

Wylder and Quill exchanged similar glares but said nothing. If all went as planned, I'd whisk Grams away from harm, meet with the pack at Ritual Rock, and perform the magics that would help both parties. *No pressure at all.*

Wylder lifted my chin to look him in the eyes. "You can do this. I believe in you, even if you doubt yourself." A firm kiss brushed my lips. "I'll be right beside you the whole time."

"We both will," Max interjected. Lowering his voice so that only I could hear, he said, "If anything goes wrong, you grab Inara and get to that cliff. Do you understand me?"

I wanted to protest on his and Wylder's behalf, but I knew that it was up to me to make sure Grams survived after living in damp dungeons with who only knew what kind of conditions.

I had to trust that Max would get Wylder back to me safely. "I swear to see things righted. You have my word."

The word of a faery couldn't be broken. I'd come to learn a lot of little things along this journey.

Mostly from Leif. I liked him, secrets and all.

Turning towards the others, I said, "Okay, Uncle Lox. Show me to that fiendish great- great grandfather of mine."

Wickedness dripped from my lips.

"Let's see who's afraid of the big bad wolf."

Chapter Fifty-Four

Wylder

Faelan did an amazing job at glamouring me and Imus. We looked like any other of the royal guard.

She allowed Loxias to place the anti-magics cuffs on her wrists, but the key lay right within her sleeve to be pulled out using just one finger.

The halls of the castle were crowded with festival activities set up along each corridor.

Jugglers and vendors abounded every few feet. The laughing and cheering of small children caught my eye as we passed a puppet show in the large waiting area before the throne room.

As the doors opened, Red was fidgeting, and I felt her anxiety sharpen through the bond.

Before she glamoured me, I made her magically bind my will. The protector bond was stronger than anything else.

If she were in danger, I didn't want to fuck things up unintentionally.

Inara might be upset by the mating bond with her grand-daughter, but I was ticked at her in return for taking my free will from me.

Right now, the magics from all of the different bonds felt like a noose. There was something to be said for having no responsibilities.

This was the polar opposite of that.

In front of the king and queen's thrones sat a long banquet table. Queen Leyashna sat to the right. Two males and a female sat beside her with small crowns upon their heads.

I assumed that they were her children, because on the left side sat the king, a male, and twin females with slightly larger crowns.

Imus's fists clenched beside me. Leif faltered in his steps.

Faelan stood beside Loxias with her head held high, but I could feel her intimidation by the royals through our bond.

Quill and Leif stood to either side and two steps behind.

That left me and Imus to stand behind them and to the side, forming a vee formation.

There were three groups ahead of us in the line waiting to approach the royals as they feasted.

Halfway through whatever the first groups query, the second of three dessert courses was brought out.

The scent of sweet honey and cinnamon wafted through the chamber. More bright yellow wine was poured into goblets. And music continued to play as courtiers filled the chamber with their merriment.

I had never met royalty before and if I'd thought it would be like that of the Brits I'd seen on the television, I couldn't have been more wrong.

Guards were posted every twenty feet around the perimeter, but there didn't seem to be any tension in their stance.

From what I could tell, they weren't worried that they'd be called upon to do anything but watch for unruly drunks.

After that group left with their judgement, the second group approached. I could barely make out what it was they were asking for but words like land rights and common decency flittered back to my ears.

"What makes you think you deserve any more freedoms than you have been given?" said the prince to the king's right.

He got to his feet and glanced down his nose at the lord and his family.

"It seems to me that you could have chosen better when it came to breeding."

The queen tsked at the prince as the king sneered. Neither of them spoke directly to the lord in question.

If this were what it was like to live under the rule of the Suilari royals, I would stay put in the Lupian Forest for sure.

The female to the Queen's side had brought a honeyed pear to her lips before Roxalus had spoken and had yet to take a bite. Setting it back down on her plate, she stood in turn.

"Lord Tovenar, you have my deepest sympathy on the loss of Lady Sofina. She was a beautiful soul. Perhaps a three-month variance on your tithes would extend to you and yours a proper grieving period. Go home with our blessings of solace."

Roxalus turned towards his youngest sister, a sneer of his own plastered on his overly handsome face. "Dear sister," he spit the word. "I did not ask for your commentary on my observations. I will remind you of your place."

At those words, the lord and his family exited the throne room as quickly as possible. They were smart for not giving Prince Roxalus the time to change the verdict of their terms.

The male closest to the Queen stood to face his brother. He was big and brutish, but his face held no contempt as he addressed his brother. *Only for show, then.*

"And I will remind you once again, Roxalus, you are not in charge here. Father still breathes and the queen still sits upon her throne as well."

He didn't make any threats but the implication of one was there all the same.

This prince was well built, a warrior under the refinement of royal garments.

From what I could see, the demeanor from which he spoke oozed natural confidence. Nothing was forced.

The intimidation that could be felt was from a lion not afraid of standing toe to toe with a jaguar. Both had teeth. Both had claws. And both had bite, but one was clearly the king of the jungle.

King Zyoden appeared bored, before the encounter with the lord, and again now that the princes were squaring off verbally.

"Approach," he motioned to our group.

Spotting Loxias with Faelan shackled at his side, the king sat up straighter.

"Loxias. What is the meaning of this?" he motioned towards Red's hand.

Why would he care if she were in chains?

"Greetings King Zyoden," he nodded. "Mother." Taking another step forward, we all followed his lead. "I request an audience with all of the royals present."

Roxalus rolled his eyes, but I noticed the female to the queen's side shooting glances towards Imus.

I didn't know if her gifts allowed her to see through our facade.

Well, shit. That would mean that the jig was up before we'd even gotten started.

Unease shimmied its way down the bond, and I pushed back confidence towards Faelan. I would lend her as much strength as I could.

Queen Leyashna flourished a hand towards the feast.

"You have our attention, my son. You should eat with us and enjoy the abundance that Luna has provided us this turn of the wheel."

King Zyoden's eyes never left Faelan's face. The full attention of the chamber had been drawn to our group because of the king's interest.

"Loxias, I ask again... why have you brought her here?"

Fear and anguish crinkled his brow, making him look the ancient age that he was.

"The First Witch was banished from our lands many centuries ago. Why have you brought her back, in chains no less?"

Chapter Fifty-Five

Faelan

That was not what I had expected the king to say.

For him to think that I was his mistress, the First Witch, his brains must be addling in his final season.

I didn't know what the First Witch looked like, but Max and the rest of them would have known. No one had mentioned my resemblance to her.

How to proceed from here, without knowing if that was truly the case, could prove crucial.

"The First Witch is long dead, Father." Loxias gestured to me, to the chains that bound my hands. "I present to the court a way to break the curse. I present to you..." he said as he touched my skin.

The act was important to make them think that he was able to control me with his gifts.

"...the Deliverer. Kin of the First Witch. From the male line of Tobias Isbith. Descendant of the Callileach daughter."

Roxalus glared at his brother. "And isn't that the same speech you gave us when you brought in the woman who now resides in the dungeons of this very castle?" he said. "What makes you so sure that this one is the Deliverer? Does she have the fabled stone?"

The queen shifted uncomfortably in her chair. "He has a fair point, my son. How do you know this one is any different than the last one?"

I stole a quick look in Maximus's direction. Giving a subtle nod, I took a step closer to the royal table.

Not missing Ayxian shifting towards his mother protectively, I turned my full attention to the king.

"Your Majesty, I would like to petition for the release of my grandmother from your dungeons."

King Zyoden appeared besotted. His attention was unnerving.

I remembered the story of his love for the First Witch. How he never looked at the woman he loved as Queen Ombriana banished her and her name from the realm of Anavrin.

Looking at him, I got the impression that he never stopped loving her.

He'd been a shell of a male before we'd all approached and now, he was slowly filling with some semblance of life.

The chamber had become quiet all around us. Dancing stilled, merriment ceased, and the crowd held a collective breath waiting on the King's verdict.

Nope. That's not ominous or anything.

It was Roxalus, once again, who saw fit to interject on his father's behalf.

"Why would the king ever consider handing over a shifting fae from the First Witch's line to another of the same? I say we lock both of them up and throw away the key."

Maximus and Wylder shifted with grunts and growls from behind me. Leif's shadows drifted around me and Prince Loxias' feet.

Signaling with a slight movement of my finger for them to hold steady, they did so begrudgingly.

The distracting smell of food and sweat hung heavily in the air all around us.

Loxias cleared his throat. "Prince Maximus had an heir with the fae witch, Eowyn, of the First Witch's line." Gasps went up around the room. "The female held in the dungeons is his daughter which he never had the chance to meet. If you will entertain the Deliverer's request, we shall give you the rest of the story."

From behind their gossiping hands, one of the twins finally turned her attentions to our little group.

"You will give us the rest of the story regardless," said one of them. "It is your duty as sworn huntsman of the royal line, dear brother. You must put duty to the realm first and family second."

"Well, therein lies the rub, dear Embla. My duty to the realm is to break the curse on our peoples. If the Deliverer won't use her magics to do so because we have given her no incentive, then I have failed Anavrin." Quill smirked in Embla's direction, but her twin took up her charge.

"Oh, foolish Loxias. If we bring her up from the dungeons, we can simply torture her until this Deliverer gives us, not only the rest of the story but lifts this curse upon our powers and the mating bond as well."

Before I could stop him, Max sauntered forward. Wylder was at my side in an instant.

This hadn't gone to plan, but we would have to make it work. Wylder took my hand and gave it a gentle squeeze before letting go.

The shackles fell from my wrists and clanged loudly as they hit the stone floor. All of the royals but the king showed their distress.

Except the female on the queen's side who had spoken up for the lord and his family before them. *Interesting*.

Maximus pulled at my elbow.

"Oh, right." I felt for my magics holding their glamours in place and let them fall.

The queen nearly fell out of her chair. Ayxian and his siblings looked dumbfounded at discovering their lost brother standing in their midst. Roxalus snarled and the twins hissed like angry cats.

Not surprisingly, the king said nothing. He actually looked bored again. Still, his gaze hadn't left my face.

"What's the matter, dear family? Not pleased to see me?" Max took a half step in front of me just as a spear of ice shot towards my head like an arrow.

He melted it before it had made half the distance.

"Tut tut tut. There will be no harm brought to my daughter or my great granddaughter. I swear it on the royal name." Gasps, once again, ran a circle around the room.

Any royal that swore an oath, especially one done on the royal name, was bound to uphold that oath at all costs.

"You were presumed dead or forgotten long ago, brother." Roxalus drew the sword from his side. "You only need ask and I will make that official."

The two males from Queen Leyashna's line stood and drew their swords as well.

"What happened to you? Why did you forsake our family?" Ayxian demanded. The other must have been Noxian.

The shifted uncomfortably but the love for her stepson shined through her sorrow filled eyes.

"Why not ask our father," he looked to the king who still had not so much as blinked away from me. "Or even ask your mother, though I do not hold her accountable."

Max inclined his head in Queen Leyashna's direction. Tears streamed down her face.

Softly, he said to her, "I forgive your neglect of my condition, as I hope you will forgive my being gone far too long."

A shuttering sob left the queen's chest and she half jump, half flew over the feasting table. Throwing her arms around Maximus, he wrapped his arms around her too, lifting her from her feet.

"Sweet boy, I have missed you every minute of every day." Wetness streaked down her face. "I do not deserve to be this happy at our reunion, but I cannot help how my heart leaps with joy at your homecoming."

Wylder leaned over to whisper in my ear. "What in the hell am I missing? I know they were working together, but she legit seems to have missed him like a lost son?"

Duh, neanderthal.

"Well, she is his stepmother. That means something to some people. Apparently, they were friends too, if all of what he told us about her trying to help and visiting him in the dungeons was the full truth."

The dungeons. Shit.

"Um, not to interrupt, but I would like to see my Grams." I said.

Max stiffened at the mention. Queen Leyashna signal to a guard and he was off towards a hall at the back of the chamber.

Wylder took my hand again. The King's head snapped to attention.

"Get your hands off of her, you dirty peasant shifter!" Standing from his seat at the table, he looked around the room. "Out! Everyone out!"

He spoke only to the crowd surrounding the chamber, not to his family. They weren't going anywhere.

"Your discomfort is not my intent, Your Majesty," Wylder said. "Faelan is my mate and I am her bonded protector."

Max stepped away from the queen and blocked me from the king's glare, but wind began to whip around the room like a bad storm. Embla and who I assumed must be Emenda stood now too.

It was Elodie, the queen's only true blood daughter who spoke up.

"Father, that is not the First Witch! That is your great-great granddaughter. You need to recognize your state of being!"

Quill and Leif had taken up flanking positions on Loxias' sides.

He tried reasoning with the king again. "We need her, Father! She is the only one who can break this curse."

Raking a hand through his hair, it tossed his locks in odd directions. "I need to have this retched curse broken." Defeat made his face pale. "I need to find my mate."

The guard who the queen had sent to retrieve my grandmother arrived in a maelstrom of activity.

Grams was overcome by the commotion, falling to her knees in her weakened state just a second before an ice spear crashed where she'd been standing only a moment before.

"Nooooo!" Maximus roared his outrage as he launched himself at Roxalus. Elodie ran towards Grams as Ayxian and Noxian came bounding towards me, Loxias, and the rest of our group.

I wanted to run to Grams, but the scene around me froze me in place. A thump came down the mating bond and I looked over to see Wylder in wolf form.

Ayxian raised his sword as Noxian notched a bolt in his crossbow.

Quill raised his own in the direction of the princes. "Ah, ah, ah. I wouldn't do that if I were you."

Shadows swirled around Loxias and Leif and he extended them to me as well.

It was sheer chaos. My thoughts all ran together, and I didn't know which way to turn.

Wylder's wolf form was large and menacing. The fae had their own powers, plus strength on their side. Grams was still down, and I could see that Elodie was trying to help her.

Thank Luna for small miracles.

The king and queen were in some sort of heated altercation and Max was battling Roxalus as if he'd gone off the deep end. His kind eyes were replaced by dark, cold emptiness. Fire and ice clashing in equal intervals.

Ayxian took a step towards me, sword raised, as Loxias grabbed for my arm. Noxian fell back to his mother's side.

Wylder's growl cut through all of the noise in the room as he leapt, open jawed, at Ayxian sword arm. A snarl left my own throat.

I took two steps in his direction when I heard a scream. *Grams.*

Embla and Emenda had subdued Elodie, and electric sparks danced across Grams and Elodie's skin as the twins cackled with glee.

Cruel fucking faery princesses!

With a last glance at Wylder, who was now in human form again, wrestling the warrior fae prince, I sent love down the mating bond.

He turned and nodded to me once before throwing himself back into the fray.

Magics dripped from my fingertips. A blast shimmered out and around the room, leaving everyone knocked off of their feet.

Teleporting over to Grams in the blink of an eye, I linked our elbows. Thoughts of Ritual Rock the only thing I allowed myself to think.

With one more blast of magics towards Roxalus, we were gone.

Chapter Fifty-Six

Wylder

The moment Faelan left the realm of Anavrin, I felt the emptiness of her non-presence like a chasm in my chest. Everyone slowly got to their feet.

Imus, otherwise known as Prince Maximus, made his way to Elodie, pulling her into a tight embrace.

The queen helped the king to his feet, and they took the throne.

The feasting table and everything else in the room had been swept to the sides of the chamber from Red's blast before she teleported Inara away.

Loxias, Quill, And Leif looked around for signs that they may still be there, but I felt it the moment they'd left.

It had been mine and Imus's plan that Faelan grab Inara and depart if anything went awry.

We hadn't filled the others in on that because of their insistence that the priority was the curse being broken.

Loxias wouldn't have agreed to let her go. He would have shackled her for real. His desperation for his full powers clouded every other thought the poor prince had.

Embla, Emenda, and Roxalus took up space to the right of the king's throne. Roxalus continued to whisper in his father's ear while the twins shot looks of daggers at the others around the room.

"I have returned to claim my court and help my people," Max declared to the room as a whole. "I can't say that I won't leave the realm to visit my girls more often than you may perhaps like, but my court will know that their prince intends to help his land flourish, and his people thrive again."

Roxalus sneered. "That really isn't your call, dear brother. I have been named heir in the wake of your absence. And I don't see why father would change his mind."

The king stared blankly. It was clear that there wasn't anybody home in that head of his.

As one, Ayxian, Noxian, Loxias, Elodie and lastly, Queen Leyashna rose to stand.

The queen's voice was quiet but firm. "With the eldest prince returned, the position of heir is in play once again."

"You have no authority to make that call, dear stepmother." Roxalus seethed.

"Oh, but she does." Max retorted. "She has every power of the king in his absent state. None here can contest that, by ancient laws and right of Luna, on this day, the festival of her namesake, it is declared."

A light shimmering sizzled around the area. The smell of burnt sugar hung in the air. Weighted power dropped low over the throne room. *Oooh. Spooky.*

"Father still holds the power here. He is not yet passed." Roxalus stomped his foot. "Undue this madness."

Queen Leyashna took her husband's hand in hers.

"By the name of the First Witch, I release you."

Roxalus' jaw dropped and the twins looked to their brother to stop her from saying it. Ayxian and Max stepped in front of her protectively.

"By Mabels own wishes, her heir and yours have prospered."

The king inhaled deeply, a guttural moan escaping his parted lips.

"Queen of witches, lover of the fae king, Mab's wish is fulfilled. I release you to your forever peace."

King Zyoden shuttered before a genuine smile overtook his face. Slumping upon his throne, the king was no more.

"I declare a bid for the throne. It will be decided in thirteen moons. The new king," she paused to look at all of them... "or queen, will be announced upon the zenith of the thirteenth cycle at the Festival of Sol. Until then, Maximus Suilari, first of the royal line, will be King Regent. So it is said, so shall it be done."

A flare of light went up as magics sealed the vow.

Max smiled but I had known him long enough to know when he was acting. He didn't want any of this. He simply didn't want Roxalus or the twin's cruelty to overtake the lands of Anavrin.

"What about the curse?!" Loxias demanded. *Greedy, arrogant twit.* "It must be lifted. Faelan must be brought back right now!"

Everyone in the room turned to glare at him.

Imus words were soft but firm. "More power isn't what this land needs. No way am I going to bring my great-granddaughter back here for you to run amuck."

Elodie was kindhearted as far as I could tell. It surprised me when she spoke up in protest. "I didn't think you cruel, Maximus."

If he felt the hurt from her words, he didn't let it show on his face.

"How is it cruel to not overburden our lands with unnecessary abundance of power, darling sister?" With tight lips, he still managed a false smile, and I wondered at the hardships that brought about that kind of necessity.

"Power isn't the only thing that breaking Mab's curse will do," she said none too shyly. "The mating bond, finding our other half, is all that some of us have ever dreamed." Her glance towards was Loxias poignant.

And the hits keep coming.

Imus flinched, my hand landing on his shoulder. Clearing my throat, I spoke to the fae royalty around me.

"Faelan is my mate. It was her great-grandmother that levied that curse against mated pairs." Some of them gaped at me. Some of them looked angry.

"Her name was Eowyn." Imus shuttered as I spoke her name. "She was Prince Maximus's mate." More gasps and denials. "When he came to the palace to get King Zyoden's blessing for their union, he was thrown into the dungeons for more than three decades."

"No. That's not possible." Elodie didn't want to believe that her father had been that cruel.

"Yes, it is" the queen interjected. "I knew and yet I was powerless to do anything." Her eyes filled with unshed tears. "I owed him so much and yet I failed him when he needed me the most."

Max took her hand and gave it a gentle squeeze.

"By the time I made my escape, Eowyn had died. I never knew that she was pregnant or bore me a child until a few days ago."

He looked at every sibling in turn. Face serious. A death glare that could bring down a mountain.

"Therefore, I will say this one time and hope that you heed my warning; if harm befalls my line, by your hand or your command, I will show no mercy. Understood?"

Queen Leyashna's children agreed quickly. Roxalus, Embla and Emenda took a few minutes and muttered a non-verbal commitment.

"Good." He held his hand out to me, and I took it. "I must take him back to the pack. His mate is waiting."

A whooshing sound filled my ears, and the micro-pinning of my being felt all encompassing. Seconds later, we arrived on top of Ritual Rock.

Red was standing with the pendant stone dangling from her one hand and Inara's book of shadows in the other.

Max yelled, "Look out!" just as Loxias lunged for my neck.

Chapter Fifty-Seven

Faelan

"The stupid knit-wit jumped the port." I heard Max yell and turned to see that Wylder and Loxias were brought to the rock together.

Loxias was running as quickly as his legs would carry him in my direction.

Luna's light was already shining on the stone pendant that hung from my hand. With the ritual half completed, I glanced towards Grams, who was resting against a tree close by.

The time spent in the damp dungeons had drained her resolve. Her body was healed, but her spirit was taking time to mend.

Reed, Piper and Blaze shifted quickly, heading to block the prince before he could interrupt the ceremony.

Zito and Lanie held back, positioning themselves in front of me as a last line of defense.

Wylder and Max raced to catch up to Loxias before he even made it to the first line of wolves, but he was challenging to get a hold of without letting him lay hands on them to force his will.

I'd told no one that I'd learned enough to alter the ritual, but I had to keep my word to Loxias, and to Leif.

The fact that I'd never really lied outright before in my life all made sense to me now. The fae cannot tell lies, and I was a full-blooded faery princess. *Tinkerbell's got nothing on me.*

What we can do is use their words to elude the truth. Omission was the easiest form of untruth, but it was difficult to get away with at times.

With my promise given, I re-read the book of shadows Grams left me upon arriving, trying to figure out a way forward that might benefit all of those involved.

I only needed to tweak what Grams had been trying to do with the ritual.

More words flowed from my lips and into the stone as the chaos around me continued to escalate.

The prince grabbed Piper on both sides of her head to stop her from ripping his throat out. The growls coming from her stopped, turning into whimpers just before she flung herself at Blaze and Reed.

Snarls and snapping teeth were all that I could hear outside of my bubble of concentration.

Fuck! I'm tryin' to wing it here. I don't need all of these distractions.

As that thought crossed my mind, Wylder cried out in pain.

My head snapped in his direction. Reed had taken a chomp at Piper and Wylder got in the middle of them before he could shift.

Max was throwing small flames in her direction to get her to back down a little, but whatever Loxias had told her to do was overriding her ability to stop herself from attacking the lot of them.

"Stop where you are, Uncle!" I shouted. The corner of his turned up at the title but he continued forward, trying to get his hands on Lanie and Zito.

"You know that I can't," he said. "Please... niece." He smiled more broadly as the sound of heavy paws came thundering up behind us. "I need this curse broken." He hung his head slightly. "I need to be whole again."

I couldn't tell if he meant his powers or if he wanted to find his soulmate. Either way, I had given my word.

"Farewell Uncle Lox. I wish you the life you deserve to live."

Before he could say anymore and before anyone registered what I was doing, I lifted the pendant towards the moon, spoke the ancient language of unmaking, and repeated the words of binding.

Loxias and Max disappeared. Lanie screamed. The stone burst into a million sparkling pieces before it vanished altogether.

Reed was the first to rush to me. "What did you do? Where is the stone?"

As the adrenalin suddenly left my system, I collapsed to the ground.

Wylder rushed to my side, almost fully healed from Piper's bite but still looking slightly pale.

Out of the corner of my eye, I saw Grams chanting something. The color slowly filtered into my mate again and he was cradling his chest.

"The protector's bond is gone. I don't feel your angst or pain like I did before."

He put my head in his lap and ran his calloused fingers through my hair. "Hi there, sweetpea."

Smiling up at him, after all that we'd been through over the last couple of weeks, it felt like taking a breath I hadn't realized I'd been holding for a very long time.

"Where's Piper!" Blaze shouted in alarm. "What the fuck did you do to her?"

The wolves were all back in their human forms and drawing closer to me, their alpha, unconsciously.

Sitting up too quickly, I looked around the area. Piper had disappeared along with Loxias and Maximus.

"The ritual shouldn't have affected her."

"What did you do, exactly?" Zito's voice was that calm, logical reassurance that I'd grown to really like. "The stone? The Fae? Piper? Where did they all go?"

Grams came to sit next to me and Wylder on the ground, and she motioned for them all to do the same.

Her face was healed from the bruises I'd seen after she emerged from the dungeons. Her color was becoming more of a natural shade rather than the sallow yellow it had been an hour ago. She hadn't shifted, so it was taking longer than I expected it to after leaving Anavrin.

Come on, old lady. Wolf out.

She dropped her glamour, and I stared in awe at my beautiful, mid-thirties looking, grandmother. *Woah.*

"Tell us, moonbeam," she said. "You broke the curse, didn't you?" There was no accusation in her tone, just a quest for answers. "You changed something, yes?"

Smiling and touching my arm, Grams helped me to focus again.

I waggled my eyebrows at the group. "I did. I swore to break the curse that held the fae hostage..."

My mischievous grin should have tipped them off that there was more to it than that.

"The fae in Anavrin are back to their full powers and they are now able to find their mates. It was only right."

"You stupid woman!" Reed spit.

Wylder growled menacingly beside me but stayed where he was.

Reed simply couldn't keep his disrespect in check. "They're cruelty knows no bounds. They'll go after every human they see and make bargains with them that they won't understand until it's too late. You've doomed us all."

Yup. I'm going to gnaw his face off. Egotistical asshole.

Pushing away from Wylder as he snarled in Reed's direction, I positioned myself directly in front of him. It didn't even take any thought now to elongate my teeth and snout without fully becoming my wolf self.

The alpha tone dripped from my voice as I spoke. "If you speak freely to me with such disrespect again, you'll be minus your balls."

Magics sparked from my fingertips, a crackling sound filled the air.

Reed's expression turned fearful. The rest of the pack coward slightly at the command in my voice, even Grams.

Good pups.

"Tell us the rest of your story, Alpha." Grams winked in my direction. "I would love to hear the constraints of your new spell."

The whole pack stilled at her words, but Wylder stood and gave me a loving squeeze.

"I, for one, would like to know what you did with my Netflix buddy." He said, barking a laugh in my ear that sent goosebumps down my spine.

"Max will be back shortly. I just have to tweak a few things first."

Lanie grimaced, but I could tell that it was only her discomfort of not knowing where Piper was that made her upset.

*Why the heck **Was** Piper sucked into Faeryland with all of the rest of the fae?*

"Grams. what do you about Piper's lineage?"

Chapter Fifty-Eight

Wylder

Looking at Inara, I'd expected judgement or at the very least, displeasure. Neither of those things showed on her face as she watched me and Red together.

If anything, she looked smug. *Did she know all along?*

Faelan smiled at her grandmother's inquiry. I was quite interested to hear what my mate had done too.

She'd really come into herself in just a few short weeks. I was realizing how smart and adept she was with handling anything that was thrown her way.

As anxiety ridden and prone to panic attacks as she was when we'd first met, it was amazing how quickly she fell into her Alpha-Witch-Fae role.

Gods, I'm in trouble with this one.

"I altered the ritual from the original binding curse."

Holding her finger up for Zito to be patient while she explained, he smiled at her gentle quashing of the questions he undoubtedly had been prepared to pepper her with.

"Gram's book of shadows seemed vague on why the curse of mated pairs was added. After meeting Max, I understood it better and something just clicked." Red looked to Inara. "Grams, Max is your father."

Inara stared blankly in disbelief. Her hand came up to cover her mouth, but words failed her. Lanie reached over and laid a reassuring hand on her former Alpha's arm.

"It was Eowyn who added the mate curse. Prince Maximus was her mate, Grams. And after he went back to Anavrin to get the blessing of King Zyoden for a formal union, he was thrown in the dungeons for over thirty years."

Alayna gasped while Blaze, Zito and Reed all hissed through their teeth.

Inara, however, was staring blankly at Faelan. Shock seemed to be her dominate feature at the moment.

"He didn't even know that she was pregnant with you when he'd left." Faelan continued. "When he'd gotten back, he found her grave marker. It crushed him, Grams."

Faelan went over to where Inara was, putting her arms around her, as silent tears streamed down her face.

Inara came back to herself at the contact. "My father lives? And he is a prince of Anavrin?"

"Well technically," I interjected.

I looked over at Faelan. She and Inara left before me and the princes.

"He is now the King Regent for the next thirteen moons. They'll all be making bids for the crown." My tone was somber as I spoke. "King Zyoden is dead. I am sorry about your kin's passing."

"King Zyoden was my grandfather?" The way that Inara asked the question made me believe that she was overwhelmed with all of the new, shocking revelations.

Hmmm, I wonder if she understands that she's a full fae?

"Ugh. That's a wrench the size of a skyscraper." Faelan rubbed at her eyes in exhaustion. "I locked the realm portal. It sucked in all full-blooded and half-blooded faeries. Even if they'd never been to their ancestorial lands, they're now in Anavrin. Only those with our," she threw a looked towards her grams,"... direct blood line can pass through the portal gate at will."

She hadn't told me anything about her plan to do away with the curse or lock the portal. Hurt stung deep in my chest.

Stop. She had her reasons, dumbass. Trust her.

Taking a breath, I calmly asked, "How did you plan for Imus to get back and forth to see you and Inara?"

Faelan placed her hand on my chest. My heartbeat steady and sure under her touch.

"I would have told you back at the castle, but I promised Leif and Max to keep their confidence's. I plan on tattooing my rune..." she said, holding out her arm to me.

In the crook of her elbow sat a symbol. It was a circle with a small wolf howling from a cliff. I realized that the circle represented a full moon.

"... onto their arms. If I bless it as it's formed, it will allow them to open the portal at will."

"Max, I understand. Why Leif? Can you speak of what he told you?" Sworn words bound fae by them.

I understood what she hadn't... or couldn't say before. As Faelan smiled at me, I got the feeling that I was finally asking the right questions.

"Leif has always been treated as common folk by the royals, lords, and ladies. He's never complained or told them anything to give them the impression that he was anything other."

Her gaze was far off, like she was recalling the walk we'd all made to the castle grounds.

"Leif is Max's son. And before you ask, no. Max doesn't know. He had loved and bedded a common fae years before he'd met Eowyn. She hadn't had a chance to tell him before he'd been sent on a mission for the good of the kingdom. By the time he'd returned, she'd died... in childbirth but he'd never known that fact."

Poor Imus. The bastard could never catch a break with women or with his offspring.

I was going to have to start calling him Max at some point, but it was all still too fresh and new for me to make the switch so easily yet.

Inara gave a little sob. I'd forgotten she was still here, reeling from all of the new information.

"I have a brother... and a father." Tears streamed steadily down her face, but they were as happy of tears as I'd ever seen. "Moonbeam! You have given me the world. I am so Luna blessed, I could burst."

As Faelan hugged her grandmother tighter, Blaze cleared his throat. "Not to be a buzz kill, but where the fuck is Piper?" *Good Question.*

Inara pulled back from the hug and took Red's hand. "Don't be angry with me."

"Alright. Why would I be, Grams? I just got you back. And our family grew by three more members." Her eyes darted to mine with a wide smirk.

"After all the truth bombs you just dropped on me, I understand that we are full-blooded fae."

She bit her bottom lip, and after blowing out a long breath, she let her hand fall from Faelan's.

"Piper is my cousin. Yours and your mother's too. She is from the line of Tobias, but of the daughter, Cloe. Our line is of the daughter, Lachie. Piper must be a fae too, Faelan."

Her hands rung out in front of her. I had never seen my friend so worried about what anyone thought of her or her choices. I guess grandmothers and granddaughters were a different kind of breed.

"I should have made you aware that she was our kin sometime in the last couple of decades, but she asked me not to and I had agreed. I suppose that it must have counted as a fae binding because, whenever I thought to mention it to you anyway, I found myself unable to do it. I'd end up doing other things or forgetting that I was going to say something. Now I understand why."

She hung her head. "She must be so disoriented. Faelan, she's my bestfriend." There was a hitch in her throat as she realized that the rest of the pack was gaping at her. "She didn't want favoritism. She liked to go unseen, and I was respecting her wishes. She has secrets of her own to keep." After another sigh, she asked, "Which court would she have been sent to in Anavrin?"

A smile donned Faelan's face that I didn't understand at first. Then it dawned on me. *This wicked little witch wolf.*

"She'd have been sent along to Leif, back at Prince Maximus Suilari's court." Red tipped her head in my direction. "The First Witch, Mab, was a common fae who lived on the outskirts of his lands."

I turned to my mate. "You trickstery little minx." Turning back to the pack, I reveled in her cunning. " If any fae from Mabel's line were sucked back into Anavrin, they would arrive to open arms by Imus ... King Maximus's court, that is to say."

"Wylder and I will teleport to his lands and make sure that all is going well. Fae and half fae that have traveled and lived in this realm that aren't from Mabel's line will be very confused and we must help them acclimate as well. It may be a week or two until we return."

She took Inara by the hands. "Grams, watch over the pack. I will return with your father and your brother as soon as we can. We all have a lot of catching up to do."

Blaze and Reed exchanged a look that I didn't miss. Zito clapped Inara on the shoulder. Lanie was nervously bouncing from one foot to the other.

"Um, I don't want to make waves, but will Piper be brought back here too?"

If I thought that the immediate answer would be yes, I'd be wrong.

Faelan thought on it for a moment. "I can't say that she will. The new binding of the gate was word specific. With all of the fae now having their full gifts restored, the danger to the human population and even the creatures of the Lupian Forest could be in jeopardy if I try to alter it again."

Reed stepped towards her aggressively. I usually let her handle herself, but I'd promised this particular wolf that he wouldn't threaten my mate again.

Shifting quickly, my sharp wolf teeth snatched him by the leg. The sound of snapping bone echoed out over the forest. A cry of pain howled from Reed's lips.

Faelan smiled but shifted into her own wolf and stood in front of Reed's body, crumpled on the ground, trying to shift himself enough to heal.

Her teeth snapped out at... me.

Chapter Fifty-Nine

Faelan

Back down, damn it! I continued to protect Reed as he lay behind me.

It was irrational. Wylder wasn't my enemy, he was my mate, but I couldn't override the instinct to defend a member of my pack from an outside threat.

A string of snarls tore their way free from both my throat and Wylder's. Taking as many deep breaths as I could, trying to calm my instincts. Finally getting control over my wolf, my white fur faded away.

Wylder's black fur began to fall away in response.

We were both standing there again in our naked human glory, staring each other down.

Grams' laugh brought us back to reality.

"Nicely done... both of you. It makes my heart sing to see you two so evenly matched and mated to boot."

She turned to the rest of the pack. "Go out and hunt us up something for a celebratory supper. Meet me back at the cottage." Her eyes met Faelan's, "... if that's all right with you, Alpha?"

Oh shit. I'm Grams' boss too.

"Perfect. Wylder and I are going to the cabin for some... clothes." I could feel his eyes trailing along my body and gave an involuntary shutter.

Blaze and Zito chuckled. Grams tutted but said nothing more.

"We'll be leaving from there for Anavrin. The rest of you will obey Gra... Inara. She is my Beta. Zito remains in his position." Reed's scathing glares were shot like daggers, but they all fell short.

Nodding to Grams and then to Zito, I closed the distance to Wylder. I hadn't noticed until now that he was still breathing hard, still angry. *Uh-oh.*

Wrapping my naked limbs around him, I felt the hard press of his cock against my stomach.

Talking a hairs breadth above a whisper, I asked, "Are you ready?"

His arms came around my waist as he leaned down to my ear, snarling. "The better question is... are you?"

Without another word, I teleported us away.

I brought us directly into the bedroom. With his naked body on full display, my fingers curled into his chest hair, and I yanked him towards the bed.

The snarl he made had my toes curling, but he was still seething and made no move to touch me.

"What the hell was that back there!?" His teeth were on full display, and I inched away from the danger roiling off him.

Subconsciously, I knew he'd never hurt me. Consciously however, my body withdrew from the threat.

His face contorted as he took in my alarm.

Shifting into a more playful crouch, I could sense his annoyance still under the surface, but he did his best to reassure me with his body language.

"I'm sorry. I just reacted. You were attacking one of my pack members and I..." That face.

His grin grew wicked, and my words failed me. I didn't understand the villainous flaunting of his pearly whites. "What's with all the teeth?"

Without warning, he pounced.

With a hand on each knee, I was spread wide, nearly to the point of pain. Looking up from between my legs, his expression dark, I gulped.

With an arch to his brow and a devilish grin, his mouth hovered just above me. His sultry voice dripping with mischief, he held me in place.

"I told you before, the better to eat you with my dear."

And then the wolf devoured me whole.

Epilogue
Maximus

The smell of popcorn, pizza, chicken wings, and chocolate chip cookies all wafted through Wylder's cabin.

Inara had insisted that we start over from the pilot episode since the entire series of Gilmore Girls was available on Netflix. She didn't want Faelan to miss anything, even though she'd seen it all before.

It had been a rough couple of months in Anavrin.

Wylder and Faelan had stayed to help with the transition and watch the first couple of the competition ceremonies take place before the start of the court competitions that would secure one of the princes or princesses the kingdom.

It had only been a few days since they'd left, and I'd missed my great granddaughter more than I ever imagined.

I'd gotten the tattoo inked on my skin by Faelan's magics that allowed me to teleport to the Lupian Forest any time I wanted or to be able to let someone pass through the gate if they had family matters to attend to.

There were restrictions to traveling to town.

The fae that had been sucked back into Anavrin with Faelan's spell were granted a one to three days pass, allowing them to tie up any lose ends and make their farewell to friends.

They would be allowed to visit, by request, until the humans that they knew passed on or where there were other circumstances.

Some fae had children with humans. The children weren't restricted while they were still under the care of a human parent, but after their parent passed on, they'd be confined to Anavrin like all of the other fae.

The hope was, that in less than a century, the faeries of Anavrin would no longer be granted access to the human realm at all.

I may not fully agree with the arrangement, but as the Deliverer, Faelan was in charge of the decision.

Faelan had been back to see Odie many times over the last couple of months. He was growing too big be in the castle anymore and to tame to be left in the wilds.

For now, we erected a stone fence around a few acres of forest surrounding the west side of the castle. He could roam as he pleased, and Faelan was helping him learn to only kill what he could eat that day.

"Does anyone want something to drink?" Faelan asked. "These wings are super spicy."

Wylder hopped up and went to the kitchen, accidentally knocking Nixie to the floor. She meowed loudly at the disrespect before going to lay in the blankets at Faelan's feet.

Inara sat in the recliner with her feet propped up while I sat on the over used couch. "Bring some napkins too, Wylder," I called into the other room.

I would catch Inara shooting glances in my direction when she thought that I wasn't looking.

The look was so like her mother that it stopped my heart from time to time.

"What?" I playfully chided.

Looking abashed, her cheeks pinked, and she turned back towards the television. "Nothing," she said.

I could just make out the grin at the corners of her mouth from the side.

When Wylder came back into the room with our drinks and napkins, he chuckled.

"Inara has always wanted this," he motioned around the room. "And now that Daddy's here, hanging out and chillin', she's probably gonna bust at the seams."

Faelan smacked his arm, and Inara gave him a good kick that made both me and Wylder laugh.

I had only been able to steal away a few hours, here and there, over the last month or so.

There was no doubt that my daughter was part me now that I was getting to know her better. She had a lot of my qualities.

Eowyn gave me the most precious gift, a daughter who was very much like her mother.

"How is Leif handling all of the new attention?" Faelan asked, interrupting the thoughts of my lost mate.

"He's doing quite well... under the circumstances. I don't know that he wants to take up my court just yet, but he is very well liked around the palace. And, thanks to you, the palace renovations are nearly complete."

I'd taken a bite of a wing and immediately regretted it. "By Luna's asshole! You said spicy, not melt your face off hot."

Inara reached for a wing and chewed it slowly without any problem from the heat at all.

"Well, Father dear, it would appear that you... are a little bitch."

Wylder and Faelan burst out laughing. Inara tossed the bone onto her plate and picked up another one. The Eowyn look she gave me while maintaining eye contact sent my heart soaring.

"Careful there, daughter of mine. My nemesis may be a hot wing today, but it could very well be wolf shank tomorrow." I tried to look menacing but that just made Faelan and Wylder laugh harder.

Inara joined in on their revelry and it took several minutes before they'd caught their breaths.

"Alright, already," Wylder turned on the tv and looked around the room at all of us. He took his Netflix addiction seriously. "Any bathroom breaks or questions should be saved until the end of each episode. Got it?"

"Um, no Mr. Crankypants." Faelan reached up and took the remote from his hand and growled. "If I have questions, I'm going to pause it." Wylder rolled his neck and took a deep breath, blowing out his frustration as he went. "Besides, I wanted to ask Max about Piper first."

Ah, Piper. The poor thing had been ripped away from her pack and realized that it meant a great deal of things that she hadn't wanted to shift through for many years.

I'd brought her back twice to talk with Inara and picked her up on my return trips.

I knew that it wasn't fair to the other fae, but I'd missed so much of Inara's life. I couldn't bring myself to deprive her of the cousin and bestfriend who'd been there for her when Eowyn died.

I didn't even know that they were that close until the first time that I'd brought her back. She and Piper had downplayed their friendship as to not show favoritism in the pack.

After she'd been in my lands for a few days, I realized that Piper wasn't even a wolf. Her line is that of jungle cats.

Tobias's daughters had made the choice to differ their lines, though, because of Mab's power over particles, they could switch them within the first few years after the onset of their abilities in this realm.

In Anavrin, the magics were too strong to deny one's dominant true form. Her black panther was stunningly beautiful from the very first shift.

"Piper is doing fine. She has been spending quite a bit of time with my brother."

Faelan dropped the bucket of popcorn all over the floor. The smell of butter filled the air with its sudden upheaval.

"What? Why would she want to spend any time at all with Loxias? She knows what he's capable of."

I let her seethe for a moment before I corrected her.

Loxias wasn't a bad guy. My youngest brother had always had it the toughest when we were growing up.

I had looked out for him when I could, but Roxalus and the twins were ruthless. Even Ayxian could be a bit of a prick at the worst of times.

"Not Loxias. Ayxian... And before you ask, I have no idea what is going on between them. She is a grown female and it's not my place to interfere."

Faelan settled back against Wylder's chest, taking in what I'd said. Inara was smirking like the cat that ate the canary but added nothing.

"With the kingdom competition in full swing, I only have a few episodes before I have to return."

I took a bite from the end of my pizza and chewed. With a mouth full of pepperoni, I motioned towards the television.

"Let's get this show on the road, Gigi."

She laughed. "What was that?"

"Well, great granddaughter is a mouthful to say all of the time. Would you prefer it if I called you Princess Faelan, Deliverer of the Anavrin Fae. Descendant of the First Witch, Alpha of the Lupian Forest Wolfpack. Burner of popcorn?" I teased.

"Hey! I did not burn the popcorn." I watched as her hands landed on her hips.

Wylder held up a piece of burnt popcorn and cleared his throat.

"Okay, so maybe one piece is a little burnt."

Inara and I shared a smile and then held up our own burnt pieces to her and she huffed as she sat back down on Wylder's lap.

"It's okay sunshine," I said, pointing at his discarded chicken wing. "We all have our short comings."

She pouted and turned on the first episode without another word.

After a few minutes, we settled into a comfortable quiet, laughing at the craziness that was Lorelai.

In this moment, all was right in each of our worlds. Time stood still and our hearts were happy.

All too soon, it was time for me to get back to my new-found son, my lands restoration, and running the kingdom of Anavrin.

This contest for the crown could be the answer to every-thing.

With Piper now part of my kingdom, Inara wanted to vis-it more often. Eowyn would have been so proud to see the woman she's become.

With Inara, my mate's loss isn't healed... it never would be, but life was more bearable.

I couldn't make it right for either of my children that I hadn't been there for them growing up. All I could do now was make the best of the times we had together.

As much as it pained me, I didn't push Inara about Faelan's mother. We all agreed that I could meet her informally, like at a coffee shop or somewhere along the way.

Faelan said that she could talk her mother into seeing me in my former office, perhaps on the pretense of investing. I'd planned to give her all of my holdings anyway. It was smart to let her think that she earned them.

Of course, Inara and Faelan would be taken care of while they were here in the human realm before the rest went to her, but my savings were beyond enough for one human lifetime.

After all, I'd been living amongst the humans for two hundred years.

My great-granddaughter was a smart cookie. I'd be able to see her mother regularly, check in on her in my own way. All while she was none the wiser.

Before teleporting home, I stole one more look at my girls. Wylder dipped his chin in understanding.

With a contented smile, I left back to Anavrin to run my kingdom and make a better life.

Kingdom Seat
Princess Embla
Princess Emenda
Prince Ayxian
Prince Noxian
Prince Roxalus
Prince Maximus
Princess Elodie
Prince Loxias

About the Author

Anexa O. Saphire

I was born in Maryland and love steamed crabs. I moved to Florida for a few decades but have moved back to Maryland recently. I love to write, create art, read, and sing. I've become extremely introverted as I have gotten older, but I do still love going out for an occasional night of karaoke. My hubby and I live a simple, quiet life with our furbabies. Life becomes simpler once you let yourself dream and let go of whatever holds you down.

Acknowledgements

Thank you to my husband. His encouragement and understanding make my writing time enjoyable. He'd tell you that I am book obsessed, but I really do find peace reading, writing, and anything else book related.

Thank you to my Booktok and Instagram community. Without you guys, I would never have found half of the courage it took to go through with my dreams.

A huge thank you to Melanie Elkins for all of her help. She has been my eyes when mine have failed me. I am so grateful for her. She has stepped up and been in my corner in a time when I truly needed a friend.

Thank you to all of my friends who check in on me, making sure that I eat, sleep, and stand up a few times a day.

My mom gets a special thanks... her love and support are the building blocks to a good foundation.

And a big shout out to my fur babies. I never feel lonely when spending hours on end with the written word because they are always a constant presence.